IN THE PRESENCE OF EVIL

A Selection of Recent Titles by Tania Bayard

Novels

IN THE PRESENCE OF EVIL *
A MEDIEVAL HOME COMPANION
SWEET HERBS AND SUNDRY FLOWERS

* *available from Severn House*

IN THE PRESENCE OF EVIL

OF EVIL

Tania Bayard

Severn House Large Print
London & New York

This first large print edition published 2018
in Great Britain and the USA by
SEVERN HOUSE PUBLISHERS LTD of
Eardley House, 4 Uxbridge Street, London W8 7SY.
First world regular print edition published 2018 by
Severn House Publishers Ltd.

British Library Cataloguing in Publication Data
A CIP catalogue record for this title is available from the British Library.

ISBN-13: 9780727829368

Severn House Publishers support the Forest Stewardship Council™
[FSC™], the leading international forest certification organisation. All
our titles that are printed on FSC certified paper carry the FSC logo.

MIX
Paper from
responsible sources
FSC   FSC® C013056
www.fsc.org

Typeset by Palimpsest Book Production Ltd.,
Falkirk, Stirlingshire, Scotland.
Printed and bound in Great Britain by
T J International, Padstow, Cornwall.

The Devil is a philosopher. He understands a man's nature, condition, and inclination, and he knows what vice he is most disposed to – either by temperament or by habit – and that is where he makes his most powerful attack.

From a book of moral and practical advice for a young wife, Paris, 1393

Prologue

As the king led his army forth to subdue the Duke of Brittany, he was overpowered by a grievous illness.

The Monk of Saint-Denis,
Chronique du Religieux de Saint-Denis, contenant le règne de Charles VI de 1380 à 1422

5 August 1392

When the king rode out with his troops on that hot summer day, he was a robust, good-natured man of twenty-four, sound of body and mind.

In an instant, he was changed.

As he led his army across a dry, dusty plain, his page, drowsy in the heat, dropped a lance. It fell against the helmet of another page, and the sharp clang of steel striking steel filled the king with terror. He spurred his horse to a charge and raced at full speed toward those around him. Knights, squires, and men-at-arms scattered in all directions as he wheeled left and right, lashing out with his sword and shouting that his enemies were attacking him. For over an hour the frenzy continued. His troops tried to seize him, but they were forced to flee as he bore

1

down on them. When he finally slumped in his saddle, exhausted and drenched with sweat, four of his men lay dead.

One of his chamberlains lifted him from his horse, lowered him to the ground, and tried to revive him. But the king lay without speaking or moving, his eyes rolling wildly. He was placed on a litter and taken to a nearby monastery, where he remained senseless for two days.

Gradually, the king recovered his reason and the use of his limbs, but his mind was shattered. Spells of unreason descended on him for the rest of his life. He lived in fear of those episodes, which he said began with pain like the sting of arrows. During times of affliction, which became more violent as the years went by, he forgot who he was and that he was the king of France. He fled from his wife and denied having any children. He tried to deface his coat of arms, and he often believed he was made of glass. He refused to wash. He soiled his breeches, ripped his surcoats to shreds, and threw his robes into the fire. He destroyed his furniture, tore his tapestries, broke his windows, and smashed his crystal goblets. He ran howling through the palace, dancing and making lewd gestures.

There were periods of relief when he seemed to be in his right mind, and at those times he was often lethargic and lost in gloom. He said he would rather die than suffer more spells of unreason.

Some of the king's doctors said his illness was caused by an excess of hot black bile. Others attributed it to poison, or the heat of that August day, or the strain of preparing for battle. Certain wise men said the king had inherited an unsound mind from his mother.

The common people knew better. It was sorcery.

One

Alas! Poor widows who have lost every-thing! Who will comfort them?

Christine de Pizan, *Ballade*, c.1405

Paris
January–February 1393

Christine didn't believe in omens and signs. But her mother did, and she talked of them all the time. Sometimes the predictions came true, and then Christine was sorry she hadn't listened. Especially on the morning when she went to the palace and discovered the first murder.

The day seemed ill-starred from the moment she was startled out of sleep by the sound of her shutters rattling in the wind, long before the bells at the nearby priory of Sainte-Catherine sounded prime. She cried out to her husband. But Étienne wasn't there beside her, never would be again. She rose from her bed, wrapped herself in a woolen coverlet, lit a taper by holding it against the smoldering embers in her fireplace, and staggered downstairs to the kitchen.

In the grey half-light, she could barely see her mother's dark shape kneeling in front of the fireplace, but she heard her call out, 'You must

5

not go out today, *Cristina.* It is snowing. And I saw a blind man in the street yesterday. That is a very bad sign.'

Christine crept across the room, wincing as her bare feet touched the cold floor, and stood on the warm hearth. 'I have to go to the palace,' she said.

Francesca jabbed a stick into the nearly dead ashes. '*Stupida!*' Christine hoped her mother was referring to their hired girl, who had forgotten to bank the fire the night before. Francesca uncovered some embers, added more sticks and a bit of charred tow, leaned forward, held her long hair away from her face, and blew until sparks caught. Flames leapt, and light swept around the room, setting reflections dancing in copper pots hanging from the ceiling and shiny pewter platters standing on the shelves. Francesca looked up and laughed. She struggled to her feet, nearly falling in her haste, and limped across the room.

'There they are, *Cristina!*' she cried. 'The spirits!'

'Nonsense! It's just the flames.'

'It is the spirits. They are trying to tell us something. And there is your father!' Francesca pointed to one of the glinting shapes. Her husband had been dead for six years, yet she found him everywhere. '*Povera Cristina.* I ask myself why she never sees him.'

Christine glared at her mother, though to be honest about it, she sometimes thought she heard her own husband, dead for several years too, talking to her.

Francesca glared back at her. 'Your father is saying to you, do not go to the palace.'

6

'Blind men in the street! Reflections in the frying pans! How can you believe things like that mean anything?'

'The king did not observe the signs, and demons took his mind away. Therefore, you must not go to the palace. There is evil there. Something terrible will happen to you.' Francesca smoothed her black dress down over her hips.

Christine ducked around her mother and stalked into the pantry. There the sweet scent of dried apples and pears soothed her – until she realized that the yellow slices of fruit hanging from the ceiling in long chains reminded her of her father's wrinkled face as he lay on his deathbed. She had the unhappy thought that perhaps her husband's face had looked that way, too, when he died, although she would never know, because Étienne had been far away in another part of the country on a mission with the king when he was taken from her. She reached up to the shelf for a cheese tart. A mouse ran across her hand. 'The devil take Georgette,' she muttered. Now she, too, was angry with the hired girl, who had left the plate uncovered.

In a temper, she strode back into the kitchen and found her children, wrapped in their bed-clothes, their faces gleaming in the firelight, clustered around their grandmother.

'You woke us up with all your arguing,' announced Jean, who was nine. He put an arm around his twelve-year-old sister, Marie, but she pushed him away, her prim little face set in a scowl. Thomas, a chubby eight-year-old, snick-ered. Five-year-old Lisabetta, Christine's niece,

7

who lived with the family, leaned against her grandmother and started to cry.

Francesca, large and round in a dress that was a bit too tight for her, drew the little girl close and shook her finger at Christine. 'See what you have done!'

Christine, who was small and thin, with none of her mother's softness, suddenly felt like a child herself. 'I'm twenty-eight, Mama. You shouldn't talk to me like that.' She stalked out of the kitchen and hurried up the stairs to her room, where she sat on her bed, shivering in the cold and listening to Francesca comforting the children in the kitchen. *She's a much better mother than I am*, she thought.

She ate the tart the mouse had tasted first, then rummaged through her clothes for her warmest chemise and a heavy blue wool cotte, which she pulled on even though it had threadbare spots she knew she should have asked her mother to repair. She started to put on a starched linen headdress, then threw it aside and shoved her black hair under a plain grey hood, feeling as she did so a tiny indentation on her cheek, left there by a recent illness. She reached for a small bowl of flour soaked in rosewater and gently applied some of the mixture to the pockmark, thanking God there were not more. By that time, it was light enough to go out. She collected quills, knives, parchment, and an inkhorn from her desk, tossed everything into a large leather pouch, and tiptoed downstairs, where she threw on a much-mended brown cloak, struggled into her boots, and hurried out the door before her mother could accost her with more warnings about the dangers awaiting her at the palace.

Francesca heard her go, but she said nothing. She waited until the older children left for school, thrust Lisabetta into the arms of the hired girl – who had arrived late, as usual – and limped up to Christine's room. Ignoring twisted covers on the bed and discarded clothes on the floor, she went straight to her daughter's desk and searched through the clutter. A small piece of unused parchment was all she needed, and when she found one, she seized it and concealed it in her sleeve. She went downstairs, told Georgette to make sure the fire didn't go out, and threw on her cloak. Francesca wasn't going to sit idly at home while Christine walked into danger. She was going out to get something to protect her daughter, something that would have made Christine even angrier than she already was, had she known about it.

Out in the street, Christine was greeted by falling snow and a fierce wind that seemed to have been waiting there to attack her. Tears stung her eyes – from the wind, and from anger at her mother, anger mingled with shame that she had been so unkind. What Francesca had said was true; the king had lost his mind, and evil seemed to stalk the palace.

Christine was no stranger to the court. She'd lived there as a child, for her family had moved from Italy to Paris after her father, the renowned physician and astrologer, Thomas de Pizan, had become an adviser to the present monarch's father, King Charles the Fifth. Everyone at the court had doted on her then. But when the old king died, things changed. His son Charles the Sixth was only twelve, and the government fell into the hands of his uncles, greedy, power-hungry men who had little use of the old king's advisers. By the time Thomas de Pizan died several years later, he had lost much of his influence at the court, and even Christine's husband, who was well established as one of the royal secretaries, had found his salary reduced. And then Étienne died, too, and Christine was left a widow with little source of income. To support her family, she'd become a scribe. She was occasionally called to the palace to work as a copyist, when the royal secretaries had too much to do, but she dreaded those times, because everyone there lived in fear of the king's attacks of unreason and distrust of the charlatans who prowled around claiming they could cure him with vile potions and spells.

The wind blew her cloak open and nearly succeeded in pushing her off her feet. She shook her fist at it. A snowstorm like this was unusual for Paris, and she was annoyed that she had to be out in it. A few years earlier, it wouldn't have been necessary. Now worries about money troubled her constantly, for she was responsible for her three children, her mother, and her niece Lisabetta, whose mother had died and whose father was away in Italy. To make matters worse, she'd been ill and had only recently been able to work again. The royal librarian, Gilles Malet, who'd been a friend of her husband's, had learned of her troubles, and he'd spoken to the queen, who wanted a copy of a book to give one of her ladies-in-waiting as a wedding present. Christine was glad to have the job, but it meant that she had to go to the palace, no matter how apprehensive she was about the perils lurking there.

Bent over against the wind, she trudged along the street where she and her family lived, in a marshy section of Paris between the old city wall and the new one King Charles the Fifth had built farther out into the countryside. It was a district with only a few houses and many open spaces planted with market gardens. She loved those gardens in summer, when they were lush with vegetables, fertile and warm like the rich farm-lands around Bologna, where she'd lived until she was four. Now the gardens were nothing but barren furrows, rapidly turning white. Shriveled leaves fluttered over the frozen ground, and there were a few dry weeds with heavy seed pods bent down by the snow; they made her think of her children, who would have said they looked like little goblins wearing white caps.

Suddenly a gust of wind burst out of a garden, and with it, as if one of those goblins had sprung to life, came a tiny white dog, fleeing from a pack of hounds. With a crooked tail, a muzzle covered with long, bristly hairs, and ears flapping like rags, the little dog was such a comical sight that Christine started to laugh. But he was about to be mauled. She leaned down, scooped him up, and stuffed him under her cloak, all the while shouting abuse at his tormenters. The hounds turned and fled, their tails between their legs.

11

Bracing herself against the wind, she walked on, holding the dog close and keeping her head down to escape the cruel blasts. She passed the enormous *hôtel* built by the King of Sicily, its innumerable gables and turrets hidden behind a veil of swirling snowflakes, and turned down the rue Saint-Antoine, the broad, paved street that led to the king's palace. This street was usually alive with the clatter of hoofs and the babble of voices – knights prancing by on horseback, couriers scurrying along with messages for the king, merchants driving mules laden with supplies for the court, street vendors hawking their wares. On this day, however, as she stumbled along through the wind and snow, her sense of foreboding increasing with every step, the street was deserted and silent. She looked in vain for the gawky man who cried the virtues of his crispy meat pasties and the snaggletooth crone who always managed to thrust one of her fragrant honey cakes right under her nose so she couldn't resist buying it. Bells chiming tierce at the priory of Sainte-Catherine reassured her, until the wind stole their intonations and smothered them with its own dismal song. The air tasted like metal. She felt comforted when the little dog reached a soft paw out from under her cloak and touched her cheek.

But when she came to the cemetery next to the church of Saint-Pol, the dog began to twist and turn in her arms. Wild dogs roamed the gloomy burial ground, and she sensed that he felt their presence. Then she remembered her mother's beliefs about the *loup-garou*, a werewolf said to

12

prowl around the city, feasting on the flesh of children and drinking the blood of dead men. *What nonsense*, she thought. She clutched the dog tighter and started to run.

Suddenly, a girl in a red cloak dashed past her, swinging a large brown sack over her head and taunting someone who came rushing out of the cemetery. When Christine tried to step aside, she collided with a man in a hooded black cloak and fell to the ground. The girl with the sack started to run in the other direction, but the man was too fast for her. He grabbed her around the neck and wrenched the sack from her hands. Then the white dog jumped out of Christine's arms and ran toward the pair, snarling and barking. The man let out a terrified scream, dropped the sack, and fled. Before he disappeared from sight, Christine, watching stupefied from the ground, noticed his feet: he wasn't wearing shoes.

The girl in the red cloak looked at the dog and laughed. 'A man like that, afraid of a runty little thing like you!' she said. She picked up the sack and hurried off. Christine knew she was a prostitute named Agnes who worked at a brothel on a nearby street. She struggled to her feet and called after her. But the girl was gone.

Christine looked down and saw that her cloak was caked with mud. She would have to go home and clean it before she went to the queen.

She hoped this was the end of the trouble her mother's signs had warned about, but she had the uneasy feeling it wasn't.

Two

Everywhere there are more brothels than any other kind of house.

From a thirteenth-century poem

The brothel where Agnes worked was in an old cottage on a little street known as the rue Tiron. Seen from the outside, the building looked neglected, for its roof tiles moldered under grey-green moss and its half-timbered walls dripped with rot. On the inside, however, it was well tended, and even on snowy winter days it was warm and comfortable. Rushes blocked the cold air seeping up through cracked wooden floorboards, oiled parchment over the windows shut out the wind, and a fire blazed in a large fireplace. Private spaces, partitioned off by cracked leather curtains, offered stained but serviceable straw-filled mattresses and hot-bodied women to go with them. Used only during the daylight hours, the brothel was a popular stopping place.

On the morning of the day of Christine's encounter with the hooded man with bare feet, a prostitute named Marion arrived late at the cottage. She was a tall girl with bright red hair bound in strings of glittering gold beads, and she wore a fur-lined purple cloak and a green

14

and yellow dress decorated with handmade embroidery. Marion cared little for laws forbidding prostitutes to wear such colorful clothes. As she strode through the falling snow, she glowed like a tropical bird.

Pushing aside the snow-covered canes of brambles sweeping over the path to the door of the cottage, Marion sang a ditty about a nun and a priest and was just getting to the bawdy part when a man in a hooded black cloak came from behind, pushed her down, and rushed into the brothel. 'Son of a whore,' she cried as she picked herself up. She ran in after him and watched in amazement as he raced around overturning everything in sight. Benches teetered on their sides, a trestle table lay on its back like a beast with its legs in the air, and drinking cups and wine jugs flew by her head. Startled prostitutes and their clients emerged from the curtained rooms and shrank back as the man dashed past them into the private spaces and ripped apart the mattresses. Finding nothing in any of those, he darted back into the communal room and hurled himself up a ladder to the loft. There he found what he was looking for. Clutching a large brown sack to his chest, he jumped down to the floor below and stood for a moment, glaring at the prostitutes and their clients with red-rimmed eyes half-hidden in the shadow of his cowl. Marion, the only one who was fully dressed, lunged at him, but he shoved her away, dropping the sack as he did so. A large book tumbled out. He grabbed it and thrust it back into the sack, but not before she had seen the book's leather cover, which was inscribed with strange symbols. The man stared at her and said, 'Tell your friend Agnes she's as good as dead if I ever see her again.' Then he ran out the door.

Marion was too stunned to cry out. But before the door swung shut, she noticed that the man's feet were bare.

Three

Many women have the courage, strength, and daring to take on and complete successfully the same noble tasks undertaken by conquerors and celebrated men of war.

Christine de Pizan, *Le Livre de la Cité des Dames*, 1404–1405

Christine returned home, her throat tight with apprehension about what her mother would say when she saw her dirty cloak. But to her surprise, her mother wasn't there, and the hired girl had no idea where she'd gone. Now Christine was no longer angry with her mother; she was worried. Francesca never went out in winter weather. Many years earlier, on her way from Italy to her new home in France, she'd hurt her leg falling from a horse in an Alpine pass, and ever since she had been terrified of snow.

16

In spite of her worries, Christine couldn't wait around until her mother came home, so she cleaned the mud off her cloak and set out for the palace again. It was still snowing, and the streets were slippery, but she walked quickly, until something brushed against her leg and she nearly fell once more. She'd forgotten all about the little white dog. He stood on his hind legs and whined.

'You scared that horrid man. I suppose you could do it again,' she said, as she picked him up and continued on her way. But when she drew near the palace, she nearly turned around and headed back home again, for in front of her was the barefoot man in the black cloak. The dog growled, but she held him close and watched until the man had disappeared into the courtyard of the queen's residence. Then she continued on. She was afraid, but she needed to complete her work.

The gatekeeper at the queen's residence recognized her and let her through, then ignored her as he watched the street. She entered the courtyard and looked around. The man with the bare feet was nowhere to be seen, but she knew there were many places where he could be hiding, places she'd hidden in herself when she was a child, because the palace, the Hôtel Saint-Pol, was like a small city in which the residences of the king and queen were part of a larger complex of gabled and turreted mansions, streets, galleries, courtyards, stables, orchards, and gardens. Hundreds of people lived or worked there, though none of them were out on that wintry morning. The only sounds she heard were the moaning of the wind and the roaring of the king's lions in their stockade near an orchard on the other side of the royal enclave.

Ignoring her fears, she started across the courtyard. The snow came down faster than before, and the wind played with the flakes, sending them dancing around her boots and nudging them into piles at the base of the courtyard wall. Intent on looking around for the man with the bare feet, she slipped on the icy cobblestones and reached out to steady herself against the basin of the big central fountain, which was empty of water but rapidly filling with snow. She looked up at the stone lion sitting at the top of a pillar in the middle of the basin and cried, 'A pox on you, *dandin!*'

Someone laughed, and the laughter was so full of mirth, she knew it couldn't be that of the ghostly man with the bare feet. She crept around the fountain and found crouched on the other side a stocky little boy in a red jacket and a red cap that only partially concealed a thicket of tawny curls.

'You spoke to the stone lion,' the boy said, giggling. He jumped to his feet, and his red cap fell off. He ran a bare hand through his unruly hair.

'Don't you have gloves?' she asked.

'For certain.' He pulled a pair of gloves out from under his red jacket, held them up for her to see, and tucked them back under the jacket. 'Where are you going?' he asked as he scooped up some snow from the basin of the fountain and made a snowball.

'To see the queen.' The white dog poked his head out from under her cloak. She held him out to the boy. 'I found him in the street. Perhaps you'd like to have him for a pet.'

The boy dropped the snowball and reached for the dog, which leapt into his arms. 'My grandmother won't let me keep him.'

'Then you can play with him for a while, and I'll take him when I come back.'

'Do you know my grandmother? She sews for the queen and her ladies.'

She nodded, for she knew that his grandmother, whose name was Blanche, was one of the many seamstresses who served Queen Isabeau and her ladies-in-waiting. A tall, silent woman who wore plain black or brown cloaks and unadorned cottes that contrasted with the richly colored brocade, damask, and silk gowns worn by the ladies of the court, she lived in the city and often came to the palace. She appeared forbidding, but Christine had seen her smile when she was with the little boy in red who stood before her, his eyes sparkling as he fondled the white dog.

'What's your name?' she asked.

'Renaut.'

She looked toward the entrance to the palace and saw the *portier* who stood guard beckoning to her. 'I must go in. Take good care of the dog for me,' she said as she walked away.

The boy called after her, 'What's his name?'

She thought for a moment, then called back over her shoulder, 'Goblin.'

The *portier*, a burly giant named Simon who'd

19

worked at the palace for many years and had known her since she was a child, smiled and said, 'You should not tarry out there in the snow. You look cold.'

She knew her nose was running, her eyes were tearing, and her face was bright red. She tried – unsuccessfully, because her fingers were stiff – to push some wayward strands of hair back under her hood. Then she pointed to Renaut, who was throwing snowballs and laughing when they broke into pieces as the white dog tried to catch them. 'Isn't that boy too young to be out there by himself?'

'For sure he is. He's only seven. But I watch over him while his grandmother is inside.'

'Where are his parents?'

'His mother is dead. The father?' Simon shrugged. 'He has an aunt, Blanche's other daughter, but she's no help, even though she lives right here at the palace.' He touched his forehead with the tip of a finger.

'She lives *here*?'

'Well, Not exactly *here*. With the lions.'

Christine had heard about the strange woman who helped the king's lion keeper, but she'd never seen her, and she suspected not many people had, because the reclusive woman never left the lions' stockade.

'That's Blanche's daughter?'

Simon laughed. 'Surprising, isn't it. You'll never see the two of them together, although her mother must go to visit her sometimes.'

Christine looked over at Renaut, who was now running around the fountain, with the dog at his heels. 'Will Blanche come to get the boy soon?'

'Probably not. There's to be a wedding ball next week, so she's working on the ladies' new gowns. Everything has to be tried on. It will take time. But he's safe with me.'

Christine turned to go into the palace, but Simon held up his hand. 'Do not go in just yet. There are no guards in the great gallery. The queen's monkey climbed up one of the tapestries and threw a turd down on them. They are chasing him all around the palace.' The big man doubled over with laughter, then straightened up and said in a worried voice, 'They should not have left their posts. There is a man in there who disquiets me. You had best wait here until they come back.'

Christine shuddered. 'A man in a black cloak turned in here just before I did. He wasn't wearing shoes. Is it he?'

'In truth, it is. I would not have admitted him, but I had orders. He is delivering something to the Duke of Orléans.'

She hesitated, then walked to the door. 'I'm not afraid,' she said, as she entered the palace.

The gatekeeper called out to Simon, 'She'll be back soon if she sees that man in there. She's not as brave as she looks.'

Simon shook his head. 'I would not be so sure about that.'

Christine hurried through the entrance hall, shook snow from her cloak, and stepped into a great gallery, a cavernous space deserted except

21

for the wind, which followed her in and set the heavy tapestries on the walls straining and grating against the metal hooks attaching them to moldings under the ceiling. Her footsteps resounded on the hard wooden floor, and the gallery echoed with the distant shouts of the guards searching for the monkey in another part of the palace. Carved basilisks, griffins, and sharp-toothed dragons leered at her from the arms and tops of high-backed chairs standing against the walls, and the place stank of monkey dung.

A group of courtiers in broad-brimmed beaver hats came in, stamping their feet and brushing snow from their clothes. In low voices, they spoke of the king.

'He's changeable, like the wind. But he seems in his right mind at the moment,' said a tall man in a blue velvet mantle.

'That may be, but he sits for hours without speaking. What will happen when the demons attack him the next time?' asked a fat gentleman in a green fur-lined cape.

They all bowed their heads and tiptoed through a side door, leaving Christine alone again.

Usually when she walked through the gallery, she stopped to admire the scenes in the tapestries, but she was hesitant to do so on a day when a hooded phantom might be lurking nearby. Still, she paused when she came to an open door. She recognized the king's high-pitched voice, and she looked into the room.

King Charles, wrapped in a voluminous red velvet houppelande embroidered with silver lilies, stood before a huge fireplace, his head bowed and his arms hanging limp at his sides. He was still the tall, broad-shouldered man Christine remembered, but he looked much older than his twenty-five years. His face was drawn, his long blond hair and beard were unkempt, and he stood hunched over like an animal that has been beaten and expects another blow. She could see nothing in him of the cheerful little boy she'd played with as a child.

Standing beside the king was his younger brother Louis, the Duke of Orléans. Unlike the king, he was clean shaven, slender and graceful in a blue-and-gold brocaded tunic lined with sable. Christine had never trusted Louis, for even as a child he'd been moody and unpredictable, and at twenty-one, he was even more so – a brilliant, tormented man who alternated between spells of debauchery and periods of repentance that sent him weeping to the nearby church of the Celestine monks to ask God to forgive his sins. Of the two brothers, Louis, sly and secretive, seemed the one more likely to be possessed by demons.

The king began to shamble back and forth on the fireplace hearth, his face glistening with perspiration, his arms twitching as if pulled by invisible strings. Several sergeants-at-arms who stood nearby were alert, ready to spring into action as they watched the long sleeves of the king's red houppelande swirl dangerously close to the tossing flames. The duke merely watched, with a curious expression on his handsome face; he reminded Christine of a cat, ready to pounce.

23

So engrossed in the scene was Christine that she forgot about the hooded man with the bare feet. Then she remembered: he was supposed to be delivering something to the duke. But he wasn't in the room with the king and his brother. Afraid he might be creeping up behind her, his cold feet soundless on the wooden floor, she turned quickly, nearly fell, and had to reach out for the wall to steady herself. Her hand brushed against one of the tapestries. She looked up and saw an alarming scene: a city was on fire, and the terrified citizens leapt from the roofs of crumbling buildings into the flames.

'Babylon destroyed by the wrath of God,' a soft voice behind her said.

Christine swung around and saw with relief that the voice came not from the barefoot man but from a young woman carrying a small harp in a blue velvet sack.

'I startled you. Forgive me,' the woman said.

'It wasn't you. It was the tapestry,' Christine said, not wanting to admit that what she'd really feared was the man with bare feet.

'I would have thought nothing could frighten you.'

'Whatever gave you that idea?'

'I know who you are. You're a scribe, and you go about the city as you wish. Most women are content to remain at home with their housework.'

Christine laughed. That was what her mother thought she should do: stay at home with the cooking and sewing.

'But the tapestry *is* frightening,' her companion said. 'Paris is like that. Sometimes I think the city

24

is doomed, like Babylon, and we will all fling ourselves into the fire.'

'Paris does not please you?'

'Not from what I have seen of it so far.'

Christine knew that this young woman, Alix de Clairy, was the bride of the knight and royal chamberlain Hugues de Précy, one of the king's favorites, who had brought her to Paris from her home in Picardy. She was a childlike person, with eyes of intense green, a dusting of freckles across her nose that made her seem even younger than her sixteen years, and an irreverent manner. Unlike the other ladies at the court, she didn't redden her lips with madder, pluck her hair to make her forehead higher, or whiten her face with wheat flour. As she looked at her, Christine put her hand to her own face, and touched the pockmark, hoping it didn't show. She adjusted her hood and noted with satisfaction that although Alix wore a proper starched linen headdress, she had trouble keeping her auburn hair under it.

Christine remembered the first time she'd seen Alix de Clairy, in the queen's chambers. It had been an enchanting scene: Alix, wearing a bright blue cotte, an embroidered belt with a large silver buckle, and a long necklace of blue and green beads, perched on a stool, singing to the accompaniment of her harp; Queen Isabeau, a small, dark woman in a green houppelande, reclining against a big red pillow on her ceremonial bed; the queen's dwarf, dressed in a similar green gown, squatting on the floor in a trance; the queen's fool, watching from the doorway, for once not babbling to herself. Even the queen's white greyhound, sitting beside the bed with his head tilted to one side, had been charmed by the music. The queen's ladies-in-waiting, however, had retreated to the other side of the room, where they stood chattering, while Catherine de Fastavarin, the queen's favorite, sat on a large blue cushion next to the bed, turning her head away from Alix and pretending not to hear.

As she'd listened to a song about lovers in a beautiful springtime garden, Christine had suddenly realized it was something Étienne had sung for her. So lost was she in the music and her memories, it was a while before she realized that the dwarf, in a voice clear and sweet and perfectly in tune, had joined in. Ignoring the scowls of the ladies-in-waiting and the disdainful looks of Catherine de Fastavarin, Alix rose from her stool, crossed the room, and sat down on the floor beside the misshapen little woman, smiling as the two of them continued the song.

Then Alix had returned to the queen and talked to her, telling her about the *trouvère* who had written the song, and confiding that she had always dreamed of being a minstrel herself. The queen had nodded sympathetically, but one of the ladies-in-waiting had said, 'Surely that is not the dream of the wife of a royal chamberlain! Nor is it fitting to sit on the floor with a dwarf!'

Alix had merely picked up her harp and started singing again. At the time, Christine had longed to ask her about the song, and she started to do so now, but Alix was no longer paying attention to her; she was staring at the floor.

Christine looked down, too. At the bottom of the tapestry, the ill-fated men and women of Babylon plummeted into a sea of flames, their hands thrust out in front of them. Below that, on the floor, was another hand – a real hand, with dirt in the creases and blackened fingernails. It belonged to someone behind a low wooden chest that stood near the tapestry.

A sergeant-at-arms entered the gallery. Christine motioned to him, but when he came over and stood waiting for her to say something, she was unable to speak. She just pointed to the hand. He stared at it for a moment, then grabbed the chest and pulled it away from the wall.

A man who was wedged between the chest and the wall slumped to the floor. His filthy black cloak was covered with blood, his scruffy beard glistened with spittle and vomit, and his eyes were open and staring – at nothing.

He wasn't wearing shoes.

Christine no longer had to wonder where the barefoot fiend who had knocked her down in the street might be hiding. He was lying right in front of her, with a dagger through his heart.

Four

*The people prostrated themselves
before the Lord, crying and lamenting,
begging Him humbly and contritely
to cure the king.*

The Monk of Saint-Denis,
*Chronique du Religieux de
Saint-Denis, contenant le règne
de Charles VI de 1380 à 1422*

Christine looked away. She couldn't breathe.
Then she looked back, praying the dead man
would be gone. But he wasn't. The sergeant she'd
summoned dashed away to get help, and she was
alone with Alix de Clairy, who reached down
toward the dagger protruding from the man's
chest. Christine gasped, and Alix drew back her
hand, as if she'd been burned.

Suddenly, the gallery, which had been so empty
and silent, was filled with people. Women in
velvet surcoats and tall linen headdresses pressed
against her, men in long, pointed shoes trod on
her feet. Above her, the tapestry billowed and
swayed, threatening to bring the terrified citizens
of Babylon down on her head. She lost sight of
Alix, and when she looked around for her, she
was gone.

Renaut, the boy from the courtyard, came running toward her, pushing past the long skirts of the women, weaving in and out of the legs of the men. He held something in his hands, and as he stood looking down at the dead man, a melting snowball dripped water into a pool of blood on the floor. A moment later, Simon appeared, followed by the Duke of Orléans and a sergeant-at-arms with a huge mastiff on a leash. Maddened by the scent of blood, the dog lunged forward, and then, as the sergeant yanked him back, turned and sank his teeth into the man's arm. The duke thrust the swearing sergeant aside. He threw open the dead man's cloak, oblivious to the spittle and vomit splattered across it, and ran his hands over the lifeless chest, thighs, and legs. When he didn't find what he was searching for, he leapt to his feet and kicked the corpse, the dagger still protruding from its chest, back against the wall.

Christine fled through the crowd toward the entrance hall, and Simon followed, dragging Renaut with him and muttering, 'Saint Peter's beard! Where is his grandmother?' At that moment, the seamstress – hood askew, strands of grey hair flying – strode into the hall. Her face softened with relief when she saw Renaut. She rushed to him, seized his arm, and started to take him away, but the boy twisted out of her grasp and ran to Christine. 'Goblin's in the fountain,' he cried. 'You promised to take him.'

Christine had a vision of yet another body, that of a drowned dog, until she remembered there was no water in the fountain. Before she could

29

say anything, Blanche took the boy in her arms, cradled him against her chest, and forced her way back through the mob.

Simon said, 'They tell me you discovered the body. I should not have allowed you to come in here alone. I hope you are not too distressed.'

'I'm all right. But Hugues de Précy's wife was with me, and she's disappeared. Did you see her leave?'

'I did. She ran out into the street without her cloak.'

'I think she has some knowledge of the dead man.'

'I am not aware of that. But I think I know why the man was killed. He was bringing the Duke of Orléans a book, and the book is gone. The murderer must have taken it.'

'What manner of book?'

'No one has told me. All I know is, the man had a large sack, and it must have been in there. The duke is raging. There will be hell to pay for the guards who left their posts.'

Someone tugged on Christine's sleeve. Startled, she turned to find a boy she knew to be the brother of her family's hired girl, Georgette. He asked, 'Were you frightened when you found the body?'

'It is discourteous to creep up on people like that, Colin,' Simon said. He gave the boy a gentle cuff on the side of the head. 'Make yourself useful. Walk home with the lady.'

Christine started to object, but she didn't want to offend the boy, who ran small errands around the palace and was much fancied by the queen, so she followed him into the courtyard. The snow had stopped, the wind was not blowing, and the sun was about to come out. Frenzied barking came from the fountain, where she found the little dog hurling himself against the sides of the basin, trying in vain to leap out.

Colin laughed. 'His legs are too short. I wonder who he belongs to.'

'I found him in the street. Why don't you take him home?'

'I have no liking for dogs.'

'Very well, Goblin. You'll come with me,' she said, as she leaned down to lift the dog out of the fountain. *At least I'll have something to give the children to make amends for my bad temper this morning*, she thought.

Out in the street, Colin pranced along at her side, pestering her with questions about the murder. When he was convinced she knew no more about it than he did, he darted away and ran around looking for the killer's footprints in the snow. *How unlike his sister he is*, Christine mused. At fifteen, Georgette was thick-set and sluggish, while Colin, a year younger, was thin and agile and growing so fast his clothes were too small for him; the sleeves of his brown fustian jacket barely reached his wrists. She wondered why the queen – who'd found him working as a stable boy and decided he should have a better job – didn't provide him with better clothes.

Colin talked too much, and Christine was afraid he'd blurt out the news of the murder to her mother, so when they reached the other side of the old city wall, she sent him back to the palace. She started down her street, then turned and then looked back when she heard loud noises. Over the snow-dusted ramparts of the wall she could see banners and pennants floating gaily over the blue slate rooftops of Paris, but the scene was not peaceful. Orange and yellow flames shot high into the air through clouds of black smoke, and she heard frenzied cries and smelled acrid fumes. Somewhere in the city, a fire raged, and for a moment she thought Paris was burning, like Babylon in the tapestry at the palace. She remembered Alix de Clairy saying the city was doomed, and it seemed possible, considering all the shocking sights she'd seen that winter, when the people realized something terrible had happened to their beloved ruler: grown men weeping in the streets; distraught crowds swarming into the churches to pray; frightened old women crawling on their knees in the mud, clutching at the robes of the priests, begging for a miracle to drive away the demons that had taken control of the king's mind. Even worse was the sight of the priests themselves bringing wax images of the king into the churches and stationing them in front of statues of the Virgin, pleading with her to cure him. Everything seemed like a hideous dream.

And now, to add to the horror, a murderer had struck at the palace.

She wondered where her mother had gone, and she hurried to get home.

Five

*There is a Latin proverb that men use
to defame women. It says, 'God created
women to weep, speak, and spin.'*

Christine de Pizan, *Le Livre de la
Cité des Dames*, 1404–1405

Hiding Goblin under her cloak, Christine
arrived home as the bells of Sainte-Catherine's
sounded sext. She was relieved to see her mother
there.

Francesca had come in just a moment before.
She sat on a bench by the kitchen fireplace,
hoping her daughter wouldn't notice she was out
of breath. Christine didn't notice, because she was
lost in her own thoughts, trying to decide how
to tell her mother about the murder at the palace.
She stood at the door and watched as Francesca
drew Lisabetta to her and started to comb her
hair, seemingly unaware that dirty pots, spoons,
and ladles were scattered everywhere, and that
the floor was littered with crumbs. Then Georgette,
untidy as usual in a rumpled dress and a grimy
apron, appeared, and Francesca began to scold
her. The girl sniffled and picked up a copper
pot that looked greasy even though she'd just
washed it. She held it by the rim, dabbed at it

33

with a towel, and set it down on the worktable, perilously close to the edge.

Francesca threw up her hands, loosening her hold on Lisabetta, and rose from the bench. The child stumbled and bumped against the table, causing the pot to fall and roll along the floor. Francesca picked it up and gazed into it, spellbound. Christine knew what she was thinking, but Georgette didn't.

'Is it dented?' the girl asked timidly.

'It is my husband,' Francesca whispered. 'Observe.'

Georgette peered into the pot. 'I cannot see him. What color are his clothes?'

'I see only his face. Why do you ask?'

'Because if he's dressed in black, he will appear to you again. If he's in white, his soul has been saved, and he's free to leave.'

'È vero?'

'In France, we know about these things.'

'Che miracolo!' Francesca sat down on the bench again and motioned for Georgette to sit beside her. 'You must tell me all about it.'

And so it was that when Christine got up her courage and walked into the kitchen, Francesca sat before the fire discussing ghosts with Georgette, completely unprepared for what her daughter had to tell her.

'Bene. You have returned home in time for dinner,' Francesca said. Tempting smells came from a pot simmering over the fire, and Christine knew her mother was making one of her favorite soups, a delicious combination of eggs, cheese, and spices. She decided to wait until later to tell

34

her about the murder. Goblin smelled the soup, too. He jumped out of Christine's arms and stood on his hind legs, wagging his crooked tail and waving his front paws in the air. Lisabetta ran over and hugged him, but Francesca looked at him in disbelief. 'Why have you brought a dog into the house?'

'He was about to be eaten by some hounds.'

'*Pazza,*' Francesca tapped her head with her finger and stalked into the pantry. Christine followed, hoping to find some tidbits of yesterday's dinner for the dog and expecting to hear loud complaints from her mother. Instead, she found Francesca tossing scraps of meat onto an old platter. 'I was going to throw these out anyway,' she said.

Christine thought the meat looked quite savory. She put her arms around her mother and said, 'His name's Goblin.' Francesca sniffed, added more meat to the platter, and took it to the dog.

When the older children came home from school, they managed to contain their excitement over the dog while Georgette set up trestles and a board for the dining table, covered the board with a linen cloth, and set out the dishes, using the plates to hide soiled spots. They washed their hands, sat down, said their prayers, and then exploded with questions about the dog. 'Can he stay?' they asked Christine over and over again. 'You have to ask your grandmother,' she said, and they all turned to Francesca, who shrugged her shoulders.

'That means "yes",' Thomas cried, and he jumped

up, nearly overturning the table. Francesca tried to scowl, but the dog leapt into her lap and licked her face, tickling her with his whiskers, which made her laugh. Then he crept under the table and went to sleep.

Jean sat at the head of the table. Tall and thin and serious, with a wisp of brown hair hanging over his forehead, he reminded Christine so much of his father, she felt tears in her eyes. But she had to smile when she looked at Thomas, who was short and chubby and ate noisily, all the while chanting '*zanzarelli, zanzarelli,*' the name of the soup, and glancing knowingly at Francesca, who was teaching him Italian. Marie, on the other hand, sat up straight and looked smug. 'That's disgusting,' she snapped at Thomas when he wiped his nose on his sleeve.

'Better a snotty child than one with no nose at all,' he announced, giggling so hard he nearly rolled off the bench. Jean smiled and put his arm around shy Lisabetta, who snuggled up against him.

'*Basta, Tommaso!*' Francesca smothered a laugh, and her dark eyes sparkled. He'd repeated a proverb he'd learned from her, and that pleased her. Her grandsons, especially Thomas, could do no wrong. It had been the same with her own sons.

Christine only half heard all this, and she couldn't eat, not with the image of the dead man behind the chest constantly before her eyes. She'd told her mother it was perfectly respectable and safe for a woman to go out and work as a scribe, assuring her there were other women scribes in Paris and nothing bad would happen to her. Now she stared at her uneaten soup and realized it was not true. She began to have doubts about her decision to take up a profession that often took her away from home. But when she looked at her mother and the children, she couldn't help imagining them all begging in the marketplace, and she knew that when the queen summoned her back to the palace, she would have to go.

Usually she escaped from the kitchen after a meal, but that day she stayed, trying not to get in the way as her mother moved around the room hanging pots on hooks and arranging platters on top of the cupboard. Georgette had washed the spoons, ladles, and knives, but most of them were still covered with grease, so Christine rewashed them and put them away, only to be told by her mother she'd put them in all the wrong places. *At least I'm not as witless as Georgette*, she said to herself as she watched the girl toss leftovers at the midden beside the fireplace and wipe her hands on an apron covered with the remnants of the week's meals.

Francesca looked at the girl with disgust and sent her to the market to buy bread for supper. 'Take the children with you. Goblin, too,' she called after her.

Christine couldn't put it off any longer. 'There is something I must tell you, Mama. A man was murdered at the palace this morning. I discovered the body.'

The pitcher Francesca was holding crashed to

the floor and broke into several pieces. Francesca didn't notice. She just stared at her daughter. Christine was sure she was going to remind her about the signs. But after a long silence, Francesca said, 'I have said to your father many times, it is dangerous to teach a girl to read and write.'

Christine was tempted to laugh. 'What have reading and writing to do with it?'

Francesca threw up her hands and raised her eyes toward heaven. 'Oh, Tommaso, why did you not listen to me? For women, the best is to stay safe at home with the cooking and sewing.'

'You know it is not possible for me to stay home, Mama. How would we live?' To hide her exasperation, Christine bent down and picked up the pieces of the pitcher. It was one of her favorites – faience decorated with blue and green vines. She put the pieces on the table. The breaks were clean, and she was able to fit the fragments together, remembering how her father had always been able to repair broken crockery. *He knew so much*, she thought, *and he taught me so much, especially how to read and write*. She pushed the pieces of pitcher aside and glared at her mother. 'Don't you want me to tell you what happened?'

Francesca sighed and sat down on the bench by the fireplace. 'I suppose you must.'

Christine sat beside her mother and told her everything, her voice trembling when she came to the moment when she'd seen the hand reaching out from behind the chest. Her mother said nothing; she just put her arm around her and held her close. Christine felt comforted – until

Georgette burst into the kitchen brandishing a loaf of bread and shouting, 'Someone was murdered at the palace! Colin told me.'

'Calm yourself, Georgette. We know about this,' Francesca said. 'Put the bread away. Go upstairs and sweep.' She stood up, went to the fireplace, and picked up a metal jug that had been warming on the hearth. 'You have had a terrible experience, *Cristina*. All the more reason for you to drink the tisane I have prepared for you.'

Because Christine had been ill and had become very thin, Francesca prepared for her a daily mixture of licorice, figs, and barley water, hoping it would help her gain weight. So far, to avoid an argument, Christine hadn't complained about the tisane, but that day, as she watched Francesca pour the warm brew from the jug into a beaker, she said, 'I've had enough of that, Mama. Who prescribed it? Your old doctor?'

'You must not say unkind things about the doctor. He restored you to health.'

'Your doctor did nothing more than bleed me. I would have had my health back sooner if my midwife had treated me. She knows as much as your doctor. Probably more.'

'The midwife is only a woman.'

With that, Christine left the kitchen and marched up to her study. She sat at her desk and seethed with anger. Her father had given her to understand that women were as capable as men, and she had always believed it. But when she thought of what had happened at the palace that morning, the doubts that had assailed her at the

39

dinner table returned. Perhaps her mother was right to say she should stay at home with her cooking and sewing.

A noise at the door startled her, and she looked up to find Marie standing there, watching her.

'I didn't go out with the others. I heard what you told *grand'maman.*' She had such a troubled expression on her face, Christine regretted having brought home the news about the murder. But it was too late now.

'What do you think, Marie?' she asked. 'Your grandmother wants me to do nothing but cook and sew. Do you agree?'

'Not at all.' She was only twelve, but she seemed very grown up.

'Why do you say that?'

'What would you do with all this?' she asked, walking to the desk and gesturing toward the jumble of quills, inkhorns, knives, rulers, and sheets of parchment that covered it.

Just then, Jean appeared in the doorway. 'What are you two talking about? Something's wrong. Tell me, too.'

'Your grandmother wants me to stay home all the time? Would you like that?' Christine asked.

'I would. But you wouldn't.'

'Of course she wouldn't,' Marie said. 'Papa taught her to be a scribe, and she likes that better than cooking and sewing. She's good at it, and she shouldn't give it up.'

That's just what Étienne would have said, Christine thought, and she remembered the encouragement she'd had from her husband, who'd taught her to be as fine a scribe as he

40

was. He'd often worked in this room, which served as a study as well as their bedroom, and she still had some of his quills. She reached for one. It felt warm, as though he'd just put it down. She took an old scrap of parchment, dipped the quill into her inkhorn, and wrote in bold black letters, *I, Christine, am an excellent scribe. Should I continue?*

Someone said, *Certainly.* It must have been Marie, or Jean. But she couldn't be sure.

When Christine went down to the kitchen for supper, she found Francesca standing at the table, holding the pieces of broken pitcher.

'There is no need for you to go out and work, *Cristina.* Your brother is going to send money from Italy.'

'When?'

The children came thundering down the stairs and into the kitchen. Francesca put her finger to her lips. 'We won't discuss this now, *Cristina.* Especially in front of Lisabetta. She misses her father.'

At the table, Thomas couldn't sit still. He giggled and nudged his grandmother, bursting with something he couldn't wait to tell. When Christine finally demanded to know what it was, Francesca reached into her sleeve and pulled out a rolled-up piece of parchment.

'I got something to keep you safe, if you go to the palace again,' she said as she handed it to her daughter.

Thomas bounced up and down. 'Open it, open it!'

41

Christine unrolled the parchment and stared at it in disbelief. 'Where did you get this, Mama?'

'She went out in the snow!' Thomas cried. 'She told me all about it, and I kept the secret, didn't I, *Nonna*?'

'You did indeed,' Francesca said.

Christine said, 'This is foolishness, Mama. Who gave it to you?'

'A friend. There is evil around. The words will protect you.'

'You can't read, so how do you know?'

'My friend who wrote it told me. Those are prayers.'

'So I see.'

'And they are written in the blood of a white dove. To make them more powerful.'

Christine sighed. 'You shouldn't believe what people tell you. Your old crone might have written magic spells instead of prayers, and you wouldn't know the difference.'

Francesca stamped her foot. 'She is not an old crone. She is my friend.'

Christine waved the parchment in front of her mother's eyes. 'You're taking a great risk with this, Mama. You could be accused of trying to conjure demons. I can't believe you involved the children in something so absurd.'

'Only Thomas,' Francesca said.

The boy was close to tears, and Christine put her arms around him. 'It's not your fault, Thomas,' she said. The other children looked relieved; they hadn't been let in on the secret.

Christine looked closely at what she held in her hand and turned to her mother. 'Where did you get this piece of parchment? It looks like something I had on my desk.'

'I put it to good use. The prayers will keep you safe. You must wear them around your neck when you go out.'

'I'll do nothing of the sort!'

'Then you must stay at home.'

'You know I can't do that!' Christine thrust the piece of parchment back into her mother's hand, marched up the stairs, and went to bed.

Six

Women know less because instead of having a variety of experiences they stay at home, satisfied with running the household. The best way for a reasonable person to learn is by being exposed to and doing many different things.

Christine de Pizan, *Le Livre de la Cité des Dames*, 1404–1405

Shortly before his marriage to Alix de Clairy, the knight Hugues de Précy had received from the king a mansion near the Hôtel Saint-Pol. The house, originally owned by a wealthy nobleman, was now shabby and nearly empty. Hugues liked to gamble, and thus had little to spend on much-needed repairs or furnishings. It was to this melancholy place that Hugues had brought his bride from Picardy.

In the early afternoon of the day she and Christine discovered the murdered man at the palace, Alix de Clairy sat alone in her bedroom, playing her harp. She had no idea where Hugues was, but that was not unusual; he was rarely at home. She knew that had he been there, he would have berated her for wearing a plain woolen shift, neglecting to put on her shoes, and letting her long auburn hair hang loose around her shoulders. Little about his young wife seemed to please Hugues de Précy.

Silk cottes, velvet surcoats, and fur-lined mantles hung on rods next to the bed where Alix sat. Golden hairnets and starched linen headdresses reposed on a large wooden chest. Hugues hoped she would become one of Queen Isabeau's ladies-in-waiting, and in spite of his straitened finances, he managed to buy expensive clothes for her to wear when she went to the palace. Alix detested those clothes. The long dresses made it difficult to walk and their high-belted waists bound her so tightly she could scarcely breathe, while the stiff headgear never stayed in place. Until she'd come to Paris, she'd rarely worn anything other than short, loose-fitting chemises, plain cottes, and simple kerchiefs. At the Hôtel Saint-Pol the air was dense with smoke from torches, candle wax, and open fireplaces; courtiers and servants alike spent their days perspiring in elaborate, cumbersome garments. She found life there suffocating.

Alix de Clairy was the only child of a wealthy

lord with extensive landholdings near the city of Amiens. Her mother had died when she was six, and she had been cared for by an old nurse-maid who allowed her to roam the woods and meadows of her father's estates and play with the children of the peasants who worked there. One day an itinerant musician visited her father's manor house, and from that moment the little girl thought of nothing but music. She convinced her father to let the man stay and teach her to sing and play the harp. The old musician told her about the troubadours and trouvères who'd written the songs she learned. 'Some of them were women,' he said, and Alix longed to emulate them. Now, in a strange city with a husband who neglected her, music was her only pleasure, a distraction from many troubled thoughts.

Music provided no comfort on the day of the murder at the palace. When she thought of the man with a dagger through his heart, a shiver ran through her body. She laid her harp aside, went to the chest, lifted its lid, and searched inside. When she didn't find what she was looking for, she let the heavy lid drop and stood holding back tears. She didn't know where her husband was, when he would come home, or what she would say when he returned.

She went to the window and looked out. She longed to walk the streets of Paris, talk to the shopkeepers, gossip with the women in the markets, learn about the city, perhaps even begin to feel at home there. But Hugues had forbidden her to go out alone. As it was, he would be very angry when he learned she'd left the palace

45

unaccompanied. It would be useless to try to explain that she'd been so frightened she hadn't realized she'd forgotten her cloak; she hadn't even noticed how cold she was without it.

She thought of the scribe, Christine, and she wondered whether she'd noticed she'd run away. She pictured the king, reacting with horror to the news of the murder, perhaps losing his reason again, and she imagined the queen trying in vain to comfort him. She liked the queen, who enjoyed listening to her music and was kind to her, and she longed to do something to ease her sorrow.

Alix's father had died shortly after her marriage, and now her only friend was her old nursemaid, Gillette. The woman had followed her to Paris, but Hugues wouldn't allow her to come to his mansion. Alix knew she was staying with a cousin named Maude in a small house in another part of the city. Once she'd even secretly visited her there.

Gillette had said she would give her something the queen could use to cure the king of his terrible malady. Remembering this, Alix dressed and left the house. She knew how angry Hugues would be, but she didn't care. If there was something that would make the king well, she was determined to get it.

Seven

The second kind of avarice is robbery.
That is when someone takes something
from someone else and refuses to give
it back, instead keeping it and hiding it
because it pleases him. And if he is asked
to give it up, he denies knowing about it
and conceals it so no one can find it.

From a book of moral and practical
advice for a young wife, Paris, 1393

The next morning, Marion sat at the trestle table
in front of the fireplace at the Tiron brothel. It
was too early for customers, and the other prostitutes were either out in the street or resting in
the curtained-off rooms. The burning logs in the
fireplace crackled and spit, the parchment over
the windows rattled in the wind, and the canes
of brambles scratched at the door, but Marion,
lost in thought, heard none of it – until Agnes
came in and climbed the ladder to the loft.
Marion woke from her reverie and listened to
the girl searching through her belongings. She
knew she was looking for the sack that belonged
to the barefoot man.

Agnes came back down and swaggered up to
her. 'Who took it?'

'It didn't belong to you.'

'That's no business of yours. If you've got it, give it back.'

'I don't have it. The man you stole it from came here yesterday and took it.'

'Liar.' Agnes grabbed Marion's hair and pulled her to her feet. Marion lashed out at her with her fists, but Agnes ducked and butted her in the stomach. Marion doubled over and fell, dragging Agnes down with her, and the two scuffled on the floor, kicking and clawing. The other prostitutes came out of their rooms and stood around urging them on, until a sergeant-at-arms from the palace, one of Agnes's regular customers, strode into the brothel. He pulled Agnes to her feet. 'What's going on here?'

'She stole my book.'

'What would you be doing with a book?' The man put an arm around Agnes. 'I've had my fill of books,' he said. 'A man brought one to the palace yesterday and got himself murdered because of it.'

A shiver of excitement went through the girls, and they all started asking questions: Who was the man? How did he die? Who killed him? What happened to the book? Delighted to have an audience, the man released Agnes and sat on the bench. 'No one knows who he was. He was dressed like a monk, but he can't have been in his right mind. He wasn't wearing shoes.'

Marion and Agnes looked at each other.

'Someone stabbed him through the heart, stuffed him behind a chest, and ran off with the book. A woman who writes for the queen found

48

him. Hugues de Précy's new wife was with her.' The sergeant looked at Agnes. '*She's* a sweet bit of ass, I can tell you.'

'I know all about Hugues's new wife,' Agnes sniffed. 'She may be sweet in bed, but that doesn't stop Hugues from abusing her.'

'What's in the book?' Marion asked.

All the sergeant could say was that the Duke of Orléans was in a rage because it had been stolen.

What if he had come here and found us with it? Marion asked herself. The Duke of Orléans was no stranger to the brothel. She felt sick. While the other girls crowded around the man, asking endless questions, she snuck out and went home.

Marion shared a room with several other prostitutes in another section of the city, near the place where the rue Saint-Honoré crossed a street known as the rue de l'Arbre-Sec because of a wooden gallows standing there. When she arrived at her lodging house that day, she found her landlord, a strange little man with a black beard who owned several such buildings, standing in the street. He was dressed, as he always was, in a black cape with a long black hood and an ermine collar. He looked so dark and forbidding, she was glad she didn't have to encounter him often. Nevertheless, she had to admit knowing him could be to her benefit. She'd heard he had ways of freeing prostitutes from prison when they were arrested for wearing jewelry or furs.

The man had come to collect the rent, and

49

Marion expected she would pay what she owed and be done with him. But he didn't leave. 'What happened to your face?' he asked.

She touched her cheek, and when she took her fingers away, she saw blood. She bowed her head to avoid his gaze, but he put his hand under her chin and lifted it up, forcing her to look at him.

'You've been in a fight.'

'One of the girls at the brothel stole a book. The man it belonged to came and got it, but she didn't believe that. She thought I had it.' She remembered how the man had raced around the brothel in a frenzy, and she saw again his red-rimmed eyes and his bare feet. She shuddered.

Her landlord stared at her for a long time, and then he said, 'You are fortunate that book is no longer at the brothel. If it ever crosses your path again, have nothing to do with it.' He turned and left her.

She went to her room and lay on her bed, trying to forget about the book and the man with the bare feet. After a while, she got up, washed the blood from her face, put on a clean cotte and a warm cloak, picked up an embroidered purse, and walked toward the market at the junction of the rue Saint-Honoré and the rue de l'Arbre-Sec. She knew there was a corpse swinging on a gallows there, and she didn't really want to see it, but she was friends with the woman who sold honey wafers at that spot, and she was hungry.

Eight

In the name of God, you women who profess Christianity and yet pervert it with such vile conduct, get up out of the filth and save your poor souls. God is merciful; He will receive you if you sincerely repent.

Christine de Pizan, *Le Livre des Trois Vertus*, 1405

That same morning, Christine stood in the street in front of her house, wondering how best to calm her anger at her mother, who didn't seem to understand how necessary it was for her daughter to go out and work, no matter where that took her. Worries about money made Christine ill-tempered and impatient, and she needed to think about something else. It was a warm day and the snow had melted, so she decided to walk to the Place de Grève and watch the wine boats dock at the open space beside the Seine. Surely it would be a pleasant distraction.

She was wrong. Throngs of people headed in that direction – housewives with baskets of carrots and turnips slung over their arms, peddlers bearing sacks of crockery on their backs, peasants

51

driving mules overburdened with panniers of pots, pans, and old clothes, kitchen boys toting bundles of faggots, bakers' boys dropping the pastries they were supposed to be delivering, university students, clerks, monks – all had forgotten the errands that had brought them out: they were rushing to see an execution. She stepped into a doorway as a nobleman charged through the crowd on a black stallion, spattering everyone with mud and knocking an old woman carrying a basket of laundry to the ground. The woman lay sprawled at Christine's feet, surrounded by her freshly washed shirts, aprons, and underclothes. 'May a canker rot you!' she screeched at the departing horseman's back. 'I hope that nag throws you into a pile of turds!'

Christine helped her up, retrieved her basket, and stuffed her mud-stained laundry into it. The woman brushed herself off, swearing all the while at the brown slush clinging to her cloak, then grabbed Christine's arm and tried to drag her along to the Grève. 'Hurry, or you'll miss the beheading,' she cried. Christine pulled free and watched her scurry away. She was tempted to call after her that she would do better to go and rewash her clothes. She'd never found executions in public places entertaining. That day, the thought of them was unbearable.

To escape the bloodthirsty crowd, she walked on the street where the glassmakers worked, slipping into the garbage-filled gutter in the center of the crowded street as she dodged the signs jutting out from the glass painters' and enamellers' shops. The contents of a chamber pot emptied from an upper window just missed her head, whereupon an old man standing in a doorway laughed and spat at her feet.

She crossed the rue Saint-Martin and went down the rue des Lombards, in the shadows of the tall buildings where Italian bankers had their counting houses. Some snow remained in the dark, narrow alleyways separating the houses, and a group of small boys played there, laughing and throwing snowballs at passersby. A group of bankers wearing elaborately shaped green, red, and brown *chaperons* swore at them as they hurried by. Christine followed them, listening to their conversation and thinking about the life she could have had in Italy, if her family had remained there. Her mother would have been happy, her father would have been a professor at the university in Bologna, and she might have been allowed to go to school. But then she remembered – if she hadn't come to France, she wouldn't have met Étienne.

As she passed the markets at les Halles, thankful she'd escaped from her house without orders from her mother to pick up a head of cabbage or a piece of cheese, one of Francesca's friends, a hunched old woman with snow-white hair, approached. Hoping to avoid her, Christine turned down a side street, but the woman called out, 'Come to the pillory!' Christine shook her head. She was in no mood to stand around in a marketplace jeering at thieves and dishonest merchants with their heads and arms stuck through holes in a revolving iron wheel.

53

'Well, tell your mother the butter seller who cheated her is in there. They've put a lump of his rancid butter on his head.' The woman cackled and hurried off. Christine walked down the rue Saint-Honoré, thinking unkind thoughts about old women who enjoyed public displays of cruel punishments.

When she came to the intersection of the rue Saint-Honoré and the rue de l'Arbre-Sec, she found herself under a rotting corpse swinging from the gallows. Shreds of the man's jerkin and leggings hung from his exposed bones, and two crows tugged at what bits of flesh remained. The vendors who used the crossroads as their marketplace ignored the cadaver as they cried the virtues of their wafers, meat pies, and onions, but for Christine the body was a gruesome reminder of the dead man at the palace. Feeling ill, she walked unsteadily to the stone cross at the junction of the two streets, and tripped and fell on the steps at its base. Strong arms pulled her to her feet and a husky voice asked, 'What's Lady Christine doing here?'

She leaned against her rescuer. 'I could ask the same of you, Marion.'

'It's not what you think. I'm just buying something to eat.'

Christine considered prostitution a grievous sin, but she had known Marion for a long time, and she liked her. The girl's mother had worked for her family as a housemaid, but when Francesca had learned the woman's daughter was a prostitute, she'd dismissed her. Christine thought this unfair, and she'd argued it wasn't Marion's fault she'd been raped when she was fourteen and wouldn't be able to find a respectable husband. She'd told Francesca she would try to convince Marion to take up another profession, hoping this would persuade her mother to keep the woman on, but Francesca had been adamant: 'I do not want people to talk about me because I have let the mother of a prostitute into my house.' Marion knew how Francesca felt about her, but she didn't care. Now eighteen, she mocked Christine's respectability, calling her Lady Christine, and usually greeting her with a curtsey. Francesca would have been appalled.

Marion eased Christine down onto the stone step at the base of the cross and sat beside her. 'If you're feeling unwell, I can understand why. Bodies.'

'I suppose you mean that,' Christine said, looking up at the corpse on the gallows.

'That, and the one you found at the palace. It's enough to make anyone spew.'

Christine had to laugh. Marion had always been able to make her laugh, even during the terrible days following Étienne's death. She wondered how Marion had learned she'd discovered the body at the palace, but she knew it would be futile to ask. Just as futile as asking about the bruise she saw on the girl's cheek. Marion spoke her mind about many things, but she never discussed her private life.

Marion rummaged in her purse and found some cloves. 'To settle your stomach,' she said as she handed them to Christine. 'I wonder what became of the pretty little lady who was with you. I pity her. They say her husband abuses her.'

'Surely that can't be true!'

'I'm certain it is. Men are all bastards, even the ones at the palace. Even the Duke of Orléans. He wants for nothing, yet he flies into a rage about some old book. He probably abuses *his* wife, too.'

'Do you know something about the book?'

Marion lowered her gaze. 'Ha! Louis, Duke of Orléans, with his padded shoulders and pinked sleeves. Look! I've embroidered him.' She held up her purse so Christine could see that it was decorated with the image of a nobleman clad in an emerald green doublet, long pink scalloped sleeves, silver hose, and a beaver hat ornamented with turquoise peacock feathers.

Christine had known Marion did embroidery, and she had seen other examples of her work, but this was extraordinary. 'You could sell that,' she said.

Marion hid the purse under her cloak and changed the subject. 'I suspect it was a book of magic.'

'So you do know something about it!'

Marion shook her head. 'I'm only guessing. But the duke believes in magic, you know. He's even asked me to teach him some.' She jumped to her feet. 'I can teach you, too. Here's how to make a love potion. Stick a rooster's head between your buns and squeeze till it's dead. Then cut off its balls, grind 'em up, and put 'em in your lover's wine. They say it works every time.'

Christine couldn't help smiling, but she turned away so Marion wouldn't see.

'Lots of people believe in magic,' Marion said. 'Even the king.'

56

'How do you know?'

'Because of something that's going to happen next week. Have you heard about the banquet and marriage ball for the queen's favorite lady-in-waiting, Catherine?

'I've heard.'

'What you haven't heard is this. The king and some of his friends are planning a masquerade that night. They're going to put pitch all over their bodies and cover it with flax, to make themselves look like hairy wild men of the forest.'

Christine was appalled. The men were planning a cruel ritual meant to humiliate a woman marrying for a second time – in this case, a third. The men would do a lewd, frenzied dance, and she shuddered to think of how the diabolical performance might affect the king, whose mind was already so unsettled. 'Why would the king agree to be part of such a thing?' she wondered out loud.

'Because the masquerade is supposed to heal him. The wild men will call out the demons in his head and drive them away. Or perhaps they are witless enough to think they can catch the demons and kill them.'

'Where do you get such ideas?'

'I'm only repeating what I've heard. The queen and her ladies don't know about the masquerade – the men are keeping it a secret.'

Christine knew better than to ask how Marion knew about it. She merely said, 'Those men are fools.'

'I know.' Marion held out a hand to help Christine up. 'Come. It's getting late, and you look ill. I'll walk home with you.' She took Christine's arm and led her firmly up the street. When they came to the secondhand clothes market by the cemetery of the Innocents, she stopped to peer at the gowns in one of the stalls. 'Nothing special there,' she sniffed. 'I'll wait until after the marriage ball.' Christine smiled, picturing Marion prancing around in a long blue velvet houppelande trimmed with gold, her red hair studded with beads and piled high on her head in imitation of the enormous jeweled hairdos so popular with the queen and her ladies.

They walked on, Marion musing about the masquerade all the way to Christine's street. 'You won't be invited to the ball, Lady Christine, so you won't be there to see the demons,' she said as she turned to go back home. 'But I think something very bad is going to happen, and we'll all be affected, one way or another.'

Nine

In those days were burned in Paris many mandrakes that had been safeguarded in secret places by foolish people who had faith in such rubbish, firmly believing that as long as they kept them neatly clothed in fine silk or linen, they would never be poor.

*Journal d'un Bourgeois de
Paris, 1405–1449*

Several days later, Colin arrived at Christine's house early in the morning with a message from the queen summoning her back to the palace. This time she put on the linen headdress she disliked, hoping it would stay in place, gathered together her writing materials and stuffed them into her pouch along with some egg-and-chestnut rissoles wrapped in one of her mother's dish-cloths – she planned not to be home in time for dinner – and left the house with Colin quickly, ignoring Francesca's protests.

It was a sunny day, and the streets were crowded with women out to do their marketing, merchants, couriers, and noblemen hurrying to and from the palace, and street vendors offering their wares. The scrawny man with the meat pasties was in his usual place, and Colin looked with longing at his basket. Christine bought two pasties and gave him one. He gulped it down, then asked, 'Aren't you afraid to go back to the palace? The last time you went there you found a body.'

She was tempted to tell him she wasn't worried, but that would have been a lie, so she merely shrugged and walked on.

In the courtyard of the queen's residence, Renaut was standing beside the lion fountain. 'Will you talk to the stone lion today?' he asked. In the distance, one of the king's lions roared. The boy bounced up and down with excitement. 'You could go and talk to them instead,' he said, giggling so hard his red cap flew off and his tawny hair swirled around his face.

Simon, who'd stepped out into the courtyard, laughed. 'He thinks you're very brave.'

Colin hovered around, whistling softly, and Simon laughed again. 'On the other hand, Colin thinks you might need him to accompany you past the place where you found the body.'

Christine shook her head and went into the palace alone. Nevertheless, she was glad the guards were back at their posts in the great gallery. The chest had been returned to its normal place, but there were bloodstains on the floor, awakening memories of rigid fingers, bare feet, and sightless eyes. She walked past quickly and came to the entrance to the room where she'd seen the king and his brother the day of the murder. Standing there were Alix de Clairy and her husband, Hugues de Précy. Alix, wearing a mantle of dark-blue velvet over a sea-green houppelande with a gold belt, carried a cumbersome black leather pouch instead of the velvet sack with her harp. The black pouch seemed out of place, but she looked elegant, nevertheless. On the other hand, Hugues, who had a reputation for having affairs with women at the court and was excessively vain, fit perfectly Christine's idea of a fop. That day he wore a cap with long turquoise feathers, a short russet-colored tunic, skin-tight hose – one leg blue, the other red – and the foot-long poulaines that were the latest fashion in shoes. When Alix touched his arm gently, he brushed her hand away and swaggered into the room, removing his cap and running his hands through his tawny curls. He was limping, and Christine thought it was because he was

60

unable to keep the excessively long points of his shoes from crossing.

Alix looking sadly after her husband. Christine went to stand beside her, and said, 'I looked for you, after we found the man who was stabbed.'

Alix turned to her. 'It was horrible. I had to leave.'

'Did you know who the man was?'

'No, no.' Alix shifted the black pouch from one hand to the other, and said quickly, 'Are you going to the queen's chambers? If so, I'll come with you.' Christine nodded, and they walked on. Before Christine could ask any more questions about the murdered man, Alix changed the subject.

'How did you come to be a scribe?'

'There is little to tell. My husband died, and it became necessary for me to support my family.' She hoped she would not have to justify her profession to this young woman who could know nothing of the trials of a widow. At sixteen, she herself could not have foreseen the difficulties she would one day face: the long hours spent in the law courts attempting to obtain what was owed her from her husband's estate, the greed and dishonesty of the people who stole money she had invested with them, the disdain of those who shunned her because she was a woman fighting for what was rightfully hers.

'Are there many women scribes?' Alix asked. Away from her husband, she seemed like a lively, curious child. She reminded Christine of Renaut.

'There are others.'

To Christine's surprise, Alix made none of the usual comments about a woman doing a man's work. Instead, she said, 'I envy you, going freely about the city. I would like to do that.'

'Would your husband approve?'

Alix looked away.

Christine wondered what was in the sack she carried, and where her harp was. 'I have heard you singing for the queen,' she said. 'I recognized one of your songs: the one you sang with the queen's dwarf.'

Alix smiled. 'I learned that song when I was a little girl. Do you know, I even sang it for the king, when he came to Amiens to be married. My father held a big banquet, and the king came and he asked me to sing. I thought it was splendid to sing for a king.'

Christine remembered that time. Étienne had gone with the king's entourage to Amiens. Was it possible he'd learned the song from Alix? It was an unusual song, not one he would have heard just anywhere. 'Do you remember any of the men who were with the king?' she asked.

'I was only eight. There were so many.'

'My husband was one of them. I'd like to think he learned that song from you,' Christine said.

They had come to an inner courtyard and Alix pointed to a glass-paned window through which they could see into a room of the palace. A bearded old man wearing a long purple robe sat there at a desk, engrossed in a large book. 'That's one of the king's physicians, looking for a cure for him,' Alix said. 'He's tried many things. I have something better.' She held up the black leather pouch. 'There's a mandrake root in here.'

Christine was appalled. Many people thought mandrake roots had mysterious powers, even her own father. Once, when she was a child, he'd showed her a picture of a hideous root in an herbal. She'd made a face. 'I know,' he'd said. 'The mandrake is not comely. And its juice is deadly poison. But it is a wondrous plant, *Cristina*, and you must not mock it. Doctors esteem it, because they know how to administer just the right amount of its juice to numb pain without killing the patient. And it has an even greater virtue.' He'd traced the outline of the root with his finger. 'Do you see how it is shaped like a man? That is because it houses a little spirit. The spirit can bring you luck, and it can drive away demons.' His voice – hushed, as if he were under a spell – had frightened her. From that moment, Christine had feared the mandrake. It seemed an evil omen that Alix de Clairy had carried one into the palace.

'Where did you get it?' she asked.

'My old nursemaid gave it to me.'

'There are many herbs that might benefit the king. Surely the doctors have tried them.'

'Assuredly. They give him potions of vervain, motherwort, and thyme, and they tie herbs around his head. None of it does any good.'

'Neither will what you have in your pouch. In truth, it may do the king harm. Do you truly believe there's a spirit in the mandrake that can cure his affliction?'

'I don't know. But if the queen believes it, she'll be happier.'

'That may be, but mandrakes contain deadly poison. People may misunderstand your intentions.'

Alix smiled and adjusted the gold cord that closed her blue mantle. 'The queen knows I want to help.'

'What about her ladies?'

'I have no concern for what they think.'

They came to a gallery where one of the walls was covered with a painting of a garden. Under a blue sky filled with billowy white clouds, children played, gathering flowers and climbing fruit trees to pick crimson apples and golden pears. Alix reached out to them, as if she longed to join in their fun. Christine was reminded of a picture she'd seen in an illuminated Book of Hours, a rose arbor where the Virgin Mary sat surrounded by angels with harps, all busy making music – all except for one mischievous angel who was picking a red rose. *Alix is like that little imp,* she thought. *She doesn't realize the court is a perilous place where it's not wise to ignore the rules.*

Feeling the need to protect the young woman, she took her arm and held it tightly as they walked across a courtyard, through a doorway decorated with a frieze of dragons and centaurs, up a winding staircase, and along a tapestried hallway to the queen's apartments.

In the queen's bedchamber, the air was warm and heavy with the smell of rose water, lavender, candle wax, and wood smoke. Queen Isabeau sat on a low-backed chair beside her fireplace, wearing a houppelande of blue silk damask shot through with silver threads that glistened in the light of the flames. From the corners of the room, braziers with burning coals added more heat, but even that was not enough for the queen, who cupped her hands around a hollow gold ball filled with hot cinders. As she stood in the doorway with Alix de Clairy, Christine watched a chambermaid dress the queen's hair, twisting the long black strands around balls of cloth, fastening them with jeweled pins, and arranging them over her ears like horns. The woman held the pins between her lips – something Francesca had advised Christine never to do – and from time to time she plucked one from her mouth and jabbed it into one of the horns. Another chambermaid waited to crown the arrangement with a padded and jeweled circlet that resembled a bowl of fruit. The queen's dwarf, who wore a similar circlet, stood nearby, leaning against the queen's greyhound.

Her hairdo complete, the queen rose from the chair and went to recline on the red coverlet spread over her ceremonial bed. Catherine de Fastavarin, perched on her large blue cushion, spoke to her excitedly in German; Christine supposed they were discussing the wedding. The other ladies-in-waiting stood idly by, and Christine thought that with their brightly colored gowns, whitened faces, and reddened cheeks and lips, they resembled exotic flowers, exuding cloying perfume as they wilted in the over-heated room. Even the flames in the fireplace seemed listless. Only the greyhound was alert. He jumped up, nearly overturning the dwarf, trotted over to Christine, and thrust his cold, wet nose into her hand.

Alix removed her blue velvet mantle, handed it to a chambermaid, stepped into the room, smiled at the queen's dwarf, and knelt beside the queen. Christine, waiting to be summoned, stroked the dog's head and gazed at Queen Isabeau, reflecting that she did not look like a queen. The daughter of a Bavarian duke and an Italian mother, she was shorter and darker than most of her ladies-in-waiting, and a little plump; she might, at first glance, have been mistaken for a child. But Christine knew her youthful appearance should not be mistaken for innocence. The queen was only twenty-two, but she was suffering. At fifteen, she'd been brought from Bavaria to marry the young French king. Now she had born five children – two of whom had died – and her husband was not in his right mind. *How lonely she must be*, Christine thought, *far from her homeland, speaking our language with difficulty*. She wondered whether Catherine might not be the only real friend Queen Isabeau had in Paris. The queen's other ladies-in-waiting, many of whom were much older than she was, seemed kindly enough, but they'd been chosen for her from the nobility at the French court, and, as far as Christine could tell, none of them conversed with her in German.

Madame de Malicorne, the lady-in-waiting in charge of the royal children, came into the room holding the queen's year-old baby. She knelt and placed the little prince in his mother's arms, then stepped back. The queen cooed and rocked her son gently. Catherine de Fastavarin moved away, a disdainful look on her long, aristocratic face. Christine wondered what her expression would be when she found herself surrounded by men dressed as hairy savages.

The seamstress, Blanche, came down the hallway. The last time Christine had seen her, the woman had been frantic and disheveled as she rushed to take Renaut away from the scene of the murder. Now she was herself again, in a neat brown cotte and a black hood, and she smelled pleasantly of cloves. She was carrying a rose-colored gown embroidered with silver leaves, no doubt made for one of the ladies to wear at Catherine's wedding ball. A chambermaid came to the doorway and took the gown, but Blanche hardly noticed; she was looking into the room and staring at Alix.

The chambermaid came back, took Christine's cloak, and indicated that she should approach the ceremonial bed. Christine adjusted her linen headdress, touched the pockmark on her cheek, went into the room, and knelt. The queen hardly noticed her at first; she was playing with the little prince. But Christine was sure her shrewd, black eyes missed nothing. As though she could read her mind, the queen looked up.

'The copying, it is going well?' she asked in her thick German accent.

'Yes, *Madame*. I am sorry it will not be done in time for the wedding.'

The queen smiled reassuringly and indicated that she should rise. Christine went to a small adjoining room where a desk had been set up for her. Mademoiselle de Villiers, the lady-in-waiting who cared for the queen's large collection of books, came into the room and placed an illustrated *Life of Saint Catherine of Alexandria* in front of her. Christine thought the little volume, one of the queen's favorites, an interesting wedding gift for Catherine de Fastavarin, who might have been named after the saint. She enjoyed her work, taking pride in the columns of text she wrote around blank spaces an illuminator would later fill with miniature paintings of the saint's life and martyrdom. She could visualize those pictures, glowing in lustrous reds, blues, and greens, and touched with gold. The finished book would be – like the original – an exquisite jewel.

But she found it difficult to keep her mind on the copying. The room was cold and damp, her fingers were chilled, and she was hungry. She got up, added more logs to a fire that fidgeted and sputtered in a small fireplace, and ate the rissoles she'd brought in her pouch. Then she stood on the hearth, rubbing her hands together to warm them, and looked through the open door into the room where the queen and her ladies sat. What she saw sent a shiver down her spine.

The queen, holding her baby, reclined on her bed. Catherine de Fastavarin, cradling something in her hands, sat beside her, while the other ladies-in-waiting hovered around her, attracted to the object she held as moths are drawn to a flame. Alix stood apart, observing them calmly, but the greyhound and the dwarf were far from calm. The dog had retreated to a far corner of the room, where he half stood and half sat, whining and trembling. The dwarf, who had thrown her arms around him, held him tightly and spoke to him in a strange tongue as she tried to quiet him.

'This is a magic root. It has in it a spirit,' Catherine said. She held the mandrake high so everyone could get a good look at it. The ladies drew back, and one of them crossed herself.

'It's the elf, *"main de gloire,"*' someone said, using one of the names by which the mandrake was known in France. 'We must treat it with respect, or it will do us harm.'

Madame de Savoisy, the wife of the queen's *grand maître d'hôtel*, said, 'Perhaps it is not necessary to believe all the things one hears about the mandrake.'

Mademoiselle de Villiers and Madame de Malicorne said they agreed, but Catherine ignored them. She looked at the queen and said, 'This is *Alraun*,' emphasizing the German name for the mandrake, but speaking in French so all the ladies would understand.

The queen clutched her baby to her breast.

'You must not be frightened, *Liebling. Alraun* has grown under a gallows, and he knows how to help you. He will cure the king. But first we must do certain things for him.' Catherine leaned over and adjusted the pillows on the queen's bed. 'Listen carefully.'

She held the queen's hand, but looked at the other ladies, as she said, 'We must prepare for him a bath of the finest wine and carefully wash him in it.' The ladies moved closer.

69

'When he is bathed,' Catherine continued, 'we will bake him in an oven, and then we will dress him in silk.'

The ladies stepped even closer.

'But most important is this,' Catherine said. 'Once *alraun* has been made ready, we will bring to him communion bread. Then we will take him to the king, and he will give back to the king his proper mind.'

Christine expected the ladies to object to the sacrilege, but no one did. They stood immobile and silent, as if under a spell.

Catherine held the mandrake over Alix's head and shook it. 'The little spirit might help you, too. It might help you have your husband's love.'

Alix grew pale, but said nothing.

Catherine rose. 'I must go to the seamstress. She will prepare clothes for the little gallows man.' She laid the root on a cushioned stool at the foot of the queen's bed and left the room, nearly colliding with Blanche, who was standing at the door.

'Come with me,' Catherine said, and the two women disappeared down the hallway.

The queen relaxed her grip on the baby, and the little prince, who was usually quiet – unnaturally so, Christine thought – struggled out of her arms and crawled to the end of the bed. Suddenly, he leaned over and reached for the mandrake. Madame de Malicorne grabbed him and lifted him high into the air. The queen gave a little cry, jumped up, snatched the baby, and fell back onto the bed. The ladies-in-waiting fluttered around her, uttering frightened cries that mingled with howls from the dog in the corner.

Christine thought the ladies might realize how foolish Catherine's words had been, but instead, they stood around discussing her instructions. They were too preoccupied to notice her, so she tiptoed into the room and stood by the stool and looked at the mandrake. It was like a parsnip, but larger, and it was black and hairy and shaped like a wrinkled little man, with a knob bent to one side for a head and something resembling a tail dangling obscenely between leg-like append-ages. She told herself it was only a root, but she couldn't help feeling it exuded evil. She could almost understand why Catherine de Fastavarin believed it had magical powers.

Catherine came back. As she went to the queen's bedside, she passed Christine and indi-cated with a toss of her head that she should return to her copying. Christine turned to go and found Alix standing beside her. Christine said to her, 'The mandrake will cause trouble.'

Catherine heard, and she glared at Christine. 'You are wrong,' she said. 'The mandrake will cure the king.'

'I do not believe any good can come of such beliefs,' Christine said. Catherine glowered at her, and the hostility of the other ladies-in-waiting was palpable. When Christine returned to her copying, she found it impossible to concentrate. She went to the doorway and watched the women: the queen propped up against her pillows, like a limp doll; Catherine de Fastavarin sitting beside her, gently stroking her forehead; the other ladies-in-waiting gathered around, whispering together; the dwarf comforting the cowering dog in the corner; and Alix de Clairy, standing alone by the fireplace, staring into the trembling flames.

Ten

Women at the court should be more honest, more courteous, and have better manners than other people.

Christine de Pizan, *Le Livre des Trois Vertus*, 1405

Later that afternoon, Christine, having completed her work for the day, rose from the desk and looked into the other room. She found the scene oppressive – the queen and her ladies, encased in ornate, burdensome garments; the red coverlet spreading over the queen's ceremonial bed like a pool of blood; the heavy tapestries shrouding the walls; the thick carpets covering the floor, smothering any sound. These were somber surroundings for Alix de Clairy, who stood to one side in her sea-green dress. The young woman looked troubled, and Christine hoped it was because she regretted having brought the mandrake.

The disgusting root, not yet dressed in silk, still lay on the stool at the foot of the bed, and the ladies-in-waiting glanced at it uneasily from time to time. As she looked at the women, Christine wondered how they could be so foolish as to believe the mandrake had magical powers to heal the king. *What would the men at the court think*, she wondered, and then she had to laugh to herself; the king and his friends had an even more foolish plan – a masquerade to drive the king's demons away.

The queen beckoned, and Christine went to kneel beside her. 'There is still more to copy, *Madame*,' she said. The queen nodded and indicated that her scribe was dismissed. Christine retrieved her cloak from a chambermaid and left quickly, glad to escape from the sinister little 'man' lying on the stool at the foot of the queen's bed.

As she went out the door, she felt a hand on her arm and looked around to find an old lady in a simple black cotte and wimple, leaning on a crutch. She recognized the Duchess of Orléans, the king's great aunt by marriage, and she felt like a child again, for when she and her family had lived at the Hôtel Saint-Pol she had often been chastised by this imperious personage for wrongdoings she didn't even know she had committed.

The duchess motioned for her to follow her. Walking slowly and painfully, she led her across the entrance courtyard, through courtyards and cloisters, up steep stairs, and along narrow passageways and dark corridors in a part of the palace Christine had never seen before, until they came to a room very different from the queen's chambers – only a few tapestries and cushions, thin rugs on the floor, a plain wooden bed with no canopy. The duchess sat down on a wooden chair by a small fireplace where a few flames fluttered against a lone, charred log, laid her crutch on the floor, and motioned toward a small bench. Christine brought the bench up to the fire and perched on it gingerly, hoping the old woman was not about to scold her for something.

The Duchess of Orléans was sixty-five, and with her heavy-lidded eyes and sallow skin stretched over sunken cheeks, she looked even older. Her face was ghostly in the flickering light of the dying flames. She leaned forward and grasped Christine's hands, imprisoning them with her cold fingers. Christine could feel her sour breath on her cheek and see the network of tiny lines covering her face as if spiders had been at work there. She pulled her hands away and drew them into the folds of her cloak. *She's going to treat me as if I were still a little girl,* she thought.

'I am told you discovered the murdered man in the great gallery. Were you not afraid to return here after such an experience?'

Christine shook her head.

'I admire your courage.'

'I must earn my living, *Madame.*'

'So I understand. That is why I have brought you here. I have work for you.' The duchess pointed to a desk in the corner of the room. On it lay a pile of manuscript pages. 'Bring those to me.'

Christine went to the table and picked up the

74

pages. She started to place them in the duchess's lap, but the old woman waved her back to her seat on the bench.

'Those are for you. I want you to copy them.'

Christine folded her hands over the pages, noticing with satisfaction that there were a great many of them. She would have plenty of work for a while.

The duchess said, 'As you probably know, I have for some time occupied myself with matters of morals and etiquette here at the court.'

I certainly do know, Christine thought, remembering her childhood.

'I am old and ill,' the duchess continued. 'Soon I will not be here to give advice. So I think what you have there may be beneficial when I am gone. It was written for a young wife, to teach her how to run a household and conduct herself properly. It might be useful for other ladies, including some of the queen's ladies-in-waiting. I have observed that they do not always act wisely.'

Christine couldn't resist smiling.

The duchess noticed her smile and added quickly, 'There are many women here in service to the king and queen. They can always use some advice. There are even a number of recipes the cooks might use.

'I understand, *Madame*. I accept the work gladly.'

'You will be well compensated.'

Christine placed the pages in her large leather pouch, knelt, and left. With difficulty, she found her way through all the unfamiliar corridors and passageways back to the great gallery, where courtiers, royal officials, and commoners milled around, talking in hushed voices. She wondered whether any of them remembered that a man had been murdered in that gallery the week before. *Would they be concerned,* she asked herself, *if they knew that in another part of the palace the queen and her ladies were under the spell of a diabolical root?*

They all grew silent as the king came in, accompanied by the Duke of Orléans and Hugues de Précy. The duke had his arm around his brother's shoulder, and the king seemed calm, but Christine, like everyone else, knew his composure could be short lived. She remembered Marion's prediction that something dreadful would happen at the wedding ball.

As she turned to leave, she nearly collided with Blanche, who was standing in the shadows, staring at Hugues. The seamstress greeted her with a little wave of her hand, then moved away toward the palace entrance. She wore her cloak, and Christine hoped she was going to take Renaut home: it was late and the boy would surely be cold and hungry.

Colin sauntered up to Christine and announced that he would walk home with her if she would wait while he ran an errand. She was glad to have someone to accompany her through the dark streets, so she agreed. But she found the smoke-filled air in the gallery suffocating, and she went out into the entrance courtyard. Simon was there, watching Blanche and Renaut leave.

'Where do they live?' she asked.

'On the other side of the river, on the rue de

la Harpe. It's about time she took the boy home. He's been here all day.'

Colin reappeared, and they walked toward Christine's street, the boy prattling all the while about the murder the week before and how he wished he'd been the one to discover the body and how much blood there had been. She was relieved when they arrived at her house and he turned back toward the palace.

Francesca stood outside the door, shivering in the cold, so lost in thoughts of possible misfortunes, she didn't even notice Christine coming down the street.

'What are you doing out here, Mama?'

Francesca snapped out of her reverie. 'I am waiting for you. The streets are full of murderers and thieves.' She took her daughter's arm and hurried her into the house, where they were met by the children, holding lighted tapers, at the foot of the stairs.

'Where were you, Mama?' Jean asked. 'We were worried, it's so late.'

'Georgette's brother walked home with me.'

'He's not very big!' Jean protested. 'How could he protect you?'

The other children moved closer and put their arms around her. She gave them all a hug and sent them up to bed.

In the kitchen, Francesca told Georgette to bring Christine bread, a goblet of wine, and a bowl of warmed-up mutton stew. She gave Goblin a piece of the mutton before asking, 'Why did you stay so late at the palace?'

'The Duchess of Orléans gave me something to copy,' Christine said, taking the pages out of her pouch and placing them on the table.

'Who wrote it?'

Christine looked at the first page. 'It seems to be by an elderly man, for his young wife. The duchess said it has to do with proper conduct and housekeeping. I'm surprised she gave the work to me. I thought she didn't like me. Do you remember how she used to scold me?'

'That was many years ago. She treated everyone that way – even your father.'

'The duchess is a good person,' interjected Georgette, who stood listening at the door to the pantry. 'Colin told me. She's given all her money to poor people.'

Christine had heard that. Despite her childhood memories of the duchess, she knew the woman had a reputation for good works.

Georgette walked to the table and leaned over Christine's shoulder, trying to see the manuscript pages.

'Why are you looking?' Francesca asked. 'You cannot read.'

'Neither can you,' the girl said under her breath.

'It's time for you to go home, Georgette,' Christine said.

Georgette skulked out of the kitchen. The front door slammed. Francesca pointed to the pages Christine was holding. 'Tell me what is written there.'

Christine put the pages on the table. It was dark now, but she could read by the light of the fireplace. 'The man tells his wife how to dress modestly, live chastely, say her prayers, conduct herself in church – things like that.'

'Poor little wife.' Francesca said. 'A husband who preaches!'

'Then comes advice for taking care of the house. And lots of recipes.'

'Are any of them for pasta?'

'No. But many kinds of sauces.'

'*Poh!* The French use too many sauces.'

'Ah! Here's something you know about, Mama. How to cure a toothache by adding sage to boiling water and breathing the steam.'

'The old man probably got a toothache because he threw bones into the fire.'

'That's one of your foolish beliefs I hadn't heard before.'

Christine knew her mother would go on about aliments and superstitions unless she changed the subject. She said, 'Tomorrow there will be a banquet and a ball at the palace.'

Francesca leaned over the table toward her. 'A banquet and a ball? Who are they for?'

'The queen's favorite lady-in-waiting, Catherine de Fastavarin. She's getting married again.'

'*Scandaloso!* That woman has buried two husbands. Now there will be a third. And a party, too.' Francesca sighed.

'The queen is giving her ladies new gowns.'

'They will have new hairdos, too, and new padded circlets, with lots of jewels. Their heads will be so big they will not be able to go through the doorways.' She sighed again.

Christine got up, went around the table, and stood behind her mother with her hands on her shoulders. 'You miss the parties at the palace, don't you, Mama.'

Francesca leaned her cheek against Christine's hand. 'I do. But it is dangerous to go to the palace now. I wish you would not go there, *Cristina*.'

'Please don't start that again. Tell me what else you remember about the parties.'

'They were splendid. There were singers and musicians – pipers, drummers, *trombe* – what's the word?'

'Trumpets.'

'That's right, trumpeters. And bagpipes.' She made a face. 'Up in the air.' Francesca looked up, as if she could see the players on the musicians' balcony. 'And down below there were acrobats, walking on their hands. Tumblers bending over backwards, their heads almost touching the ground. And jugglers, with plates on their finger-tips and knives on their chins. Once there was a little white dog that jumped through a hoop. He had a crooked tail, just like Goblin.'

At the mention of his name, Goblin, who'd been lying under the table, stood up and gazed at Francesca. She gave him another piece of mutton.

'I'm sure this party will be just as splendid,' Christine said. 'The queen always provides the best of everything for her favorite lady-in-waiting.'

Lost in her memories, Francesca continued. 'Tapestries covering the walls to keep the room warm. Tablecloths as white as snow. Saltcellars shaped like lions and dragons and ships. Gold and silver dishes on a sideboard, polished so you could see your face in them.'

'I pity the servants who had to do all the polishing,' Christine said.

Francesca went on as if she hadn't heard. 'Masked dancers disguised as birds.'

'There will be another kind of disguise at Catherine's ball,' Christine said. 'The king and some of his friends will be dressed up like hairy wild men.'

'*Mio Dio!* A masquerade!' Francesca cried. She sprang up from the bench, nearly knocking it over, and stood facing Christine with alarm in her eyes. Goblin began to bark, and she lifted him into her arms, clutching him so tightly to her chest that he yelped. 'Have the people at the court lost their minds along with the king?'

'I think perhaps they have.'

Francesca sat down heavily on the bench, and Christine decided to say nothing more about the masquerade. The room became very quiet. The fire crackled as burning logs settled into a bed of ashes, shadows on the wall took on ghostly shapes, and somewhere in the night, a dog howled. Francesca shuddered and put her hands over her ears. 'There's evil nearby,' she whispered.

Christine shivered, even though she didn't believe in such things. She sat down on the bench beside her mother and put her arms around her.

'The masquerade must be part of the evil,' Francesca wailed. 'It will bring more disaster – for the king, for everyone at the palace, and for us, too.'

'That can't be true,' Christine said. She went to the hearth to get her mother a beaker of the licorice, fig, and barley water tisane, hoping that would calm her. But when she went back to the table, her mother had disappeared. She saw a faint light moving around in the pantry, and heard grumbling as Francesca tripped over something. After a while, a dark shape came back into the kitchen, holding a small dish. Christine knew what was coming; she resigned herself and settled down on the bench. It would take time, and she was tired, but she couldn't leave her mother alone when she was so agitated.

A pot of water sat on the hearth, and Francesca ladled some of this into a bowl. Then she sat on the bench, dipped a finger into the dish, and let a drop of oil fall into the water. She repeated this action again and again, waiting a long time for each new drop to settle. Finally, she sighed and pushed the bowl to one side.

'It is the evil eye, *Cristina*. You know what that means.'

'That's absurd, Mama. There's no such thing as the evil eye.'

'It *is* the evil eye, *Cristina*. Someone must have cast it upon you, when you went to the palace.' She wrung her hands. 'It is because of the masquerade. The masquerade is the devil's work.' She got up and stood in front of her daughter. 'This evil has already affected you, *Cristina*. Soon it will affect everyone.'

Christine threw up her hands.

But Francesca persisted. 'Cannot the queen do something to stop it?'

'The queen hasn't been told. Her ladies don't know, either. It will be an unpleasant surprise for them.'

Francesca looked at her daughter suspiciously. 'If the queen and her ladies have not been told, how do you know?'

Christine picked up a taper and lit it against one of the logs in the fireplace. 'It's very late and I must go to bed now,' she said as she started out the door. She wasn't about to tell her mother she'd been talking to Marion.

Eleven

Among the ladies-in-waiting who served the queen, there was one named Catherine who enjoyed particular favor. The queen loved her dearly, because she was German and spoke German as she did. The king decided to marry this lady to a rich German lord, and to stage an event of unparalleled magnificence and liberality . . . Alas, no one knew that the festivities would end in a horrible tragedy.

The Monk of Saint-Denis,
Chronique du Religieux de Saint-Denis, contenant le règne de Charles VI de 1380 à 1422

When Christine woke the next morning, it was nearly sext, and she could hear her mother in

83

the kitchen preparing the midday meal. She wanted to stay home and rest, but it was Catherine de Fastavarin's wedding day, and she needed to finish the wedding present. The illuminations would have to be added later, but at least the text would be ready. She dressed, grabbed a few rissoles, and told her mother she'd probably be home very late.

'I'll find someone bigger than Colin to walk home with me,' she assured her.

As she walked slowly down the street, she met her children coming home for dinner. '*Eccola*,' Thomas cried as he saw her.

'Yes, I'm here,' she said, laughing as she took him in her arms.

Marie said, 'You look tired. You should stay home and rest.'

Jean took his mother's hand and stroked it, as if to say he understood why she had to go on with her work.

Her steps were lighter as she continued on her way to the palace.

In the royal bedroom, the queen sat holding her baby while her ladies-in-waiting, attended by a host of dressmakers and seamstresses, paraded around in their new finery. The room was awash in color and light: long, trailing gowns of scarlet, violet-blue, rose-red, olive green, and azure, belts with buckles of glittering gold and silver, necklaces of rubies, diamonds, and emeralds. It was all a blur to Christine. She tried to slip through the crowd unnoticed, nearly tripping over the queen's dwarf, who sat on the floor in the center of the room. A hand reached out to steady her, and she was startled to find it belonged to Blanche.

'You look very tired, mistress,' the seamstress said.

'So I am,' Christine said, remembering Marie had said the same thing.

'This will help,' Blanche said as she handed her a sliver of licorice root.

The smell of the licorice reminded Christine of her mother's tisanes, but she thanked the seamstress and hurried to the room where she did her copying.

Although she had difficulty concentrating, she was able to work steadily for a while. But the copying went more and more slowly as the effects of having stayed up so late the night before took their toll. She ate the rissoles she'd brought, and they made her even sleepier. There was a small bed in one corner of the room, and she crept over to it and lay down, thinking she would take a brief nap. When she woke, it was dark.

She sat up and looked around. She had no idea how long she'd slept, but she knew it was late, because there were lighted candles in the queen's bedchamber, although no one was there. *They've all gone to the wedding banquet*, she thought. Then she heard loud music in the distance; the ball had started. She stood up, walked into the queen's bedchamber, and took one of the candles from its gilded holder. Holding it carefully in front of her, she stole out of the room and started down the deserted hallway. Some of the buildings at the Hôtel Saint-Pol were connected, and when she came to a passageway that seemed to lead in the direction of the music, she followed it. She had no idea where she was going, but her way was lit by torches that sat in brackets on the walls, and she was not afraid – until the music suddenly stopped, and other, terrifying, sounds replaced it.

She turned a corner and came to a gallery with an elaborately carved balustrade on one side. Through the openings in the balustrade she could see across a wide space to a musicians' balcony. The musicians weren't playing. They'd dropped their shawms, sackbuts, clarions, and trumpets, and they were leaning far out over the railing of the balcony, looking down into a hall below, shouting and gesturing, their faces glowing in a fitful light.

She stepped up on one of the balustrade's lower railings and peered down through an opening. She couldn't believe what she saw. The center of the hall was on fire. Flames crawled along the floor and leapt up toward the ceiling, and inside the flames were shapes, shapes that fell to the floor, rolled around, jumped up, and lurched from side to side. The shapes were men, five writhing men imprisoned in hairy costumes, screaming in agony and tearing at themselves as flames consumed them. The men who had dressed up to look like wild men of the forest were burning alive.

Christine closed her eyes. The screams rang in her ears. The smell of burning flesh choked her. She lost her footing, slipped off the railing, caught herself, and climbed back up, clutching the balustrade with clammy hands. She looked again at the scene below and saw sheets of fire stripping away the masqueraders' costumes. She saw hot pitch pouring down naked bodies, peeling away the skin. She saw blood and charred flesh covering the floor. She saw bystanders darting toward the burning men and jumping back to avoid the flames. Jewels in headdresses, necklaces, and belts flashed. Gold plates, goblets, and ewers tumbled from a sideboard. Tapestries caught sparks and went up in flames. Servants hurried to put out what fires they could, but they were helpless to save the men doing a grotesque dance of death in the center of the room.

Christine cried out when she saw one of the burning men break away from the others and race to a passageway next to the hall. He jumped into a large barrel of water that had been set up there for washing dishes, then climbed out, naked but free of the flames. Christine remembered that the king was to have been one of the wild men, and she felt the blood rush to her face as she stared at the saved man, hoping it was the king. But it was someone else.

She looked back at the center of the room and saw the king's brother standing near the flaming men with lighted torches in his hands and an expression of anguish on his face. Behind him, on a dais, the queen lay back in a faint, with her ladies gathered around her, wailing and wringing their hands.

Below the dais sat a group of noblewomen. One of them wore a voluminous blue-and-gold gown, and Christine was astonished to see a hairy head emerge from the folds. With a start, she realized there had been a sixth wild man, and he'd been saved, because the young woman had thrown the train of her gown over him to put out the flames. The man looked around, dazed and seemingly unable to comprehend what was happening. Christine couldn't see his face, it was so covered with soot, but she prayed it was the king.

The acrobats, jugglers, and tumblers who'd entertained the guests earlier in the evening stood huddled together at the back of the room. One of them held a small white dog that jumped out of his arms and raced around the room in such a frenzy that he got too close to a burning tapestry. A spark fell onto his fur, flames sprang up, and he, too, was consumed, howling as his little body was charred beyond recognition.

Christine turned and ran back along the gallery, sobbing and stumbling and reaching out to support herself against the tapestried wall. Somehow she found her way back to the queen's chambers, where she had just enough presence of mind to retrieve her cloak and her writing materials before she rushed out of the palace.

In the courtyard, people were running toward the street, frantic to get away from the fire. She covered her face with her cloak and ran with them. It was a clear, cold night, and a full moon lit her way as she raced toward home. News of what was happening at the palace had preceded her, and the streets were clogged with groups of people talking excitedly. She hoped her mother was not among them. Or standing at the door of their house, waiting for her. But Francesca was in the kitchen, asleep on a bench, her head on the table. Christine pulled her to her feet, half carried her up to her room, and laid her gently on her bed. Then she staggered to her own room, fell to the floor, and wept. The full horror of what she had seen descended on her like a shroud. She longed to go in to her mother, wake her, and ask her to comfort her.

But if there was anything she knew for certain, it was that she would never tell her mother, or anyone else, that she had been at the palace that night.

Twelve

Don't let your maidservants swear or speak coarse, lewd words.

From a book of moral and practical advice for a young wife, Paris, 1393

It was dawn when Christine finally got to sleep, and she was almost immediately wakened by Georgette, who rushed into the house shouting incoherently. She heard Francesca and the children and Goblin go pounding down the stairs, but she didn't follow. She knew what Georgette was going to tell them. She covered her head with the bedclothes and tried not to listen to the excited voices below, until she realized from her mother's impatient outcries that the girl was being more exasperating than usual. She stumbled out of bed, pulled on her chemise, tiptoed down the stairs, and peered into the kitchen.

Georgette stood babbling in the center of the room, her eyes wide with terror. Everyone crowded around, trying unsuccessfully to calm her. Finally Francesca pushed the children away, took the girl by the shoulders, and eased her down onto a bench. '*Piano, piano,*' she said. 'Speak so we can understand.'

'Colin told me. It's the devil's work.' Georgette was so short of breath she could hardly utter the words.

Francesca went to the pantry, filled a goblet with wine, and made the girl drink it. She choked on the first swallow, coughed, spat wine out onto the floor, and then drained the goblet in noisy gulps. Finally she managed to say, 'Last night at the ball. Colin was hiding behind the door. He saw it.'

'Saw what?' Francesca asked impatiently.

'The wild men.'

'The masquerade!' Francesca cried.

'They burned to death.'

'*Madonna!*'

Christine crept back up the stairs, hid under the covers again – until she heard Thomas shouting, 'The king! The king is dead!'

She jumped up.

'No,' Georgette said. 'The Duchess of Berry threw her skirts over him and put out the flames.'

'*Grazie a Dio!*' Francesca said.

Christine stepped into the kitchen again just as Georgette became calm enough to tell about the man who had dived into the vat of water. Then she became agitated as she told about the four other men, one of whom had died on the spot. 'Three of them are still alive, but not for long,' the girl wailed. 'They're at the palace, and everyone has to listen to them screaming.'

'Enough!' Christine cried, and they all turned to look at her. They'd been so engrossed in Georgette's story, they hadn't seen her come in.

'But there's more,' Georgette announced. 'That handsome knight Hugues de Précy is dead too, and he wasn't even at the masquerade. They found him lying in the street outside the palace. He'd been poisoned.

Christine gasped. 'When was he murdered?'

'Just before all the people ran out of the palace, running away from the fire.'

'A knight! Poisoned! Who would do such a thing?' Francesca asked.

'His wife,' Georgette said. 'She was lying right there beside him, with the flask she'd brought the poison in under her hand.'

When Georgette was more composed, Francesca sent her out to learn what was being said in the streets. Soon she returned. 'I met my friends. They told me men went to the palace and tried to break the doors down. They wanted to kill the Duke of Orléans, because they thought the king was dead, and that it was his fault, because he brought lighted torches into the room where they were having the masquerade. Then the king came out and showed them he was alive, so they went away. But it's dangerous out there – people are angry. The king could have died.'

'What do they say about Hugues de Précy?' Christine asked.

'Poor man. They've arrested his wife. God's bones, she must be an evil woman.'

'Georgette!' Francesca cried. 'I will not allow a servant of mine to take the Lord's name in vain!' She was about to give the girl a slap, but Georgette dodged the blow, sniffling and wiping her eyes with the back of her hand.

'Don't cry,' Christine said. 'Tell us what else you've heard.'

'They say the queen is very angry. She liked the wife, and now she's sorry she was so kind to her. But mostly everyone's talking about the fire. The king and his brother and his uncles are making a procession of repentance to the cathedral.'

'They have no concern for those unfortunate men who burned,' Francesca said. 'But they must pretend.' She went into the hall and came back with two cloaks. 'It will be a great spectacle. We will go and see, *Cristina*. You will stay here with the children, Georgette.'

And so it was that Christine and her mother and hundreds of other Parisians stood in the cold and watched as the king, dressed in black and riding a black stallion, approached the cathedral. The horse danced along the street, drops of bloody foam flying from his mouth as he strained at the bit, trying to pull away from two grooms who held his bridle. The king, oblivious to everything, slumped in the saddle and looked at the ground, while his uncles limped along behind him, barefoot to show they were penitent. The crowd watched in silence until the Duke of Orléans appeared. Then someone shouted, 'Devil's scum!' and others took up the cry. Francesca joined in, adding her own cry, *'Diavolo! Diavolo!'* She shook a fist at the duke as he passed. Everyone thought the fire was his fault. Christine didn't want to believe he'd intended to harm his brother, but she wasn't sure. She remembered the agonized look on his face as he watched the burning men. She also remembered the lighted torches he'd held.

The king stumbled as he dismounted. He seemed truly distraught. His uncles, however, looked cold and in a hurry to be done with the performance. Christine took her mother's arm and led her away. 'We're going home,' she said. 'I have no patience for this.'

At the house, they found the children in the kitchen with Georgette. They hadn't finished dressing, because there was no school that day, and they crowded around the girl, hanging on every word as she regaled them with details Colin had provided about the fire. Then she told them what she'd heard about Hugues de Précy. 'His eyes were hanging out. His lips and tongue were all swollen. There was vomit everywhere.' The children's eyes sparkled, and they moved closer to the girl.

'I don't think it's necessary for them to hear how he looked, Georgette,' Christine said.

'But it's important! Because his eyes and his

lips and his tongue were like that, the doctor knew what kind of poison it was, and that was the only way he could tell because there wasn't any more poison in the flask, and the stopper was gone, too, and Colin said the sergeants at the palace searched all over for it, and they couldn't find it.' Georgette said all this without pausing to catch her breath, so caught up in her story she was nearly unintelligible.

'I don't see what the stopper has to do with it,' Christine said.

'Never mind that,' said Francesca. She drew Georgette away from the children. 'Calm yourself, Georgette. You may now tell us what kind of poison the doctor said it was.'

'Wolfsbane,' Georgette announced as if she'd made the discovery herself.

'That is a bad plant.' Francesca tended a small garden behind the house, and she knew about herbs; she used them for cooking, and for the potions she administered to the children at the slightest hint of a cold or a stomachache. 'You can make a very bad poison from wolfsbane.'

'Everyone says the wife knows how to make poisons, because she's a witch,' Georgette announced.

'Why do they say she's a witch?' Christine asked.

'Because she brought the queen a mandrake.'

At the mention of the disgusting root, Christine shuddered. 'Where is Alix de Clairy now?' she asked.

'They've locked her up at the Châtelet.'

'The dungeon, the dungeon,' Thomas chanted when he heard the name of the notorious prison.

'They'll ask her a lot of questions, and then they'll burn her at the stake,' Georgette said, raising her hands over her head and flapping them to imitate flames.

'The dungeon, the dungeon, the lady's in the dungeon,' Thomas cried.

'That's enough!' Christine cried. Vexed by the mindless chant and irritated by all the talk of poison and witches and dungeons, she felt ready to lash out at everyone. But just then Goblin crept out from under the table where he'd been hiding to get away from the excitement, and she remembered a little white dog going up in flames. She remembered the burned men lying in agony at the palace. She thought of Alix de Clairy, imprisoned in the Châtelet, probably being tortured.

She drew Thomas to her and whispered, 'There's an old proverb that says, "It's better to let the foot flip than the tongue trip." Try to remember that when you're tempted to say foolish things.'

Then she swept out of the kitchen, pleased that, for once, she'd been able to control her temper.

Thirteen

To make a poison for killing a stag or a wild boar, take the root of wolfsbane, pound it in a mortar, put it in a sack or a small cloth, and squeeze out the juice. Put this juice in a dish in the sun, and keep it dry at night. When it is like thickened wax, put it in a tightly closed box. When you want to shoot an arrow, put some of it between the barbs and the iron socket, so the beast will be struck down when it hits and makes contact with the flesh.

From a book of moral and practical
advice for a young wife, Paris, 1393

Christine went upstairs, sat at her desk, and thought about the burned men. She'd learned their names from people in the street, and she realized that the man who had saved himself by jumping into a vat of water had been one of her husband's friends. She also recognized the name of Huguet de Guisay, the supposed instigator of the masquerade, who was still barely alive, lying in pain in the king's apartments at the Hôtel Saint-Pol, cursing everyone around him. Of the others she knew very little except that she had seen them in their moment of agony.

Then her thoughts turned to Alix de Clairy. She remembered her song, and how kind she had been to the dwarf. Surely she was not a murderess. The thought of the young woman locked away in a dungeon was so dreadful that she sprang to her feet, hitting her leg against the side of the desk and sending the pages the duchess had given her flying to the floor. As she gathered the leaves together, she remembered something she'd seen there, and she hunted through the manuscript until she found it: a page where the man told his wife how to extract juice from the root of wolfsbane and apply it to arrowheads to kill wild stags and boars.

She flew back down to the kitchen.

Francesca had a fish stew simmering over the fire, and she was making little tarts to cook in the gravy. Thomas and Lisabetta were poking their fingers into the dough, while Goblin sat under the table, waiting for scraps to fall.

'Tell me what you know about wolfsbane, Mama,' Christine said.

Francesca took a long-handled spoon, jabbed it into the stew, and stirred impatiently. 'Why do you want to know?'

'It's mentioned in the manuscript the duchess gave me to copy. Do you grow it in your garden?'

'Certainly not! I do not need to make poisons. Not like the young woman who murdered her husband.'

Georgette, who'd been out buying bread, ran in and held up the loaf triumphantly. Francesca snatched it out of her hand and squeezed it. 'This is not baked in the middle. Where did you get it?'

'The bread shop just on the other side of the old wall.' The girl shuffled her feet and looked at the floor. 'I was afraid to go all the way into the city. All those angry people.'

'*Cretina!* That baker is a criminal. Last week the other bakers pulled him through the street in a wheelbarrow, to show everyone what a bad man he is. They hung some of his bad bread around his neck.' She thrust the loaf back into the girl's hand. 'You must return this to that *cafone* and make

97

him return the money. And after you do that, go and buy another loaf at the shop on the rue des Rosiers. It is nearby, and that baker is honest.'

Thomas asked, 'Does she have to wear bread around her neck, too?' Lisabetta giggled.

Francesca raised her hand and stamped her foot, sending the children scuttling out of the kitchen, followed by Goblin with his crooked tail between his legs.

In tears, Georgette turned to go, but Francesca called her back and handed her a coin. 'From the honest baker you may buy for yourself one of those little white rolls you like.'

The girl wiped her eyes with her sleeve and went into the hall to put on her cloak again. The front door closed with a bang. Francesca made a face, returned to her tart dough, and began working it furiously.

Christine put her hand over her mother's to keep her still for a moment. 'Do you think a woman like Alix de Clairy could make poison from wolfsbane?'

Francesca pushed her hand away. 'You said the old man tells his wife how to do it.'

'Yes, but I can't believe he wants her to do it herself. He probably wants her to teach her servants.'

'He just wants to show how much he knows,' her mother sniffed, breaking off pieces of dough and shaping them into tarts.

'If you intended to poison someone, would you grow wolfsbane?'

Francesca threw down the dough. 'I would not. If there is a cut on your hand and the juice of the wolfsbane gets into it, you will die very quickly.'

'So where would you get some if you needed it?'

'Apothecaries sell it. Your midwife who thinks she is a doctor probably has it. There are old women in Paris who know how to make poisons.'

Christine ignored the remark about her midwife. But she couldn't help thinking of the old woman who'd given Alix de Clairy a mandrake – her nursemaid.

At dinner, Christine tried to turn the conversation away from the burned men and the lady in the dungeon, but to no avail. Thomas made Georgette repeat many times everything she'd heard from Colin about the men burning in their hairy costumes. Then he wanted to hear again all the details of how Hugues de Précy had looked as he lay dead in the street outside the palace. And after that, Jean assailed Francesca with questions about the poisonous qualities of wolfsbane, and Marie wanted to know where it grew so she could avoid going near it. Only Lisabetta, leaning against Jean, was quiet. Christine's head ached, and when she tried to savor the fish stew she'd watched her mother prepare that morning, the food seemed to stick in her throat. Tired of all the morbid chatter, she left the table and went up to her study to work on her copying.

But instead of working, she sat at her desk thinking about Hugues de Précy. Everyone seemed to believe his wife had poisoned him, and she had to admit she could understand why, since the flask had been under her hand. But she suspected there were many people at the court who would not be sorry Hugues de Précy was dead. She was trying to remember something she'd heard about Hugues when her thoughts were interrupted by Georgette, who staggered in with a pile of logs. Filthy apron askew and hair covered with bits of wood bark, she wobbled to the fireplace, dumped the logs onto the fire, and started out the door.

'Come back here,' Christine called after her.

Georgette turned and walked slowly to the desk.

'Do you really believe Alix de Clairy is a witch?' Christine asked.

'All my friends say so. And Colin knows, because he's always at the palace and he hears things.'

'Colin has a very long tongue! You and your friends would be wise to have compassion for the lady. She's no more a witch than you or I.'

'Only a witch would poison such a husband.'

'He was an adulterer. And he abused his wife.'

'But he was so handsome! Just last week, I saw him in the street, riding a black stallion. He wore a green jacket, pleated down the front, with padded shoulders and a fur collar. And he had a lovely hat with peacock feathers, blue and green, blowing in the wind. Like this.' The girl waved her hand over her head.

'While you were busy admiring his clothes, did you happen to notice his shoes?' The points of Hugues's poulaines had been so long,

Christine doubted he would have been able to mount a horse while wearing them, though she supposed he might have been vain enough to try.

Georgette, who didn't understand the question, looked puzzled.

'Never mind,' Christine said, making an effort to control her temper. 'Colin told you something about Hugues de Précy. I heard you and my mother gossiping about it the other day. What was it?'

'Hugues wrote love letters to one of the ladies at the court. I don't know which lady it was.'

'How did Colin know about it? Did he deliver the letters?'

'No. He never saw them.'

'So how did he know?'

'Georgette blushed and bounced up and down on her toes, trying not to look Christine in the eye. 'Somebody told him.'

'Who?'

The girl turned away and walked over to the fireplace. 'I'll put more logs on,' she said.

'The room is too warm already.' Christine had reached the limit of her patience with the girl. 'Listen to me, Georgette. Last week you dropped my mother's best saltcellar, the silver one shaped like a seashell.'

Georgette was about to cry. 'I did what you told me. I put it at the back of the cupboard so she wouldn't notice the dent. You promised not to say anything.'

'I'll keep the promise if you tell me how Colin learned about the love letters Hugues wrote.'

Georgette stared at her feet for a moment, then blurted out, 'It was the queen's brother, Ludwig. He wanted Colin to go to the lady's husband and tell on Hugues.'

Christine knew about Ludwig, who'd come to Paris several years earlier to be with his sister. A handsome man who dressed in the latest French fashions and was excessively proud of his beard, which he combed into two sharp points, he'd ingratiated himself with some of the king's advisers. Most people were wary of him, however, because he had a violent temper. It was well known that the queen gave him expensive jewelry and a great deal of money so he would stay in Paris.

'Do you know why Ludwig wanted to make difficulties for Hugues?'

'Hugues discovered something bad Ludwig had done. Colin knows what it was, but he won't tell anyone, not even me. Ludwig gave him a new knife so he'd keep the secret.'

Georgette shuffled her feet, twisted her hands together, and gave Christine a pleading look that said 'please don't ask me any more questions.' She was saved by Francesca, who called up the stairs for her.

Ludwig could have poisoned Hugues, Christine thought, to prevent him from revealing something he didn't want anyone to know. And then there was the husband of the woman who'd had a liaison with Hugues. Surely he would have wanted to rid himself of his rival. But since Alix de Clairy had been found with the flask, people assumed she was the poisoner. Her plight was made worse by the fact that she'd brought the queen a mandrake.

Christine shuddered as she thought about all the trouble caused by superstitions and belief in witchcraft. She remembered hearing one of the queen's ladies tell a pregnant chambermaid that if she had twins, it would prove there were two fathers. The poor girl had rushed from the room in tears, and she'd had a miscarriage the next day. Christine had longed to admonish the lady for repeating such a vile superstition, but she knew it would have done no good.

All afternoon, she thought about the murder, and about Alix de Clairy. She didn't join the family for supper. She couldn't endure any more talk of the lady in the dungeon and her possible fate. She'd begun to think of Alix as a friend, the only friend she had at the court. The thought that she might never see her again saddened her greatly.

Fourteen

The world is a forest replete with lions, a mountain replete with serpents and bears, a battle replete with perfidious foes, a dark valley replete with tears, and nothing there is certain.

From a book of moral and practical advice for a young wife, Paris, 1393

The Châtelet, the seat of the provost of Paris, stood on the banks of the Seine near the Grand Pont, casting a pall over that part of the city. A hideous, fortress-like structure with mismatched towers, surrounded by slaughterhouses and the shops of fishmongers, skinners, tanners, and butchers, it was a place of foul air, putrefying carcasses, and the cries of terrified animals. Not even the sweet sound of bells peeling at the nearby church of Saint-Jacques-la-Boucherie, the parish church of the butchers, could lessen its sinister aura.

Everyone knew what lay behind the thick walls of the prison: cells where prisoners were crowded together like cattle, sleeping on floors with only the thinnest layer of straw to protect them from the cold; dungeons with air so thick with dirt no candle would stay lit; and, most feared of all, a pit in the shape of an inverted funnel where those accused of heinous crimes were forced to stand in water up to their knees, unable to sit or lie down.

It was to this dreaded prison that Alix de Clairy was brought on the night of Hugues de Précy's murder. At the Hôtel Saint-Pol, the palace guards had found her lying on the ground next to the body of her husband, dazed and confused, and they had summoned the sergeants from the Châtelet, who had carried her to the prison. She was brought before the jailer, who asked her for her name and wrote it in a large register. He looked at the sergeants and asked, 'What charge?' One of the men stepped forward. 'Arrested for the murder of her husband.' The jailer wrote that in a second register. Then she awoke from her stupor.

'I don't understand. What has happened to my husband?'

'You know very well. Your husband is dead. You poisoned him.'

'I did not!'

The jailer looked up from his books. Short and bald, he had not at first seemed threatening, but now he twisted his face into a nasty grimace and repeated, 'Arrested for the murder of her husband.'

'No!' She tried to shake off the hands of the sergeants, but they grasped her arms more tightly than before.

'Take her away,' the jailer said. The sergeants dragged her to a tiny room and locked her in. After they had left, a fat guard opened the door and set a beaker of water on the floor.

The room was pitch black, alive with mysterious rustling noises in the corners, but Alix had never been afraid of the dark or of sounds in the night. She sat on the floor and held her head in her hands. *I did not kill Hugues*, she said to herself. *Sometimes I wanted to. But I did not.*

She repeated this over and over until she fell into a troubled sleep.

Sometime later she awoke, trembling, her bones aching. At first she didn't know where she was, but then she realized she was lying on the hard floor of the prison. The cold sent waves of pain through her body. There was nothing to protect her or warm her, for all she wore was a silver brocaded gown Hugues had bought for her to wear to the ball. She couldn't see anything in the dark, but she knew the gown was in tatters.

Perhaps it was the gown that started all the trouble, she thought. Hugues had refused to go to the banquet, but after supper he'd said they would go to the ball. Then he was in a hurry, and he became angry because she wasn't dressed.

It had taken her time to get ready, and it was late when they arrived at the palace. She remembered how surprised she'd been when Hugues told her to go in and find the ballroom by herself. She could picture the courtyard – footmen with glistening faces holding burning torches, shadows dancing against the walls of the palace, lights sparkling in the glazed windows. She remembered the *portier* opening the door and a footman taking her mantle. She'd walked quickly through the entrance hall and the great gallery and stepped out into the inner courtyard, where she could hear the king's lions roaring in the distance. She remembered hastening along the corridor leading to the great hall where the ball was held, and how she'd listened for the music. But all she'd heard were screams and the shouts and cries of people who came running toward her. She'd tried to step out of the way, but she'd been swept up in the crowd, lifted off her feet, and carried back through the palace. She could still feel the people pressing against her, nearly smothering her, and she remembered how frightened she'd been and how, out in the street, she'd tried to run. But that was all she remembered. The next thing she knew, she was lying

106

on the ground and the palace guards were leaning over her.

If Hugues had stayed with me, I would have been safe, she thought. *Yes, he was unkind to me. Sometimes I wanted to kill him. But I didn't.*

In the morning, shortly after the bells of Saint-Jacques-la-Boucherie sounded prime and the faint light of dawn crept into her cell through a narrow barred window, guards appeared and took her to a room so dimly lit she could barely discern men dressed in black sitting on benches, staring at her. Exhausted from the ordeal of the night before and from lack of food and sleep, she swayed and nearly fell. The guards ordered her to stand tall before *Monseigneur le Prévôt* and his officials.

One of the men – she thought he must be the provost, because his seat was higher than the others – asked whether she understood the charge against her. 'Yes, but it is not true,' she said softly.

'You would do better to confess.'

'I am innocent.'

'Your husband was poisoned. The flask containing the poison was under your hand. How do you explain that?'

'I cannot explain it, I remember so little of what happened that night.' The solemn men sitting before her looked at each other and sighed. 'Then tell us what you do remember,' the provost said.

She looked down at her torn gown. Ashamed, she drew the shreds of cloth together so her legs would be covered. If any of the men who sat before her took note of this, they didn't show it.

'We were late,' she began.

'There is no need to tell us that,' the provost said. 'Simply tell us how you came to be lying next to your husband's body with the empty flask beneath your hand.'

'I cannot tell you how it happened. I only know that I did not poison him.'

The provost and his officials looked at each other. *They don't believe me*, she thought. She couldn't catch her breath. She swayed, and the guards caught her as she fell.

The provost shook his head and announced that they would learn nothing more from her that day. 'The next time, we'll have something to make her confess,' he said as the guards lifted her and carried her away to the dungeon.

Fifteen

Slander is like a sword that kills the man who throws it as well as the man at whom it's aimed.

Christine de Pizan, *Le Dit de la Rose*, 1402

Christine slept badly, dreaming of men enveloped in flames, stretching out their burning hands to set her on fire, too. She forced herself awake and then lay in bed thinking about Alix de Clairy and all the horrors she would be experiencing at the Châtelet. When a pungent smell drifted up the stairs, she finally rose, dressed, and went down to the kitchen, where she found her mother seated at the table, holding Lisabetta in her lap and leaning openmouthed over a large bowl filled with sodden sage leaves and hot water.

'That won't help, Mama,' Christine said. 'Why don't you have that tooth taken out?'

'It does help,' Francesca sniffed. She pointed to a kettle sitting on a trivet over the fire. 'You could help, too, *Cristina*. Get me that.'

'Where's Georgette?' Christine asked as she picked up the kettle and poured more boiling water into the bowl. A cloud of steam rose, and she had to back away.

'She took the children to school and she has not returned. The lazy girl probably stopped somewhere to talk to her friends. I need her to go to the market.'

Christine disliked shopping, but she wanted to get out of the house. 'I'll go,' she said.

Francesca laughed. 'You?'

'Why is that so funny, Mama? What do you want?'

'Ribs of beef. We will have them for dinner. I suppose you can manage that.'

The air was damp and heavy as Christine walked toward the market. The street vendors watched the sky for rain as they cried their wares. 'I have good cheese, good cheese of Brie,' chanted a toothless old woman she'd seen gossiping with Francesca. 'Where's your mother, Christine?' she lisped. 'Does a little bad weather keep her at home?' The woman broke off a piece of hard cheese and handed it to her.

A candle seller approached, singing the praises of cotton wicks 'so fine they give light as good as that of the stars.' It sounded so poetic, Christine bought one of his tapers; only after he'd walked away did she realize that she'd paid far too much for it. But she forgot about the candle seller when a waferer offered her a sample from his basket. The aroma of ginger and honey cheered her, and she couldn't resist buying two. She ate them both, and then bought some almond cakes from a third vendor, who'd watched her purchasing the candle and the wafers. After that, she hurried to the butcher, where she bought the beef her mother wanted – without haggling over the price, as Francesca would have done – and started for home.

At the corner of the rue Tiron, she was startled to see Marion, who rushed up and cried, 'I've been waiting for you, Lady Christine!' Her purple cloak was open to show off a peacock-green cotte with flowers embroidered down the front – no doubt another example of her handiwork, Christine thought. She also wore a belt with a large gold buckle.

'Aren't you afraid you'll be arrested?' Christine asked, pointing to the belt.

Marion closed the cloak, which was lined with fur, and like the rest of her clothes, off limits to prostitutes. She stared at Christine, her brown eyes wide with mock fear. 'I didn't steal it.'

'I'm sure you didn't. You know what would happen if you got caught.'

'You're right, I do. My friend Colette swiped a few *écus* from a scurvy old monk, and now she's in prison.' Marion's eyes filled with tears. The punishment for prostitutes convicted of theft was burial alive. Then she remembered what she was about. 'I have something important to tell you, Lady Christine. Too bad you aren't sitting down.'

'Can it be so shocking?'

'It is. I saw who murdered Hugues de Précy. It wasn't Alix de Clairy.'

Christine grabbed her arm. 'What are you saying?'

'I was outside the palace.'

'Prostitutes aren't supposed to be out in the street after dark!'

'It was still light when I went there; I wanted to see all the people in their fancy clothes come to the ball. After they'd all gone in, I went across the street to the queen's stables and played dice with the stable boys. When I left, it was night. There was a full moon, though, and I could see everything.' She thrust out a hip, put her hand on it, and took a few mincing steps.

'What are you doing?' Christine asked impatiently.

'Showing you Hugues de Précy coming to the ball, wearing those stupid *poulaines*.'

'He came so late? Was his wife with him?'

'Yes. She had on a white dress and a blue mantle. She looked beautiful, but Hugues didn't care. He gave her a shove. He was carrying a big package, and he nearly dropped it.'

'Package? What was it?'

'I couldn't see. But he made her go into the palace by herself. Then he had to put the package down.'

'Why?'

'Because he met someone in a black cloak who gave him a flask, and he had to put the package down so he could take a drink.'

'This isn't making much sense, Marion.'

'It will when I tell you what came next.'

'So get on with it.'

'After Hugues drank from the flask, he fell down. Then a lot of people ran out of the palace.'

Christine shuddered, remembering she had been one of those people. Marion looked at her strangely. 'Do you know something about this?'

'No, no. Go on with your story.'

'Alix de Clairy was with them. She'd forgotten her blue mantle, and her white dress was all glittery in the moonlight. Something made her trip, and she fell down beside her husband. Nobody else noticed; they were all too anxious to get away. After they had all gone, the person in the black cloak put something under her hand and took the package. I don't know what happened after that, because I realized that there was a fire, and I ran away too. So you see, Alix de Clairy didn't poison her husband. The person in the black cloak did.'

'And made it look as if Alix had done it!' Christine cried. 'You must go to the Châtelet and tell the provost.'

'Where are your wits? That saintly old man would never listen to me.'

She's right, Christine thought. She believed Marion's story, but the provost of Paris, Jean de Folleville, would not, and even if he did, a statement by a prostitute would have no legal standing.

'Do you know who the person in the black cloak was?'

'No. The cloak had a hood, and I couldn't see the face.' Marion thought for a moment. 'Perhaps it was the Italian. The one who's married to the king's brother. She's got lots of poisons.'

Poor Valentina Visconti, Christine thought. There were rumors the Duke of Orléans's Italian wife had brought powerful poisons from her home in Milan and given them to her husband so he could murder his brother and take his place as king. Christine resented the assumption that Italians walked around with poisons tucked into their sleeves. 'The poison didn't have to come from Italy,' she said. 'It was wolfsbane, and it grows right here in France. It acts very quickly, according to my mother.'

'Perhaps it wasn't the Italian. The person I saw was too tall anyway. But the Italian could have given the poison to her husband so he could do it.'

'Why do you think it might have been the duke?'

'The duke didn't like Hugues. He was jealous because he was so friendly with the king.' Marion considered this for a while, and then clapped her hand to her head. 'That's not right. The duke couldn't have done it. He was at the party, setting them all on fire.' She cocked her head and shook

113

her finger at Christine. 'People say he started the fire on purpose, you know. He's always trying to harm the king.'

'Who told you that?'

'My friend Colette. The one who robbed the old monk. The monk told her about a friend of his who helped the duke turn his sword into an evil charm to use against the king. They got the Devil to curse the sword, and then they cut a hanged man down from the gallows and stuffed the sword up his . . .'

'That's enough, Marion.' Christine had already heard the disgusting story from her mother, along with a host of other stories about Louis's association with magicians and sorcerers, and she didn't want to hear it again. 'We're talking about poison, not charms.'

'I'm only trying to help.'

'You are helping. What you saw proves Alix de Clairy didn't poison her husband.'

'I know. And I can't do anything about it. Just think of her in the prison. I know what they do to people in there – my friends tell me. It shouldn't happen to such a pretty little lady, especially when she's not even guilty. Can't you do something to save her?'

Perhaps I could go to the provost, Christine thought. *But he wouldn't believe me either, since I got the information from Marion.*

Marion was looking at her with tears in her eyes. 'You could go to the king. You know him, don't you?'

Christine had to smile. Just because her family had lived at the court when she was a child didn't mean she and the king were friends. Quite otherwise. There were good reasons why her mother warned her constantly about the court; it was a treacherous place. If she involved herself in Alix's troubles, she'd probably lose her chances of getting any more work there. But that would be the least of it. She could imperil her life and perhaps the lives of her children and her mother, too.

Nevertheless, she said, 'I'll try to think of something.'

'You'd better do it quickly.' Marion turned and ran down the path to the brothel.

But I have no idea what to do, Christine said to herself as she walked on, so lost in her thoughts, she nearly collided with three courtiers on their way to the Hôtel Saint-Pol. She let them go ahead and followed, listening to them discuss Hugues de Précy's murder.

'There's no doubt his wife poisoned him,' said one. He was a tall man wearing a blue cloak and a small hat with a large peacock feather that flopped to one side and threatened to fall over his face.

'How do you know that?' asked a slender man in an ermine-trimmed green cloak who bounced along with quick little steps, like a nervous palfrey.

'Because she's a witch, or so I've heard.'

'Of course. She's a witch. She should be put to death immediately.'

'But she hasn't had a trial yet!' exclaimed a stout little personage swathed in furs who had to run to keep up with the others.

'There will have to be a trial,' the man in the

green cloak assured the others. 'But she won't be able to save herself.'

The man in the blue cloak took off his feathered hat and waved it about. 'I tell you, my friends, she's like all women, capable of every kind of evil!'

'You're slandering Alix de Clairy, and all women, without even knowing what you're talking about. I hope your words come back to haunt you,' Christine whispered, as she watched them strut toward the palace.

Sixteen

Some tasks are beyond women because of their delicate bodies. But when women set out to do something, they are smarter and shrewder than men.

Christine de Pizan, *Le Livre de la Cité des Dames*, 1404–1405

Christine sat on a bench by the fire and watched her mother and Georgette prepare the ribs of beef for dinner. The girl stood on one side of the worktable, wielding a large knife like a weapon as she sliced carrots and brushed stray pieces onto the floor. Francesca sat across from her, her eyes tearing as she chopped onions.

Goblin stood at attention under the table, waiting for something to fall.

'You do not look well, *Cristina*,' Francesca said. 'I was wrong to send you to the market so early in the morning.'

'I'm thinking about that poor young woman in the dungeon at the Châtelet.'

'That is where she should be, if she murdered her husband. They say she is a witch.'

'I know her. She's not a witch.'

'Then why did she give the queen a mandrake?'

'Because she thought it would help the king. You must believe me, Mama. She's a good person.'

'People are not always what they seem.'

Christine thought about what Marion had told her, and despaired. What could she do with the information? She couldn't take it to the provost. Or to the king.

'I think I'll go and talk to Alix de Clairy,' she said. 'I might learn something that would prove she is innocent.'

'You can't go into the Châtelet!'

'Why not?'

'You must have some sense, *Cristina*. The prison is a terrible place. The air is very bad. You will be ill again.' Francesca brought the knife down hard on an onion, and some pieces flew to the floor. Goblin sniffed them and turned away. 'And besides, you need a letter from the provost to visit someone there.'

I'd forgotten about that, Christine thought. *Who would give me such a letter? Certainly not the king. Or the queen, since Georgette says she's so angry.*

Francesca said, 'You must stop troubling yourself about Alix de Clairy. Have you copied those pages for the duchess? You could take them to her.'

'I haven't finished them yet.'

'Then go and work on them. Or read a book; you have a lot of them scattered around your room.'

'That's it!' Christine cried, remembering that one of those books belonged to Gilles Malet, the royal librarian. 'I'll go to the Louvre and return the book I borrowed from Gilles. And I'll ask him to write a letter to the provost for me.'

'I am sure he will not do that.' Francesca flung the pieces of onion into a frying pan and slammed the pan down on a trivet over the fire. 'Gilles will tell you it is wrong for a woman to associate with murderers.'

'Gilles spoke to the queen and got her to give me work. Perhaps he'll help me again.' Christine hurried up to her study, searched through the clutter, and found the book. She wrapped it in a large kerchief, placed it in her pouch, and went back downstairs.

Francesca was waiting for her. 'You have not had anything to eat!'

'I'm not hungry.'

'It is going to rain.'

'No it isn't,' Georgette said. 'The sun's out now.'

Christine put on her cloak and boots.

Francesca threw up her hands. 'Wait here,' she said. She limped up the stairs and came back

118

with a pair of old shoes. 'Your boots will get all muddy. Put these on before you go into the library.'

Christine didn't want another argument, so she slid the shoes into the pouch beside the book.

Everyone seemed to have come out to enjoy the change in the weather. At the Grève, she found throngs of day laborers seeking work and thrill-seekers hoping for an execution. The wine boats were in, and a wine crier held out a bowl, inviting her to sample his wares. But even though she knew a bit of wine might improve her spirits, she shook her head and walked on, making her way over to the muddy quay beside the Seine. The river was crowded with boats, some laden with more wine casks, others with charcoal and lumber; and as she approached the Grand Pont, the cries of the boatmen and the shouts of moneychangers on the bridge rang in her ears. She turned down a street that passed the Châtelet, taking shallow breaths to lessen the effects of decaying carcasses and putrefying hides, then stopped and stood looking up at the forbidding walls of the prison, wondering in which of its horrible cells Alix de Clairy was confined. When the provost and his mounted guards came thundering over the Grand Pont, she shook her fist at them, turned down the rue Saint-Germain-l'Auxerrois, and pushed her way through crowds of shoppers until she reached the narrow, winding streets that led to the Louvre, a massive structure rising behind a thick wall beside the river.

Originally the Louvre had been a fortress, and

it still resembled one, even though King Charles the Fifth had made it into a palace. But no matter what its appearance, it seemed like a second home to Christine, because her father had often taken her there, to the library the old king had established in one of the towers. The royal librarian, Gilles Malet, had always welcomed her kindly.

A man in a black cape with a long black hood and an ermine collar walked in front of her, and she followed him across a bridge over a moat, past the guards at the entrance to the central courtyard, and up a spiral staircase to the tower room that housed the library. The man went in, but she stopped at the door to take off her cloak, remove her muddy boots, and put on the clean shoes Francesca had given her, reflecting that her mother was right about some things. Then she took the book out of her pouch and went into the library.

Gilles Malet, wearing an elegant but rumpled fur-lined doublet, paced up and down, carrying a stack of books and muttering to himself. Tall and thin, with a lean face and bushy eyebrows that shaded his eyes like wings, he seemed to care nothing for the condition of his clothes. Christine had always imagined they were wrinkled because he carried books around all the time, hugging them close to his body, like a mother with a child.

Gilles saw her, set the books down on his desk, and said, 'I did not anticipate a visit from you today, Christine.'

'I'm returning this.' She handed him the book

she'd brought and looked around for the man she'd followed up the stairs. Above them, on a balcony where scribes worked, a chair scraped.

'A man in a black cape arrived here just before I did. Is he one of the scribes?'

'Yes. Henri Le Picart,' Gilles said in a low voice. 'You are much indebted to him, Christine. It was the Duchess of Orléans's wish that he do some copying. He declined, because much of it had to do with housekeeping, and he said he had no interest in that. He told her to give the work to you.'

So that's why, Christine thought. *Not because she likes me any better than she did when I was a child*. But she couldn't help wondering how Henri Le Picart knew who she was.

'What were you grumbling about just now, when I came in, Gilles?'

Gilles sat down at the desk, moved the pile of books to one side, and held his head in his hands. 'Murders, men burned to death, a king who has lost his mind. The world is in a grievous state.'

'Surely there's nothing amiss in the library.'

'Most especially in the library. Just look around. The place is in disrepair. And what is worse, the king's uncles have carried off a great many of the books. You must remember how numerous they were, when you were a little girl.'

She remembered. There had been books everywhere, books of all sizes, shapes, and colors, some fat, some thin, some as large as table tops, some as tiny as belt buckles. They'd perched on desks and benches, peered out of cupboards, and reposed in stacks on the floor.

121

Some of the largest had even hovered overhead like big birds, hung from the ceiling on chains that could be lowered when someone wanted to read them. There were still many books, but there were many empty spaces, too.

Christine thought of everything about the library that had fascinated her as a child – the ceiling inlaid with tiny pieces of painted wood; the chandeliers that stayed lit all the time because the old king had liked to read at night; and the sound of birds – the sparrows, finches, and starlings that lived in the roofs and turrets of the palace. The chattering of the birds had been like music – to her, at least – but the windows had to be covered with wire mesh to keep them from flying in.

Gilles broke into her reverie. 'This library is of no importance to our unfortunate king.' He pointed to the floor. 'Take note of the tiles.' She could see that many of them were chipped. He pointed up. 'And observe the ceiling.' She followed his gaze and saw that pieces of the inlaid wood were missing. 'Even the windows are deteriorating,' he moaned. 'Some of the mesh has fallen away. Come spring, the birds will be constructing their nests withindoors.'

'Is there nothing you can do, Gilles?'

'Nothing. I take some consolation in the fact that the Duke of Orléans has charged me with the supervision of his own library at the Hôtel Saint-Pol. The duke respects his books and ensures they are properly cared for. His wife values them, too. Valentina Visconti is an estimable woman.'

Christine appreciated Gilles's regard for her

countrywoman. She was widely read, fluent in four languages, and certainly not one to conspire with her husband against the king, as many people believed. But before she could echo Gilles's praise for Valentina, he slapped his hand on his desk, and said, 'Unfortunately, she hasn't been able to convince the duke to rid the court of all those sorcerers and magicians. Everyone there seems to be under an evil spell. And now we learn that there has been a murderess!'

'So you, like everyone else, believe Alix de Clairy is guilty?'

'Of course I do.'

'Do you not think it possible someone else poisoned Hugues de Précy? A jealous husband, for example? There are rumors about Hugues and women at the court.'

'How do you have knowledge of that?'

'It is impossible not to hear what our hired girl tells my mother.' She hoped he wouldn't think she spent her time gossiping.

'There is no question the woman poisoned her husband.'

'*I* question it, Gilles. That's why I'm here. I want to go to the prison and speak with her. Would you write a letter to the *Monseigneur le Prévôt* for me?'

'Surely you don't intend to go into the prison!'

'I do. I want to talk to Alix de Clairy. I can't believe she's a murderess.'

Gilles looked at her in astonishment. 'She *is* a murderess! Such a woman is capable of all manner of evil, and you should have nothing to do with her.'

'Do you know her?'

'I have seen her. She is cast in the same mold as all the other women at the court, with her fine clothes and painted face.'

'She doesn't have to paint her face, Gilles. That's her natural complexion.'

He leapt up from his desk, shaking with anger, his bushy eyebrows jumping up and down like hairy little animals. 'I have been well disposed to help you find work, Christine. But you are a woman. Prisoners in the Châtelet are not your concern.' He picked up a large book and clasped it to his chest, like a shield.

'She *is* my concern, Gilles. I'm going to learn the truth.' Her voice trembled – Gilles was frightening her. He slammed the book down on the top of his desk, and at the same moment, Henri Le Picart came stomping down the staircase from the balcony. He frowned at Gilles, glared at Christine, and stomped back up the stairs.

Christine ran out of the room, grabbed her boots and cloak from the bench where she'd left them, and fled, stuffing the muddy boots into her pouch as she went.

Seventeen

The Highest Judge is the One who will examine and try us in the end.

From a book of moral and practical advice for a young wife, Paris, 1393

With Gilles's angry words ringing in her ears, Christine marched up the street away from the Louvre, sloshing through the mud and ruining the shoes her mother had given her. As she crossed the rue Saint-Martin, her head down, she bumped into a large woman who was unsteady on her feet. '*Accidenti!*' the woman cried, and she made an angry gesture with her hand. Then she laughed. 'Oh! It is you, *Cristina*. Why do you not look where you are going?'

'I'm sorry, Mama. I was thinking.'

'You think too much.'

Christine looked at her mother's flushed face. 'What are you doing here?'

'I have just seen a miracle, *Cristina*. At the church of Saint-Martin. You must come and see it, too.' Francesca grabbed Christine's arm and tried to pull her back along the way she'd just come.

'What are you talking about?' Christine pulled her arm away.

Francesca said, 'There is a baby lying on the altar. It's mother smothered it and buried it in a dump. Someone found it and brought it to the church, and the Holy Mother brought it back to life so it could be baptized. Then it died again.'

'Then it probably hadn't really died in the first place.'

'*Madonna!* You are a foolish girl. I have seen this baby with my own eyes. I do not expect you to believe me. You never do. But if you will not go with me to Saint-Martin, at least come with me to the cathedral. We can give thanks to God for this miracle.'

The cathedral was not far from where they stood, so Christine didn't object. If Francesca believed there had been a miracle, it might drive from her mind thoughts of the evil eye. They crossed the Planche-Mibray, the wooden foot-bridge leading across the Seine to the Île and hurried up the rue Neuve. Francesca, who had tired herself in all her excitement about the dead baby, was more unsteady on her feet than usual, and Christine took her arm. 'You are a good daughter,' Francesca said. 'But I wish you would believe in the miracle.'

'Don't you want to know what happened with Gilles, Mama?'

'I had forgotten all about that. What did he say?'

'He won't help me.'

'I told you he would not.'

'He's convinced Alix de Clairy is guilty, and he says it is none of my business, because I'm only a woman.'

Hearing the bitterness in Christine's voice, Francesca stopped and looked at her.

'I am sorry Gilles spoke to you like that,' she said. 'But you should know better than to involve yourself in affairs at the court. How many times have I warned you about that?'

Christine walked on quickly, so her mother wouldn't see she was fighting back tears.

They passed down the narrow street, which was hemmed in by tall, gabled houses, and then they were under the stern gaze of Christ presiding over the Last Judgment in the central portal of the cathedral. Christine looked up at Him, the happy saved on His right and the despairing damned on His left, and thought of the provost

126

and his officials at the Châtelet, deciding Alix de Clairy's fate, forgetting who the real Judge is.

She turned to her mother. 'I don't care what you or Gilles or anyone else says. I may be only a woman, but I'm not afraid, and I'm going to discover the truth.'

Francesca looked up at the figure of Christ and silently begged Him to change her daughter's mind.

They went into the cathedral and knelt before one of the altars, where Francesca thanked God for the miracle she had just seen, and Christine asked God to be merciful to the souls of the burned men. Then they turned down an aisle to a statue of Saint Thomas, lit candles, and said a prayer for Thomas de Pizan. 'I will say a prayer for you, too, *Cristina*, because you are going to put yourself in great danger,' Francesca said.

Christine took her mother's arm and led her toward home.

When they arrived at their street, they found it nearly deserted. The sun was out, and its rays illuminated fat white clouds. Christine remembered the billowy clouds over the garden painted on the wall at the palace, and she remembered Alix de Clairy standing with her arms outstretched as if she would embrace all the happy children.

'Where are all the people?' Francesca asked, then looked at Christine when she didn't respond. 'You are so silent.'

'I was thinking about Alix de Clairy. You have never met her. She isn't like the other ladies at the court. You'd understand if you could see her.'

'I have heard she sings and plays the harp.

That does not mean she could not have murdered her husband.'

'But even if she had wanted to poison her husband, why would she have done it in the street? She could just as well have done it at home.'

'You are very stubborn, *Cristina*. Just like your father.'

'You want me to believe you have seen a miracle, Mama. So I'm asking you to believe someone other than Alix de Clairy could have murdered Hugues de Précy.'

Suddenly, the sound of the cathedral bells chiming nones pierced the silence. The bells of all the other churches in the city joined in, and a flock of startled birds rose from the ground. Francesca stood looking up at them as they soared over their heads.

'If I look deeply into my mind,' she said softly, 'I have to admit it is possible that Alix de Clairy is innocent.'

Eighteen

If rats are spoiling your grain, bacon, cheese, and other supplies, you can kill them by making cakes of fried cheese and powdered wolfsbane and putting these in their holes.

From a book of moral and practical advice for a young wife, Paris, 1393

When Marion arrived at the brothel, she found that most of the other girls were entertaining customers in the curtained-off rooms. Agnes, however, sat morosely in front of the fireplace. She'd forgotten the fight they'd had a few days earlier, and she held up something for Marion to see. It was a book, and most of its leaves were in shreds, though it had once had many pictures, brightly colored and tinged with gold. Marion couldn't read, but she knew the book had been valuable, if for nothing else than the gold.

Agnes said, 'This was in the loft. We have to do something about the rats.'

'Someone put poison up there last week. I guess it didn't help.'

'I've asked Margot to prepare something stronger.'

'I'll go and get it,' Marion said.

Margot was an old woman who lived in a hut behind the brothel. Once she had been a prostitute, but now that she could no longer practice her profession, she grew herbs in a small garden just outside her door and sold them. Marion liked to visit her because she could learn about magic, love potions, and secret recipes thought to be useful to prostitutes. Margot also dealt in poisons, but the old woman didn't discuss those, or the people who came to buy them.

The hut was barely warmed by the few flames licking feebly at logs in a small fireplace. Margot leaned on a crutch, grinding something with a mortar and pestle. 'One of these days, Agnes will be arrested for stealing from her customers,' she said as she removed powder from the mortar with a long-handled spoon and mixed it with something she'd heated over the fire. 'Last month she took a gold chain and a ring. Now it's a valuable book. I suppose she showed you what happened to it.'

'She did. Most of its pages are ruined,' Marion said. 'What was she going to do with it?'

'If the rats hadn't gotten it, she'd have sold it to a shopkeeper on the rue de la Harpe who doesn't ask questions. He trades in books, though he'll sell anything he can lay his hands on in that filthy shop of his.'

'If you mean the big man with the ugly red scar on his cheek, he's a thief, too. Last week I saw him take something from a stall on the Grand Pont.'

'That's the one.' Margot finished preparing the rattraps and put them into a basket for Marion to carry back to the brothel. 'Take care you don't get any of what's in there on your hands,' she said.

'What is it?'

'Wolfsbane.'

'That's the poison that killed the knight at the palace!'

Margot turned to the fireplace and began to rearrange the logs.

'Has anyone from the palace bought wolfsbane from you recently?' Marion asked.

The old woman looked into the fire and remained silent.

Nineteen

The wise princess attends to her husband's health.

Christine de Pizan, *Le Livre des Trois Vertus*, 1405

The day after her disappointing conversation with Gilles Malet, Christine told her mother she had copying to do for the queen and left the house carrying her writing materials. Her real reason for going to the palace was to see the Duchess of Orléans; she'd decided to put aside her awe of the old woman and try to persuade her to write the letter to the provost.

The weather had turned cold again, but the sun was shining, and Renaut in his red jacket and cap was skipping around the fountain in the courtyard. When he saw her, he looked up at the stone lion and giggled. She still had in her purse two of the almond cakes she'd bought the day before, and she gave him one.

'I hope you aren't planning to go to the queen,' Simon said. 'I'm told she's too distraught to receive anyone.'

'No. I want to speak with the Duchess of Orléans. Is there someone to ask whether she'll see me?'

131

'Colin is around somewhere. I'll go and find him.'

He didn't have to go far; the boy was hovering just inside the palace entrance. Simon sent him off to the duchess.

While she waited, Christine stood and watched Renaut, who sat on the ground, his face covered with crumbs, spinning a small red top. The boy seemed content, but she thought it sad he never had anyone to play with. She heard the lions roaring in the distance and wondered out loud why the woman who helped care for them couldn't help care for her own nephew.

'From the little I know of Loyse, I don't think I'd trust her with a child. Anyone who would live with the lions all the time must be as beset by demons as the king,' Simon said.

'But surely Blanche could find someone to be with the boy while she's in the palace.'

Simon shrugged his shoulders. 'Blanche probably doesn't know anyone here to ask. You don't know about her, do you?'

She looked around, hoping Colin would come back soon, because she sensed that Simon was about to tell her something distressing. He leaned against the doorjamb and crossed his arms over his chest.

'Blanche used to know people here. Her mother was a widow who sewed for the old queen and her ladies, and she always brought Blanche to the palace with her. Such a happy child, laughing and skipping around, hiding in places where no one could find her.' He sighed. 'Then everything changed.'

A group of courtiers came out. Simon stood

tall as they passed, then leaned against the door-jamb again.

'It was terrible.' He wiped his eyes. 'One night while Blanche and her mother were sleeping, robbers broke into their house. The mother woke up and accosted them. They stabbed her. The little girl slept through it all, and the next morning she went downstairs and found her mother lying in a pool of blood, dead.'

Christine shuddered.

Simon wiped his eyes again. 'After her mother died, Blanche was left on her own. Naturally, she didn't come to the palace anymore, and later we learned she had married and gone north, to Amiens. She had two daughters. The older one was Renaut's mother; she died giving birth to him. The other one was Loyse.'

'Why did Blanche come back to Paris?'

'Her husband died. She'd become a seamstress, like her mother, and I suppose she thought there would be more work here.'

'What about Loyse?'

'The lion keeper needed help, and Blanche told him Loyse was good with animals.'

Colin returned. 'The duchess will see you.'

'Go with her,' Simon said to the boy, and Colin led the way through all the confusing courtyards, cloisters, passageways, and corridors, talking all the while about the men who had burned, and sniffing the air as though he could still smell the smoke. When they reached the duchess's room, Christine told him not to wait; she'd find her way back by herself. She couldn't stand any more of his prattle.

133

The old woman, looking very tired, sat by her little fire, fingering her beads. She didn't seem surprised to see Christine. 'I suppose you have brought me the pages I asked you to copy,' she said.

Christine knelt and said, 'No, *Madame*. I am still working on them.'

'Then why are you here?'

'I have a request, *Madame*. The wife of the knight who was poisoned is in the Châtelet, awaiting trial, and I am worried about her.'

'What concern is she of yours?'

'I'm not convinced she poisoned her husband.'

'How could one doubt it? At first I thought her worthy of the queen's regard. I was deceived.'

Christine knew this was the moment to say she had information that could prove Alix's innocence. But she didn't want to tell the duchess she'd obtained the information from a prostitute, so she said simply, 'I know Alix de Clairy, *Madame*, and I don't think you were deceived. She has no friends here in Paris, and I would like to visit her in the Châtelet. Will you write a letter to *Monseigneur le Prévôt* asking him to admit me?'

The duchess stared at her. After a long silence, interrupted only by the sharp crackling of a log falling in the fireplace, she said, 'You always were a willful child. I thought you had learned some sense. Of course I will not write a letter asking that you be allowed to visit a murderess.' She picked up her crutch and banged it on the floor. 'Affairs at the court are not your business.'

Christine felt her face burning, yet she persisted.

'But *Madame*, she might tell me something that would prove she is innocent.'

The duchess bent over her rosary. 'You may go now.'

Humiliated and at the same time angry with herself for having failed so miserably, Christine rose from the bench, curtsied, and hurried from the room.

In spite of what she had told him, Colin was waiting just outside the door. She wondered how much of the conversation he'd heard, but he accompanied her back to the entrance courtyard without uttering a word.

Renaut was still there, playing with his little red top. 'Why do you look so sad?'

Too disheartened to answer, she just smiled and gave him the second almond cake from her purse.

'The queen has summoned you,' Simon said.

She was in no mood for the queen, but of course she could not refuse her summons. At least she knew the way and could go without Colin. She walked slowly. She needed time to collect her thoughts.

When she came to the door of the queen's chambers, she saw Isabeau lying on her ceremonial bed, surrounded by her ladies-in-waiting. The queen's eyes were closed, and she lay so still, she seemed to have fainted. But Catherine de Fastavarin, who sat beside her, whispered something to her, and she moaned.

Beside the fireplace sat a man – the queen's brother, Ludwig. He looked toward the door, shifted uneasily in his seat, and ran his fingers through his two-pointed beard. Wondering what he'd seen, Christine turned and found Blanche standing beside her, holding a torn brocaded dress – a casualty of the disastrous masquerade, she supposed. The seamstress handed the dress to a chambermaid and stood staring at Ludwig. He rose from his seat, crossed the room, and brushed past her, out the door. Blanche turned to watch him go, and Christine caught the faint smell of cloves on her breath.

The queen lifted her head, looked around, and beckoned. Christine went in and knelt beside the bed. 'You sent for me, *Madame*?'

The queen, her face wet with tears, said, 'Alix de Clairy gave to me a mandrake with which to make my husband well. It is gone. Catherine has told me that Alix de Clairy took it back.'

'Why would she do that?' Christine asked in amazement.

'She needed it to poison her own husband,' Catherine said.

'Hugues de Précy was poisoned with wolfsbane!' Christine cried.

The queen said, 'Catherine has told me it was the mandrake.'

Christine looked at Catherine. 'I heard you tell the queen that the little spirit in the mandrake would *heal* the king.'

Catherine said, 'It could. But it can also do bad things.' She stroked the queen's forehead. 'I know you liked Alix de Clairy, *Liebling*, but she is evil, and you must forget her.'

The queen sat up and said to Christine, 'Please

go to the prison and ask Alix de Clairy where is the mandrake. You can get it and bring it back to me.'

Madame de Malicorne stepped up to the bed. 'If the witch has the mandrake, *Madame*, let her keep it. We will get another one for you.' The other ladies-in-waiting nodded in agreement.

'No, no! That is the mandrake I must have!' the queen cried. 'I know the little spirit in it; that is the spirit that will make Charles well.'

Christine realized that in her distress the queen was willing to believe in anything she thought might help her husband. She could hear her mother warning her that she was walking into danger, but she couldn't help herself; this was the opportunity to obtain what she needed. She asked innocently, 'How could I gain admittance to the Châtelet, *Madame*?'

'I will give to you a letter for *Monseigneur le Prévôt*.'

The queen rose from the bed, went into the other room, and sat at the desk. She beckoned to Christine. 'Give me something with which to write.'

Thankful she'd brought her writing materials, Christine placed a piece of parchment, a quill, and an inkhorn on the desk. The ladies-in-waiting standing behind her protested, but only among themselves, in whispers.

Christine heard them. She turned and asked, 'Why shouldn't I go? It can't do any harm.' They all glared at her, and she felt chilled.

The queen dipped the quill into the inkhorn and laboriously scratched out a short letter.

Reading over her shoulder, Christine could see that although the French was awkward, it would serve its purpose. Out of the corner of her eye, she also saw that Blanche had crept into the room.

The queen folded the letter, wrote the provost's name on it, and handed it to her. 'Seal it.'

Christine took her knife and a ribbon out of her scrip. With the knife, she made two holes in the parchment, and through these she passed the ribbon. She found a wafer of wax, warmed it in her hands, and flattened it against the two ends of the ribbon. The queen took the letter and pressed her ring with her official seal into the wax. Then she handed the letter back to Christine. 'Go to the Châtelet tomorrow. Find out where is the mandrake and get it for me.' Tears flowed down her cheeks as she added softly, 'Please.'

Twenty

In France, it is the custom that any prospective bride for the king, no matter how eminent her family, must be seen completely nude and examined by ladies so they can know if she is in good condition and correctly formed to bear children.

Froissart, *Chroniques, Livre II*,
1376–1385

The next morning, Christine told her mother she was going to the Châtelet. 'The queen has written a letter to the provost,' was all she said. Her mother didn't need to know the queen had written the letter because she expected her to retrieve the mandrake.

The fire had burned low, and Francesca knelt on the hearth, furiously working the bellows. She looked up and said, 'It is Candlemas. I had hoped you would go to the cathedral with me.'

'That won't be possible,' Christine said, and to avoid an argument she hurried into the pantry. She found some cheese wafers, ate one, and stuffed a few more into her purse, hoping she would be allowed to give them to Alix. When she returned to the kitchen, she found her mother pacing around the room, toying with any object that came within her reach. She overturned the saltcellar, upset the pepper mill, and pushed a carving knife to the floor. She picked up spoons and dropped them back onto the table. Then she went to the corner where she hung herbs from her garden to dry, reached up, yanked down a sprig, and handed it to her daughter. 'If you must go into the prison, at least hold this to your nose while you are there.'

'What is it?'

'Rue. Perhaps it will protect you from disease in that horrible place.'

Christine took the rue. It had a disagreeable odor, but if it appeased her mother, she didn't mind. Francesca watched as she tucked it into her sleeve, and then followed her into the front hall and said nothing more until she reached for her fur-lined cloak.

139

'Have you taken leave of your senses, *Cristina*? That cloak is old, and I have mended it several times, but it is the best you have. You cannot wear it into the prison!' She grabbed an old, plain woolen cloak, threw it over Christine's shoulders, and fastened it with a large bronze brooch, all the while muttering to herself, 'My daughter has not got the wits she was born with.' Then, while Christine was putting on her boots, she disappeared into the pantry and came back with a handful of the cheese wafers. 'Alix de Clairy will be hungry,' she said.

Christine took the wafers, hugged her mother, and left quickly. But once she was out of the house, her steps faltered. She dreaded the thought of going into the infamous prison, and she feared that even if she did see Alix, the young woman would be in no condition to talk to her. Moreover, she didn't for a moment believe Alix knew anything about the mandrake, and she feared what would happen when she returned to the queen without it. She thought perhaps her mother was right to say she'd taken leave of her senses.

The day was warm, and it was difficult to walk. Her unpaved street flowed with mud that sucked at her boots and glued them to the ground. On the other side of the old wall, the streets were cleaner, but her steps were heavy nevertheless. She walked slowly, her head down, hardly noticing when a housewife hurrying to the market or a peddler crying his wares jostled her. Shopkeepers had set up their stalls in the windows in front of their houses, and the smell of fresh baked bread, spices, fish, and candle wax mingled

140

with the stench of dung and garbage. On the rue des Lombards, stray dogs darted in and out of the gloomy alleyways, and the tall houses seemed to close in on her. She turned down the broader rue Saint-Denis, and put her hands over her ears to block out the racket of chickens and geese tied outside the poulterers' stalls and the din of hammers from the shops of helmet makers and armorers. When she finally reached the square in front of the Châtelet, she looked at the ugly building with its mismatched towers and considered turning back.

Two little girls dressed in rags stood near her, gazing up at the prison, weeping and calling for their mother. She pulled them out of the way as a group of mounted sergeants rode by, oblivious to everything but the shackled prisoners they herded before them. The sudden activity revived her courage. She held her head high and walked to a vaulted public passageway that cut through the center of the building. The provost's headquarters were to the right of the passageway, and on the left was a small door, the entrance to the prison itself. She approached two guards standing at this entrance and held out the queen's letter. One of the men, a giant with a wart-covered nose, took it and disappeared into the provost's side of the building. She waited. The other guard, a bald man with a harelip that gave him a constant sneer, leaned against the side of the building and glared at her. For something to do, she removed the sprig of rue from her sleeve and sniffed it. The acrid smell stung her nostrils.

The guard with the warty nose returned. 'You must come back later,' he said with a smirk.

She walked back through the vaulted passageway and wandered over to the street where scribes worked in tiny wooden booths against a wall of the church of Saint-Jacques-la-Boucherie. Thinking that one day she might have to work there herself, she glanced into several of the booths to see what they were like. Most of them were empty at that hour of the morning, but in one she found a scribe with a black beard who wore a black cape with a long black hood and an ermine collar. It was Henri Le Picart, the man who had glared at her in the library at the Louvre. He looked up from his work and scowled. She hurried away.

Disturbed by thoughts of the disagreeable little man, she wandered aimlessly around the streets near the church and stumbled into one of the neighborhood's infamous culs-de-sac, surprising the prostitutes, beggars, and derelicts who loitered there. After she'd been stared at, commented upon, and approached by the beggars, she decided to walk down to les Halles, to the better company of shopkeepers and their customers.

As she passed the secondhand clothes market Marion was so fond of, near the cemetery of the Innocents, she looked into one of the stalls and saw a short red wool cape with a high fur collar. The shopkeeper took it down from the rack and handed it to her. There was a tear in the lining – something her mother could easily fix – but since the man was asking for only a few sous, she bought it, thinking she could wear it when she went to the market. She didn't want to go into the prison carrying it, so she threw it over her shoulders, hoping the guards wouldn't notice she wore a cape over her cloak.

She walked back toward the Châtelet, deliberately passing Henri Le Picart's booth at Saint-Jacques-la-Boucherie so she could look in and show he didn't intimidate her. But he was no longer there.

The same guards stood at the prison door. 'Wait here,' the one with the wart-covered nose said, and he disappeared inside. His companion whispered, 'Better take out your herbs, *Madame*. You never know what might sicken you in there.' He threw back his head and roared with laughter, then snapped to attention when the warty guard reappeared, followed by a jailer who stared at her for a moment and then indicated that she should follow him. He led her through a turnstile and along a narrow corridor. It smelled of moldy straw and excrement and echoed with moans and cries from deep within the prison. She stumbled after him, wondering where he was taking her, until he turned, smiled, and said in a nasty voice, 'We've brought your friend to a lovely room reserved for visitors like yourself.' He was short and bald, and when he smiled, he displayed a mouth full of black, rotting teeth.

They came to a heavy wooden door with a peephole, guarded by a fat, red-faced man holding a cudgel. The man leaned the cudgel against the wall, selected a large key from among the many hanging on a chain around his waist, unlocked the door, and pushed it open. She hesitated, and the jailer grinned, showing all his horrible teeth. She forced herself to walk past him. The door closed behind her, and the key turned in the lock with a sickening clang.

She was in a small room with one tiny, barred, cobweb-blanketed window that let in a faint glimmer of light. The thick walls shut out the cacophony of the rest of the prison; the place was as silent as a tomb.

On the other side of the room stood Alix de Clairy, barely visible in the gloom. She remained motionless until Christine spoke her name, and then she came slowly toward her, like a specter. Her auburn hair was matted and sprinkled with bits of straw, and she had on a tattered silver-brocaded gown, obviously the one she'd worn the night of the fire. The dress was so thin it couldn't possibly keep her warm, and a thin, ragged brown blanket thrown over her shoulders wouldn't be of much help, either. Christine was wearing a heavy woolen cotte, a warm woolen cloak, and the red cape she had bought at the clothes market, but she still felt cold.

'It's Christine. Do you remember me?'

'How did you get in here?'

'The queen sent me.'

A faint look of hope crossed Alix's face, but it disappeared when Christine said, 'The mandrake is gone. The queen thinks you took it, and she asked me to come and find out where it is.'

'The queen thinks I took the mandrake?'

'I know you didn't. But there was no other way I could get into the prison.'

Alix put her hands over her face. 'They think

144

I stole a book, too. They say Hugues was bringing it to the palace.'

That must have been the package Marion saw, Christine thought.

The sleeves of Alix's gown had fallen back, and Christine could see there were no cuts on her arms. 'Have they tortured you,' she asked.

'No. They just questioned me. The next time will be worse.'

'What did you tell them?'

'Nothing. I don't remember anything. All I know is, I didn't poison him. No one believes me.'

'I believe you.'

Alix turned and Christine saw that one of her cheeks was badly bruised.

'Did you hurt your face when you fell in the street?'

Alix put her hand on her cheek. 'Perhaps. I don't remember.' She was shivering. Christine took off the red cape and draped it over her shoulders, but she didn't seem to notice. 'What day is it?' she asked.

'Candlemas.'

'Candlemas,' Alix repeated softly. She looked around the room as if she expected to see it illuminated by the hundreds of candles that would be blessed in churches that day.

Christine clenched and unclenched her fists to keep her fingers warm. *She's been here for four days*, she thought. *How much can she endure?* She remembered the cheese wafers, and she took them out of her purse. Alix stared at them, then took one and ate it slowly.

'Tell me what happened the night your husband died, Alix.'

'I've told it so many times. Ai!' Her pained cry brought a rattling of keys and the fat guard with the cudgel.

'Please leave us,' Christine said. He backed into the corridor and locked the door again.

'His name is Hutin,' Alix said. 'He's kind. He gave me this.' She reached up to touch the ragged blanket over her shoulders and found the red cape instead.

'But this is not mine.' She started to take off the cape, but Christine pulled it back over her shoulders and fastened it with her mother's brooch.

Alix began to shake, and Christine put her arms around her. 'I know you didn't kill Hugues.'

'How do you know? No one else believes me.'

'I know because a friend of mine saw someone else give him the poison. Unfortunately, she couldn't see the person's face. That's why I'm here; we have to find out who it was. Did Hugues have any enemies?'

Alix sighed. 'I suppose he did.'

'But the king was very fond of him. Do you know why?'

'Hugues was in Amiens with the king when he was married. There was a plot, you know. Hugues told the king he'd helped arrange it.'

Christine knew all about the deception that had brought about the king's marriage, eight years earlier. Francesca had talked of nothing else for days. The king's uncles wanted him to marry Isabeau, a young German noblewoman, but her father, Duke Stephen of Bavaria, wouldn't allow his daughter to travel to Paris to meet the king, because he knew that when she got there she would have to show herself naked before the ladies of the court so they could decide whether she was fit to bear children.

'That duke is smart,' Francesca had said. 'What if the ladies reject her? No one else will marry her.'

The uncles wouldn't give up. The king had moved his court to Amiens, and a plot was devised so that Isabeau would be brought there to meet him. Everyone hoped the king would fall in love with her as soon as he saw her, and he did. Three days later, they were married in the cathedral.

'What did Hugues have to do with the conspiracy?' Christine asked.

'Nothing. He lied.' Alix buried her face in her hands. 'If only he hadn't gone to Amiens with the king.'

'Was that when your marriage was arranged?'

'Yes. Do you remember, I told you about the banquet where I sang for the king? Well, Hugues saw me there with my father and he asked whether he could marry me. I was only eight, but Father agreed that he could, when I was sixteen.' Tears ran down her cheeks. 'Father was at my wedding, but he is dead now,' she said.

Her father probably had a great deal of property, and Hugues knew she would inherit it, Christine thought. That was all he cared about. It must have been different for Alix. She remembered the look of sadness on her face as she watched her husband saunter away from her that day in the queen's residence. 'You cared for Hugues, didn't you, Alix,' she said.

147

Alix sighed. 'I wanted him to love me.'

Christine thought about her own marriage. She thought she saw Étienne smiling at her from the shadows in a corner of the room, reminding her that, so far, she'd learned nothing to help her discover who the murderer was. But before she could ask Alix any more questions, Hutin returned. 'They've ordered me to take her back now,' he said.

'Just one moment more,' Christine said. Holding the young woman close, she whispered to her, 'You must think. Who hated Hugues enough to kill him? No matter what they do to you, try to answer that question. Then perhaps I can help you.' She pulled the sprig of rue out of her sleeve and thrust it into her hand. 'I know it has a bad odor, but it might keep you safe from disease.'

Alix clutched the rue, and Hutin drew her away. As she went out the door, Christine noticed that the matted hair on the back of her head was covered with blood.

Twenty-One

Think of the Blessed Mary of Egypt. She gave up her sinful life and turned to God. Now she is a glorious saint in Paradise.

Christine de Pizan, *Le Livre des Trois Vertus*, 1405

After Alix had gone, Christine stood at the window of the dark room and peered out through the cobwebs. Lost in thought, she was startled when the jailer with the decaying teeth came in.

'What have you done with your little red cape, *Madame*?'

'Please let her keep it. She'll die of the cold.'

'She will die regardless. But if you wish to part with your clothes, that's your concern.'

She followed him down the dark, foul-smelling hallway to the prison entrance, longing for a cudgel like Hutin's so she could strike his bald head with it. The two guards were still at the door, and they grinned at her as she stepped into the street. The jailer called after her, 'Hurry home, *petit chou*.'

Before she could think of a suitable retort, he'd gone back inside. The two guards laughed. She was so upset by their loathsome behavior and the jailer's mocking words, and so troubled by the thought of the blood on the back of Alix's head, she turned the wrong way down the vaulted passageway, emerged at the entrance to the Grand Pont, and didn't realize where she was until she heard the rumble of the mill wheels under the bridge. She started to go back, but she could hardly move. Hands clawed at her from all sides – touching her face, pulling on her arms, tugging at her cloak. She tried to brush them away, but it was no use; she had strayed into a crowd of beggars gathered at a water trough near the river.

A voice rasped, 'You'll dirty your clothes out here, lady.' Someone held up an arm wrapped

149

in a bloody bandage, and when she tried to step around him, she collided with a ragged man on crutches. Then she nearly fell over a dwarf-like creature, apparently legless, pulling himself along on wooden sticks tied to his hands. 'Spare a coin. A little bread,' he pleaded in a pitiful, whining voice.

She wasn't deceived. The bandages, crutches, and sticks would disappear that night in one of the muddy courtyards not far from les Halles where the beggars of Paris gathered after dark to throw off their disguises. But when she remembered her fear that her children and her mother might be reduced to a similar condition, she reached into her purse, drew out a few *deniers*, and pressed them into the outstretched hands. The wretches grinned and bobbed their heads. One held his coin in front of his face like a prize and said to the others, 'Here's to strong drink, comrades.'

'You would be wise to spend it at the bathhouse rather than the tavern,' she said, backing up against the side of the water trough as she tried to escape from the smell of sweat and urine.

Two toothless old men in tattered jackets and greasy leggings sat on the edge of the trough. One stuck out a foot to trip her, and as she turned away to keep from falling, she bumped into a woman who reached out and clutched her arm.

'Praise God I've found you, Lady Christine.'

'What are you doing here, Marion?'

'I saw you at the old-clothes market, and I followed you. Where's the little red cape you bought?'

'I gave it to Alix de Clairy. If you saw me, why didn't you say something?'

'I knew you were going to the prison, and I didn't want the guards to think I was with you. They might not have let you in.'

Christine looked at Marion's purple cloak, which was lined with fur. 'It's more likely they'd have arrested you.'

Marion pulled the cloak around her. 'Did you see Alix de Clairy in there? Has she been tortured?'

'Not yet. But when she is, she won't be able to help herself. She doesn't remember anything. You know more about what happened than she does. But there's something strange. Tell me how Alix fell.'

'On her face. It must have hurt.'

'I'm sure it did. She has a big bruise on her cheek.'

Marion winced and put her hand on her own cheek. 'I hope it doesn't leave a big scar. She's so pretty.'

'Are you sure you've told me everything you remember about that night, Marion?'

The girl looked hurt. 'Of course I have. Why would I leave anything out?'

'Because Alix has blood on the back of her head.'

'I told you, she fell on her face.'

'Did you actually see her fall?'

'No. There were too many people around. But after they'd gone, I saw her, face down. How could she have gotten blood on the back of her head?'

'I think it's because someone hit her there.'

'Who?'

'The person in the black cloak.'

Marion clapped her hand to her forehead. 'I know! To knock her out, so she wouldn't be able to get up and run away.' She did a little dance around the water trough. 'The provost wouldn't believe anything *I* say. But he'll believe *that*, when *you* tell him!'

'I'm not so sure,' Christine said, imagining the conversation. What if the provost didn't believe her? Would he throw her into the Châtelet with Alix?

'I have something to tell you that may help,' Marion said.

The old men sitting on the edge of the trough, amused at the sight of a short, proper-looking woman in a plain brown cloak talking to a tall prostitute swathed in purple, laughed and slapped their thighs. A woman in a shimmery red skirt slipped out of the crowd and pranced around making obscene gestures.

Marion said, 'We need a better place to talk.' She took Christine's hand and dragged her back through the vaulted passageway and up the street in such a hurry they were soon out of breath. Christine pointed to the church of Saint-Jacques-la-Boucherie and said, 'We can go in there and sit.'

Reluctantly, Marion followed her into the church. It smelled pleasantly of incense and beeswax and was empty except for an elderly woman lighting a candle before an altar. Sitting in the shadows on a bench at the back of the nave, trying to catch her breath, Christine watched a ray of light filter through a stained glass window and fall on a statue in one of the bays, the figure of a haggard woman with a mass of long tangled hair barely covering her naked, emaciated body. When she saw Marion looking at the statue, she was tempted to remind her that Mary of Egypt had been a prostitute, too, and that she had changed; but she held her tongue.

'Wait until the old sacristy bug leaves,' Marion said, watching as the woman finished lighting her candle and left without glancing in their direction. Then she announced, without bothering to lower her deep voice, 'An old woman named Margot lives in a hut behind my brothel. She grows herbs for medicines and love potions. And poisons. Men from the palace go to her. I think one of them may have bought the wolfsbane that killed Hugues de Précy.'

'Do you know who her customers are?'

'No. But she might tell you, if you are willing to go and talk to her.'

'Certainly I'm willing. Find out if she'll see me.'

'I'll ask her today.' Marion grabbed Christine's arm and pulled her off the bench and out of the church in such a rush they nearly collided with a man standing near the door. He walked away, but Christine recognized the black cape with the long black hood and the ermine collar. She was surprised to see Marion staring after him. 'Do you know Henri Le Picart?'

'He owns the lodging house where I live,' Marion said. 'I wonder what he's doing here.'

'He's a scribe. He works in one of the booths beside the church.'

'He seems to have many talents.'

The bright day had turned gloomy, and huge clouds rolled across the sky, promising a winter thunderstorm. Marion shivered. 'I don't want to be out in this.' She hurried away, and Christine had to run to keep up with her. On the darkening streets, merchants bustled about, gathering up their wares and slamming down the shutters of their booths. Peddlers prodded stubborn mules to a trot, and old women with heavy market baskets scuttled toward home. When Christine and Marion reached the rue Tiron, thunder crashed, lightening flared around them, and the rain came pounding down.

'I'd better leave you now, Lady Christine,' Marion said. 'I'm sure you don't want your mother to see you walking with me.'

'Have some sense, Marion! We're not near my house.'

Marion laughed. 'Of course I know that.' Water dripped from her nose and puddles formed at her feet, but she didn't seem to notice. 'You've found proof that Alix de Clairy is innocent. Now all you have to do is find out who the real murderer is. Perhaps Margot can tell you. I'm going to talk to her right away.' She made a little curtsy and splashed up the street to the Tiron brothel.

As soon as Christine reached to the door of her house, her mother opened it. She hurried in and slipped off her cloak, hoping Francesca wouldn't notice something was missing.

But of course she did. 'Where is the brooch I gave you?'

Christine knew there was no way to conceal what she'd done. 'I found a cape in the old-clothes market. It was cold in the prison, so I gave it to Alix de Clairy. She had to have something to fasten it with.' She expected an outburst of anger, but it didn't come. Francesca was too relieved her daughter had made it home safely. The streets were dark and deserted because of the thunderstorm, and as far as she knew, Christine had been alone, making her easy prey for any of the phantoms she worried about – thieves, murderers, the *loup-garou*, and, worst of all, a bestial monk who roamed around Paris looking for people to strangle.

At supper, the children were awestruck when they learned their mother had been inside the prison. Jean put down his spoon and announced, 'You should have taken someone with you.'

'No one else had a letter from the queen.'

Marie asked, 'How could you talk to a murderess?'

'I don't believe she's a murderess.'

Thomas wanted to know all about the prison: how thick the walls were, what the guards wore, how many cells were in the dungeon, how many prisoners, whether everyone slept on the floor.

'It's dark and cold and not as interesting as you think,' was all Christine would say.

'Jean would have been scared,' Thomas said, and he stuck his tongue out at his brother.

'*Basta, Tommaso*,' Francesca said.

He went on with his questions. 'Where have

they put the lady? In the Butcher Shop?' He drew his finger across his throat. 'The Pit? The Well?' He made gurgling sounds. Lisabetta giggled, Jean laughed, and even Marie couldn't help smiling. Christine sent them all upstairs to bed.

Francesca's curiosity was not so easily turned aside. She put her elbows on the table, leaned on them, and waited.

'She was very weak, and her clothes were tattered,' Christine said. 'But she hasn't been tortured yet.'

'Did she eat the cheese wafers?' She smiled when Christine said she had.

'There was someone other than Alix de Clairy outside the palace with Hugues de Précy the night he was murdered,' Christine said, letting her mother assume Alix had told her this. 'That person gave him the poison, and I must find out who it was.'

'That is the criminal lieutenant's job.'

'He won't pursue the matter further, now that the provost has made up his mind that Alix is guilty.'

'So there is nothing you can do.'

'There has to be something.'

Francesca's dark eyes were moist. 'I know I am not able to stop you, *Cristina*, but I am frightened. Especially today, because of the thunderstorm. At this time of year, a thunderstorm is a very bad sign.'

Christine's head ached. She said, 'I'm going to bed.'

Twenty-Two

The Feast of the Purification of Mary has three names; the third is Candlemas, because on this day the faithful carry lighted candles.

Jacobus de Voragine, *The Golden Legend*, thirteenth century

After Christine's visit, Alix de Clairy sank to the floor of her cell and wept. Then, ashamed of herself for giving in to her misery, she sat up, leaned against the damp, moldy wall, and watched dust motes float on a sliver of light that worked its way in through a tiny window. Christine had said it was Candlemas. That meant the churches would be filled with the glow of candles and the fragrance of beeswax. Her father had always taken her to the cathedral in Amiens for the Candlemas procession, and for a moment she imagined her cell resplendent with candle-light. She felt her father lifting her onto his shoulders to carry her above the crowd, and herself smiling down at Gillette, who walked beside them, her white hair glistening.

Where is Gillette now? she wondered. *Does she know I'm here?* She was certain her old nursemaid would come to the prison to comfort her if she

157

were allowed to do so. Gillette had been her companion for as long as she could remember, taking her along everywhere she went – to the market, to church, to visit her friends. Alix tried to remember all those friends of Gillette's: the fishwife in the market with her baskets of eel, lampreys, and herring, haggling over prices with her customers; the aged crone who sat in the square with her distaff, drawing out a seemingly endless stream of woolen yarn as she promised to make it into a hat for the little girl; the widow who brewed ale for the villagers and sometimes gave her a taste; the shepherdess shearing her sheep, letting the fleece fall into soft, fluffy piles. She had liked all of Gillette's friends except one, a woman who lived in a cottage near one of her father's estates. 'She's a midwife, but she's fallen on hard times,' Gillette had said, and one day she'd decided they should go to visit her. Alix recalled every detail of that sunny winter afternoon. They'd walked across an open field, crunching snow under their feet, leaving a trail of icy footprints, and then they'd followed a winding path through snow-laden trees until they'd come to a yard where a pig, its breath turning to mist in the frigid air, rooted in the mud under the snow, and chickens, shadowed by a flock of chattering blackbirds, scratched at the frozen ground. She remembered how the midwife's one-room cottage, attached to a cowshed, had smelled of hay and dung and a cow's fruity breath, and how the woman had stared at her with eyes sunken in a pockmarked face, and how she had tried to touch her hair. Terrified, she'd turned away and demanded that Gillette take her home. Afterward, she'd felt sorry for the woman, whose house contained nothing but a barrel chair, a table made of rough boards, a bed covered with a tattered brown cloth, and sooty pans hanging on nails driven into the wall. Now, as she sat in a prison cell thinking of that long-ago day, the midwife's cottage with rays of sunlight filtering in through a crack in a broken shutter seemed like a shining palace.

Despair almost overtook her, but she refused to give in to it. She tried to remember everything about her home near Amiens: pale green leaves in springtime, flowered meadows in summer, autumn forests dressed in orange and gold, snowflakes glistening in crisp winter air. She recalled running through mowed fields, wading in sparkling brooks, smelling roses in her father's garden, listening to hunting horns and barking hounds, tasting sweet red apples in the orchard. She pictured herself opening the door of the large manor house, stepping in, touching the cool stone walls, running her hands over the smooth, dark wood of benches and chairs, looking at her reflection in the polished copper plates on the shelves. In her mind, she entered a room with a large tapestry depicting elegant ladies playing vielles and psalteries in an enclosed garden. That was the room where she'd learned to sing and play the harp, and she imagined herself sitting there again with her teacher as he reminisced about the minstrels of the past and taught her their songs.

Forgetting her grim surroundings, she sang softly to herself, smiling as she remembered the words to a song about a beautiful lady who loved a brave knight. She'd sung it for Hugues, before they were married. Then she remembered a song about a woman who had given herself to a man who did not love her, a woman so sorrowful she hoped to die. She thought of her marriage, and she awakened from her reverie. Hugues was dead, and Christine had said she should try to think of someone who might have wanted to kill him. She wasn't sure she cared.

She stretched out on the cold floor of her cell and tried to sleep, but thoughts of her old home kept her awake. Her father was dead, and everything belonged to her now. She'd been planning to go there in the spring. *If they kill me, I'll never see it again*, she said to herself. *Perhaps I should try to help Christine discover who poisoned Hugues.*

She thought of the people she knew in Paris: the king, who, even after demons had conquered him, had loved Hugues; the king's brother, who had been resentful because the king was so fond of Hugues; the queen's ladies-in-waiting – perhaps one of them was bitter because she'd had an affair with Hugues and he'd abandoned her; the queen, who had no reason to dislike Hugues. Alix was fond of the queen, and she couldn't understand why she had accused her of stealing the mandrake. She pictured her in the royal bedroom, surrounded by her ladies. She saw someone else there, too – the queen's brother, Ludwig. She remembered something she knew about Ludwig, something she'd told Hugues. Hugues had been pleased to hear it.

That is something to tell Christine, if I ever see her again, she thought before she finally slept.

Twenty-Three

*This deplorable calamity had been fore-
told by an omen . . . it was a sign that
a great catastrophe was about to break
forth in the kingdom.*

The Monk of Saint-Denis,
*Chronique du Religieux de
Saint-Denis, contenant le règne
de Charles VI de 1380 à 1422*

As she was making her way home from Mass early Sunday morning, walking slowly through the gloom of a windy, damp day, Christine saw a dark figure moving toward her. An image flashed before her eyes of the monk her mother believed roamed around Paris strangling people. After a moment she realized with relief that this was a very different sort of religious – Brother Michel from the abbey of Saint-Denis. A friend of her husband's, he'd often come to her house. Her mother liked him, because he loved her cooking and always managed to arrive just in time for dinner. He also enjoyed talking with

Francesca about omens and portents. Christine was intrigued that a monk would be interested in such things.

Brother Michel, his black habit whipped around his legs by the wind, came scurrying along with his head down and almost bumped into her. He waved his hands in her face and tried to shoo her back the way she'd come.

'This is no time for you to be out here, Christine. Two more burned men died this morning. The king and his uncles are afraid there will be more unrest in the streets.' His pale blue eyes blinked and his round cheeks twitched.

'Has the king lost his reason again?' she asked. The wind tugged at her cloak and set dry leaves and pebbles capering around her feet.

'Praise God, no. But he is more distracted than ever. His uncles confuse him with all manner of advice, most of it meaningless.' His hood blew off, and he pulled it back over his head. 'And to make matters worse, the king's brother wanders about the palace weeping and saying everything is his fault. He promises to build a chapel at the church of the Celestines, to make amends. I fear his regrets are more for himself than for those unfortunate men who burned. The queen is very upset, too. The only one at the court who remains calm is the Duchess of Orléans. Very calm. Admirable woman.'

Christine had other thoughts about the duchess, but she said nothing. Obviously, she was a friend of Brother Michel's. He was close to everyone at the court, because the monks of Saint-Denis had for years been writing the history of France, and the current abbot had given him the task of chronicling the reign of the present king. Christine had been astounded when her husband told her about it. 'It will be a great work,' Étienne had said. 'But Michel won't affix his name to it. A hundred years from now, no one will remember who wrote it.'

'Were you at the masquerade?' Christine asked. She knew he stayed close to the court at all times so he could witness events firsthand. He'd even been with the king the previous summer when he'd suffered the attack that led him to kill four of his own knights. But she couldn't picture Brother Michel at a masquerade – not the little man who stood before her with his hands tucked into the sleeves of his habit.

'No, I was not. But the people who were can describe the catastrophe so vividly, I am able to write about it as if I had seen everything.'

She shuddered. *How shocked he'd be if he knew I could add my own description*, she thought. She couldn't resist asking, 'Did you have any premonitions beforehand? Were there any signs or omens?'

'I hope you are not mocking me, Christine. Even the ancients knew that certain signs come before certain events, and although I myself had no premonitions, there were indications, if one had known how to interpret them. One such occurred at the church of Saint-Julien in Le Mans last summer, shortly before the king went out of his mind. Surely you have heard what happened there.' His hood fell back, and gusts of wind fretted with the tufts of thinning hair around his tonsure.

Christine shook her head. Francesca must not have heard, either, or she would have talked about it endlessly.

'I write about it in my history. In that church, there is a little statue of the Blessed Mother, much venerated by the people of Le Mans. One day, not long before the king fell ill, this statue began to turn around and around on its pedestal, all by itself. No one had touched it. No one had even been near it. Yet it revolved like that for at least half an hour.' He made a slow, circular motion with his finger. 'That was a truly significant sign, you must admit.' He looked at her expectantly, his blue eyes blinking.

'My mother says she saw a dead baby brought back to life at the church of Saint-Martin. Do you believe that, too?'

'I know all about it.'

Christine sighed and turned the conversation to another subject. 'Will you include the murder of Hugues de Précy in your history?'

'No. It is painful enough to have to write about the tragic masquerade. The murder is a minor event compared to that. God have mercy on the young woman who did it, though. She seemed to be an altogether different sort of person.'

'Are you convinced she poisoned her husband?'

'She has said nothing to defend herself, even under torture. The provost and his officials have tried her and judged her guilty.'

Christine was stunned. 'When?'

'Yesterday afternoon. She will die the day after tomorrow.'

'She can't!'

'You don't believe she's guilty?'

'I'm sure she's not. Someone else gave her husband the poison.'

'Someone else? How do you know?'

She hesitated to say it to the monk, but there was no other way. 'A prostitute from the brothel on the rue Tiron told me.'

'Surely you don't speak to prostitutes!'

'Christ spoke to them.'

'But not a respectable woman like you. If anyone is going to converse with prostitutes, let it be a priest.'

'Some priests are only too eager to do so.' The words were out of her mouth before she could stop them. Michel stared at her for a moment, drew himself up to his full height, which made him only slightly taller than she was, and said, 'I always wondered how Étienne could put up with your sharp tongue, Christine.'

She felt herself blushing, and she knew she should apologize. But then Michel added, 'Still, I cannot be angry with you for speaking the truth. Many priests have fallen into sin. Many monks, too. Even some from my own abbey.' He sighed. 'Tell me about this prostitute.'

'Her name is Marion. I've known her for a long time. She has many faults, but she's not a liar. She was outside the palace the night of the murder. She saw the real murderer give Hugues the poison and put the flask under Alix de Clairy's hand.'

Michel started to say something, but she interrupted. 'She can describe it all accurately.'

'Then she must know the identity of the murderer.'

'That's the unfortunate part. She couldn't see who it was.'

'Has she told anyone else about this?'

'She knows no one else would believe her. Certainly not the provost.'

'He wouldn't believe you either. You'd be foolish to go to him with something a prostitute told you.'

'There is something else, Michel. I went to the Châtelet and spoke to Alix de Clairy yesterday morning.'

Michel stared at her in disbelief. 'How did you manage that?'

'It's too much to explain right now. I thought I might learn something that would prove her innocence, and I did.'

'She told you something she didn't tell the provost?'

'No. It's something I saw. Blood.'

'That's not surprising. She had a bad fall.'

'Marion says she fell on her face, and that's true; she has a big bruise on her cheek. But she has blood on the back of her head, too.'

'Probably from the torture.'

'She hadn't yet been tortured when I saw her.'

Michel's eyes widened.

'I think someone hit Alix on the head, to make sure she wouldn't be able to run away before she was found lying by her husband's body, with the flask under her hand.'

The monk stared at the ground and kept silent for a long time. Christine waited, scarcely breathing. Then he looked up, and said, 'I think you may have discovered something very important.'

She breathed in deeply. 'There's something else, Michel. An old woman who lives behind Marion's brothel sells poisons. Marion thinks the murderer may have been one of her customers. I'm going to visit this woman and try to find out who it was. Marion is arranging it for me.'

'It may be too late. You must speak with someone right away. Not the provost, though. He's already condemned Alix de Clairy to die, and I'm sure he won't change his mind. You will only anger him. I think you must speak with the king. He might listen to you, because he will remember the days when you were children together at the palace. In spite of his illness, he is a compassionate man, and when he hears what you have to say, he might ask the provost to spare Alix de Clairy for a few more days. I will do my best to arrange an audience for you.'

He looked at Christine thoughtfully. 'But you must not be disappointed if the king spurns your request. He may not even fully comprehend what you tell him. Sometimes he is just like a child. He even had the flask that contained the poison brought to him, and he plays with it all the time, like a toy.'

Over the monk's shoulder, Christine could see the buildings of the Hôtel Saint-Pol, shrouded in fog and gloom. The wind had subsided, and the pennants and banners adorning the towers drooped, as if dispirited by what was happening inside the palace – the pitiful king, his mind shattered; the king's brother, weeping for his sins; the queen, distressed because she'd lost the mandrake she thought would restore her husband to health.

Michel said, 'You will be taking a great risk, Christine. You know what they say: nothing is heavier than the wrath of kings.'

'I'll be placing you in danger, too.'

'That is of no consequence,' he said, and Christine realized that this man who looked so meek was just as obstinate as she was. She could hear Étienne chuckling.

Michel interrupted her thoughts. 'This prostitute seems to have told you many things. Do you see her often? I can't imagine what your mother thinks.'

She wanted to tell him to stop troubling himself about what her mother would think and instead have sympathy for a woman who had fallen into the only profession open to her. But she resisted.

'In any case, I will go to the palace now,' he said. 'Then I'll come to your house and let you know whether the king will see you.' He turned and started back toward the Hôtel Saint-Pol.

She knew he'd arrive just in time for dinner. As she watched him hurry along the street with his black habit flapping around him, she asked herself how it was possible that this unprepossessing little man was writing a great history of their times. She heard Étienne say, as clearly as if he were standing beside her, *Don't be deceived by appearances, Christine.*

Twenty-Four

If little girls were sent to school, they would learn and understand the fine points of all the arts and sciences just as well as boys.

Christine de Pizan, *Le Livre de la Cité des Dames*, 1404–1405

Christine walked to the rue Tiron, hoping to meet Marion. The wind began to blow again, but the chill she felt wasn't caused by the weather. It was caused by the fact that she'd pledged to help a woman accused of murder, and the realization that she was placing herself, and now Brother Michel as well, in peril. She came to the path leading to the brothel and gazed at the old cottage half hidden by bare, tangled brambles, writhing in the wind. Marion was nowhere in sight. If she wanted to speak to her, she would have to go to the door and ask for her, and that was impossible. She would try to find a murderer, but she would not go into a brothel, not even to defy her mother. Or Brother Michel.

So she turned around and went back to her own safe, respectable home, where, although they had to count every denier, there was always a cheerful fire and something delicious for

169

dinner. She took off her cloak and stood for a moment in the front hall, comforted by familiar sounds and savory smells – the children taunting each other on the stairs, her mother and Georgette arguing in the kitchen, dishes rattling, the fragrance of her mother's cooking. She couldn't blame Michel for always arriving at dinnertime.

She went into the kitchen, where she found Georgette grinding something with a mortar and pestle and her mother preparing a compote of dried pears and wine. 'Where have you been?' Francesca asked.

'I met Brother Michel. He told me two more of the burned men died this morning. The king and his uncles are very distressed. They fear more unrest in the streets.'

'*Cretini!* Those uncles should be run through with daggers, like the man you found at the palace.' Francesca drove her knife into one of the pears.

'Michel also told me Alix de Clairy has been sentenced to die the day after tomorrow.'

Francesca set the knife down. 'You must not upset yourself too much over this, *Cristina*.'

'I'm going to speak with the king, Mama. Michel went to the palace to arrange an audience for me.'

'How did you convince him to do that?'

'It doesn't matter. He'll come here later and tell me when the audience is to be.'

Francesca shook her head. Then she brightened and said, 'Michel will stay for dinner. We are having civet of hare. Georgette, you must break

170

up some bread. *Christina*, you will bring the spices.' She handed her the key to the small cabinet where she kept those expensive items.

Christine unlocked the cabinet and stared at the shelves, knowing she should be able to remember which spices were required for the hare recipe. But she couldn't.

Her mother sighed. 'Cloves, pepper, and mace. And also ginger, saffron, and cinnamon for the pears. How is it possible that my daughter, who enjoys eating so much, has no interest in cooking?'

Christine found the spices and set them on the table. She could have informed Francesca that she had no time for cooking now that she was working to support the family, but she didn't, because she knew that was a paltry excuse. In truth, she hated cooking.

Georgette tossed some pieces of bread into a bowl and then stood with a blank look on her face until Francesca told her to bring the hare. The girl shuffled into the pantry, came back with a skinned carcass, and threw it onto the table. Francesca started to cut it into pieces, and Christine looked away until her mother had added them to the onions in the skillet. By that time, she was tired just from watching, but her mother wasn't finished. She said, 'For Michel, we will have pasta with a sauce of marjoram and cheese. No one in France knows how to make pasta.'

'That's because they don't know how to eat it.'

'They should learn to use these,' Francesca said, going to the cupboard and bringing out some bone-handled forks she'd brought from Italy. She wiped each one lovingly with a linen cloth.

Christine snuck up to her room to rest.

Before long, there was a knock at the front door. She went down to let Brother Michel in, eager to find out what the king had said.

'I reminded him who you are, and he agreed to receive you early tomorrow morning.'

'Did you mention Marion?'

'That is up to you.'

'Please say nothing about her to my mother.'

Francesca came in. 'Michel! You are just in time for dinner.'

He smiled. 'An empty stomach rarely refuses food. At least, that is what they tell us at the abbey.' He followed her into the kitchen, where she'd laid the table as if for a banquet, covering it with a crisp linen cloth and setting out her silver wine cups. Prominently displayed in the center stood the shell-shaped saltcellar Georgette had dropped, the dented side turned away from the monk's place. Francesca glanced at Christine to make sure she'd noticed.

Michel rubbed his hands together in anticipation and greeted the children, who raced in, laughing and pushing Goblin back into the hallway; they knew what their grandmother would say about a dog at the dinner table when they had a guest. Georgette brought a basin and towels so they could wash their hands, Michel said the blessing, and they sat down. When Georgette served the pasta, the monk smiled and looked pleased with himself. He'd learned how to use a fork.

It didn't take long for Francesca to begin her interrogation. 'Tell us about the men who died at the palace this morning, Michel.'

'That is not a subject for young ears,' he said, looking at the children.

'Tell us about the king then,' she said.

'He is distraught, too upset to pay any attention to the queen, though she is as upset as he is. She has to look to her ladies-in-waiting for comfort. And to her brother, Ludwig.'

Francesca sniffed. 'That brother – not worth a peeled onion. He does not belong here in Paris. The queen is always giving him expensive gifts so he will stay.'

'Have you heard anything about a mandrake, Michel?' Christine asked.

'Unhealthy things, mandrakes. Last week, Alix de Clairy brought one to the queen, and now it has disappeared. The queen is unhappy about it. Very unhappy. She thought it could be used to cure the king.'

Thomas had been squirming in his seat, and he could no longer contain himself. 'The fire. Tell us about the fire. And how Hugues de Précy got poisoned.'

Michel looked at Christine, and she shook her head. 'There's nothing you don't already know,' the monk said to Thomas.

'I'll be a knight someday, and I won't let anyone set me on fire,' Thomas said. 'Or poison me.'

Jean said, 'Georgette says if you dip a unicorn's horn into your drink, it takes out poison.'

'Surely you don't believe that,' Christine said

to the girl, who had served the hare and was standing behind her, listening to every word.

'Colin told me. He says the king and his brother carry unicorn horns so they can't be poisoned. Most of the king's knights have them, too. Hugues de Précy must have forgotten to get one.'

'Many such things are believed at the court,' Michel said. 'Some people have diamonds that are reputed to turn black when they are near poison. The king has a sapphire that is supposed to cure diseases of the eye – he inherited it from his father. It is set in a band of gold, and it is very valuable. Unfortunately, it has recently disappeared, and he is upset about it. But he still has another stone, a magic one that cures gout.' Christine frowned at him. 'Or, so they say,' he added.

'A tortoise foot is better for gout,' Georgette said.

'No. Henbane,' Francesca said. 'But you must be careful. It is also a very strong poison.'

Thomas squirmed in his seat. 'I want to know about wolfsbane. The poison the witch used to poison her husband.'

'She isn't a witch,' Christine said.

'She *is* a witch,' Georgette muttered under her breath.

'Bring the pears, Georgette,' Christine said.

The girl went to the pantry and came back balancing the bowl of pear compote and all the necessary dishes and spoons against her chest. She set everything in the center of the table and stood behind Christine as before.

'What do they say at the court about the murder, Michel?' Francesca asked. 'Do they all believe the knight's wife is guilty?'

'Yes. But I'm not so sure she is. There was a witness.' He looked at Christine, who shook her head. To change the subject, he said, 'And one must not forget the other terrible crime, the murder of the man who was bringing a book to the Duke of Orléans.'

'Why is that book of such consequence?' Christine asked.

'It is not a book the duke should have,' Michel said. Something in his voice deterred Christine from asking any more questions.

Georgette was leaning over the table. 'The compote,' Francesca said. The girl straightened up, spooned the pears into the bowls, passed them around, and resumed her listening posture.

'Why would anyone poison a man for a book?' Thomas asked. 'There are books in my school, and I'd be glad to give them all to the murderer. I'd give away all the teachers, too.'

'Only the ignorant despise education,' Michel said.

'I wouldn't give away any books,' Marie announced.

'That's because you realize how lucky you are to be able to learn to read,' Christine said, looking fondly at her daughter, who was determined to learn as much as she could, no matter how often her grandmother and her brothers told her girls didn't need to be taught about anything other than housekeeping. Over Francesca's objections, Christine had found a school that accepted girls as well as boys, and she sent all her children there. Marie loved it.

'Books,' Francesca groaned. 'They cause trouble. Do you remember, *Cristina*, when that young theologian from the university came here and accused your father of using books to work magic?'

'If you're referring to the time Papa made those tin figures of the Englishmen and buried them in the gardens at the Hôtel Saint-Pol because he thought that would cause the English to leave France, he didn't get the idea from a book. He heard about it from a friend. He told me.'

'You are right. It was a friend.' Francesca thought for a moment. 'I do not remember his name. But no matter. If your father had not been reading books all the time, that young man from the university would not have been able to accuse him of finding recipes for magic in them. I do not care for books.'

Brother Michel looked up from his pear compote. 'It is said, "No book is so evil that some good cannot be found in it."' Then he sighed. 'Unfortunately, I'm afraid that saying doesn't apply to the book stolen from the dead man you found behind the chest at the palace, Christine.'

Twenty-Five

Ladies, see how men accuse you of the most terrible sins. Expose their deceit by the splendor of your virtue; by doing good, disprove the lies of all those who slander you.

Christine de Pizan, *Le Livre de la Cité des Dames*, 1404–1405

Early the next morning Christine went to the Hôtel Saint-Pol. Although she had tried to conceal her misgivings from her mother, she was troubled. She was well aware of what would happen to Alix de Clairy were she unable to convince the king that she was innocent. And what would be her own fate then? And that of Brother Michel? The king was a compassionate man, but when he was not in his right mind, he was capable of terrible things.

Freezing rain had glazed the streets during the night, and although the sun was shining, the cobblestones in the courtyard of the king's residence were still wet and slippery. As she crept across them, a man ran past her, bumping into her and sending her to her knees. He rushed off without an apology, and as she picked herself up she couldn't help thinking of the mysterious man with the bare feet who'd knocked her down on his way to the palace to be murdered.

She stumbled to the entrance of the king's residence, where she was surprised to find Simon standing guard, with Renaut at his side.

'Why aren't you at the queen's residence?' she asked.

'I was instructed to come here for the day, and Blanche asked me to bring Renaut along. She's over there attending to the gowns damaged the night of the ball.'

'Who was the man who made me fall? I couldn't see his face.'

'You know him – the duke's favorite knight, Guy de Marolles. He's been in a disagreeable humor for days. I think it's because his wife is ill.'

'That seems to be his customary demeanor,' Christine said. Guy de Marolles was a rude, unpleasant man who followed after the Duke of Orléans, complying with his every wish and disdaining everyone else. In addition to his loathsome manner, he was exceedingly ugly, with a short, thick neck and bulging eyes. Christine had often wondered how he could fancy himself so superior.

Renaut pulled on Simon's sleeve. The *portier* reached into his burlap sack and brought out a tart that smelled of herbs and strong cheese. The boy ate it in a couple of bites, then looked at Christine. 'Do you have more almond cakes?'

'Not today.'

'Would you like one of my tarts?' Simon asked

her, reaching into his sack again. The burlap looked a bit unclean, but she accepted the tart gladly. She'd been too apprehensive about her coming ordeal to eat anything at home that morning.

'I have an audience with the king,' she said, her mouth full.

'I know. But I was instructed to tell you he cannot see you for a while. He is very distressed today. You must wait while his brother calms him.'

'Brush the crumbs from your face before you go to the king,' Renaut said, and he skipped out into the courtyard.

Christine laughed. She watched the boy take his little red top out of his sleeve and set it spinning on the cobblestones. 'He's always by himself,' she said.

'He has friends,' Simon said. 'Everyone who comes to the palace stops to talk to him. But Blanche worries about him. She worries about Loyse, too. I think that is the reason she chews on cloves all the time – to soothe her stomach.'

'How old is Loyse?'

'Sixteen.'

Christine was too uneasy to stand talking with Simon. And she was curious about the seamstress's daughter. 'I'm going to look at the lions,' she said.

'You won't see Loyse,' Simon called after her as she walked away.

Christine wandered through cloisters and court-yards she hadn't seen since she was a child. First, she came to the royal kitchen – a large building close to the palace with a high, vaulted ceiling and four fireplaces. The door was open, and she could see the king's chef and a multitude of lesser cooks and perspiring kitchen boys rushing about as they prepared the noon meal for the hundreds of people who lived or worked at the palace. For once, the smell of roasted meat and freshly baked bread didn't tempt her.

She walked through a courtyard with a fish-pond and ran her hand over a layer of ice coating the water, imagining she could see the salmon swimming lazily beneath it. She came to aviaries, pigeon houses, and dovecotes, and she made cooing sounds, hoping the birds would answer her. She paused beside kennels and listened to the muffled barks of the dogs, and she looked into a stable where the horses pawed the floor as grooms brushed their long winter coats. The warm, moist odor of manure and hay drifted out into the cold air. One of the grooms tossed a saddle over the back of a large brown stallion and led him into a courtyard. The sharp sound of hooves striking the paving stones startled her, and she moved away.

She continued on through bare gardens bordered by fig trees wrapped in straw for the winter and entered the orchards, where leafless branches traced lacy patterns against the sky. Beyond, she could see the new wall King Charles the Fifth had built, and the fortress they called the *Bastille Saint-Antoine*, which he had constructed to provide protection for the royal residence. To the right of the *Bastille* stretched a field dotted with sheds and barns for storing catapults, battering rams, and canons. She was glad to see no movement there, because that signified the weapons were not being readied for war.

Then she came to the lions. She thought there had once been ten, but she wasn't sure, because although her father had sometimes taken her to see them, she'd been afraid to go too near. Some had died; she didn't know how many remained. She heard them shuffling around in their stockade, an area enclosed by trees and a thick fence, but when she peered through an opening in the palings, everything became quiet. She could see several of the animals standing motionless near the entrance to the den and someone in a ragged chemise hovering nearby. The woman's long auburn hair obscured her face, but Christine sensed she was watching her. 'Loyse,' she called softly. The woman vanished into the den, and the lions padded after her.

She heard something move in the trees, and she hurried away.

'Did you see her?' Simon asked with a grin when she arrived, breathless, back at the entrance to the king's residence.

'Just a glimpse. But I didn't stay. Someone was following me.'

'I know. I told one of the sergeants to watch over you. Did you think I would let you roam about by yourself, after all that has happened?'

She wanted to be annoyed, but she was too relieved.

'Have another tart,' Simon said. 'Then you can go to the king. Colin is here, and he'll go with you.'

She refused the tart, still tasting the one she'd eaten earlier, and went into a long gallery, where she found Colin waiting for her. She tried to be calm as they walked toward the chamber where she was to have her audience, but her heart was beating wildly and her palms were sweating. At the door of the audience chamber, she stopped and wiped her mouth with her sleeve, but, for once, she forgot about the pockmark on her cheek. The *huissier* guarding the door stepped aside and let her pass into the room.

Just inside, Guy de Marolles slouched against the wall, one leg crossed over the other, his short arms folded across his thick chest. He eyed her insolently. She took a deep breath, held her head high, and swept by him. Then she saw the king, slumped in a high-backed chair at the far end of the cavernous room, and she didn't feel bold anymore. She crossed what seemed like an endless space to reach him. The cold floor tiles chilled her feet, and she could feel no warmth from the flames in a huge fireplace near where the king sat.

The king was not alone. Next to his chair stood the Duke of Orléans, and beside Louis was the queen's brother. She wasn't surprised to see the duke, but she was astonished to see Ludwig.

The duke, wearing an emerald green houppelande with wide, ermine-lined sleeves, looked, as usual, elegant and proud; nothing in his expression indicated that he might be feeling remorseful about the tragic fire. The king, dressed in the same red houppelande she'd seen him in the week before, grasped with one hand a carved lion's head on an arm of his chair, squeezing it so tightly his knuckles turned white. In the other hand, he held a shiny red object, and he gazed at it intently, seemingly unaware of her presence.

She knelt on the cold floor. The duke spoke first. 'You have something to say to the king, Christine?'

Without looking at her, the king said, 'Rise, Christine. Don't be shy. We are friends, are we not?'

'In happier times, Sire, when we were children,' she said, as she struggled to her feet. Perhaps he did remember the days when he'd played at tops and cherry stones and hide-and-seek with the court astrologer's daughter in the gardens and courtyards of the Hôtel Saint-Pol. But there was no friendliness in his voice, and he seemed to be in pain. She remembered hearing that whenever he was about to have one of his attacks, he suffered as though arrows were piercing his flesh.

She looked away, to a tapestry on the wall behind him, where ancient heroes sat proudly on their thrones, strong and virile, mocking her ailing king, hunched and shrunken in his chair.

The duke, on the other hand, was imperious and very sure of himself. He said, 'I am told you visited Alix de Clairy at the Châtelet, Christine.'

'It was at the queen's command, *Monseigneur*.'

'Before you spoke with the queen, you asked the Duchess of Orléans to write to *Monseigneur le Prévôt* on your behalf. Why were you so eager to visit Alix de Clairy?'

183

'I want to help her. I believe she is innocent.'

'She is not innocent!' the king cried, suddenly sitting tall in the chair. 'She poisoned my friend. She used this.' He leaned forward and thrust the object he held to within a few inches of her face.

She stared at it in horror. It was a glass flask, the color of blood.

'Mark it well,' the king said. 'It is the vessel she filled with the poison.' He began to weep. Christine studied the floor. There was a large crack in one of the tiles, and she wanted to sink into it and disappear. But she knew what she had to do. She looked at the king and asked, in a voice she hoped was calm, 'How can you be certain, Sire, it was Alix de Clairy who gave her husband the poison?'

The king rose from his chair and lifted the flask high over her head. 'This is the proof.' She backed away. 'There is no need to be afraid,' he simpered. He turned the flask upside down and shook it. 'There is no poison in it now. The stopper is gone.' She remembered Georgette babbling about how the sergeants at the palace had searched for the stopper in the street.

The duke put his arm around his brother's shoulders and eased him down onto the chair. The king buried his face in his hands. Louis turned to Christine. 'What have you to say to the king that will prove the woman's innocence?'

She moved closer to the king. 'Sire, one of the women from the brothel on the rue Tiron saw someone give Hugues de Précy the poison. It was not his wife.'

The king raised his head and looked at her

184

through narrowed eyes, as though he were taunting a childhood playmate. 'You would speak with a prostitute?'

'I have known her for many years. Her name is Marion.' She glanced at the duke, but he turned away.

'Marion cannot say who the person was,' she continued. 'She only knows it was not Alix de Clairy. And what's more, that person hit . . .'

But she never got to say anything about the blow Alix had received, because Guy de Marolles stepped into the room and shouted, 'Of course it was the woman. Women are evil!' The duke strode over, took him by the shoulders, and pushed him out the door.

Christine fell to her knees again. 'Please, Sire, ask *Monseigneur le Prévôt* to let Alix de Clairy live for a few more days. An old woman at the Tiron brothel may have sold the poison. I will go there and find out who bought it.'

The king glanced at his brother, a puzzled look in his eyes, before fixing his gaze on the blood-red flask again.

The duke spoke. 'Brother Michel said you would have us believe Alix de Clairy is innocent, Christine. The queen's brother knows she is not.'

Ludwig stepped forward. He looked at the floor and hesitated before he said in halting French, 'I was there that night, outside the palace. I saw Alix de Clairy give to her husband the poison.'

Christine jumped to her feet. But before she could protest, the duke said, 'Your prostitute is lying.'

'Why would she tell such a story if it isn't true?' She looked at Ludwig, who was rubbing his hands on his thighs. Beads of sweat dotted his forehead.

Gripping the lion on the arm of his chair as though he would crush it, the king said, 'Stop trying to defend the murderess, Christine. Alix de Clairy will burn for what she did. You may leave us now.'

She backed away, knelt so hastily she almost fell, turned, and stumbled from the room. Guy de Marolles smirked as she went out the door. She ducked her head – and walked into Gilles Malet.

'I know why you are here, Christine,' he said. 'Have done with this foolishness.' His bushy eyebrows twitched as he strode away.

Close to her in the gallery stood a high-backed chair, and she sank down onto it, grateful that she could hide behind the large rampant lions carved on its massive arms. After she'd rested there for several minutes, attempting to regain her composure, she heard the duke and Gilles conversing just inside the door of the audience chamber. 'It's a large book with symbols on the cover – a circle with a sword, a scepter, a ring, an oil vessel, and a tablet with crosses on it,' the duke said. She shivered. He was describing the symbols in a necromancer's manual. Her father had told her about such books. They contained instructions for conjuring demons.

Not wanting the two men to know she'd over-heard the conversation, she rose from the chair and walked away quickly. But not quickly enough.

She heard footsteps behind her. It was the duke. He grasped her arm. 'If you want Alix de Clairy to live for a few more days, you must do something for me.'

She tried to speak calmly. 'Is it something that will help her, *Monseigneur*?'

'Nothing can help her. But she had a book. I want you to find out where it is.'

She froze. 'What book, *Monseigneur*?'

'The man you found behind the chest was bringing me a book. Alix de Clairy refuses to tell us where it is.'

She wrenched her arm out of his grasp. 'Are you blaming Alix de Clairy for the first murder, too? Of what else do you accuse her?'

'Like most women, Alix de Clairy is capable of every kind of vice.'

This from a man who consorted with magicians and sorcerers and who may have caused four men to burn to death! It was all she could do to control her voice as she said, 'She couldn't have stabbed the man behind the chest. She was with me.'

'Perhaps she didn't kill him, but she stole the book, and she has hidden it somewhere. We've searched Hugues de Précy's house, but we cannot find it.' The duke's voice had risen, but then he added calmly, 'I will persuade the king to ask *Monseigneur le Prévôt* to let Alix live for a few more days. Since you are her friend, you will go to the Châtelet and find out from her where the book is. I've written another letter for you.' He held out a slip of parchment. In a daze, she took it and tucked it into her sleeve.

'The book will help restore the king's health,' he said. 'That is to be desired, is it not?'

'Of course, *Monseigneur*.'

'Then you will do what I ask! But if you don't succeed . . .' The look on his face told her that if she failed, Alix de Clairy was not the only one whose life was in danger.

Twenty-Six

There is no excuse for the sin of slander.

Christine de Pizan, *Le Livre des Trois Vertus*, 1405

The duke walked away, and Christine hurried down the gallery, ignoring the sergeants-at-arms who stared at her as she passed. She had to fight the urge to lash out at men dressed in royal livery who were willing to serve a king who believed Alix de Clairy capable of murder.

Colin came running toward her, and announced, 'The queen's been asking for you.'

She'd forgotten the queen. Colin dashed off on another errand, and she stepped into the court-yard, where she found Simon and Renaut finishing the last of the cheese tarts. Simon offered her one, but she shook her head and walked away without speaking, so preoccupied with her troubled thoughts that when she came to the courtyard of the queen's residence she slipped on the wet cobblestones and fell. Someone picked her up as if she weighed no more than Renaut and set her on her feet. She smelled cloves, and she realized it was Blanche, who'd come in behind her. Christine was glad to see her. She'd had enough of royalty that day, and the sight of an ordinary person in a plain black cloak, even a person as dour as Blanche, was comforting.

The seamstress was carrying several gowns over her arm. 'I suppose you're on your way to the queen's chambers,' she said. 'I'll go with you.' Without waiting for Christine to reply, she took her arm and led her across the courtyard, into the queen's residence, and through the great gallery.

At the end of the gallery, just as Christine was about to step into the inner courtyard, the seamstress said, 'I know another way.' She went to a small door, stooped to pass under the lintel, and beckoned for Christine to follow. Beyond the door was a dark, narrow, airless passageway, which smelled of dust and mold. Blanche charged through it, and Christine followed. They came to a tiny courtyard where someone had stacked empty flowerpots, the containers used in summer for the plants that decorated the window ledges and doorways of the palace. Beyond, there was a spiral staircase in a tower, and as they climbed, they could look through slit-like openings in the walls and see the gables and turrets of the other buildings of the Hôtel Saint-Pol shimmering in the winter sunlight.

The banners and silken streamers adorning pinnacles, spires, and weathervanes fluttered in the wind, and in the gardens below, the leafless branches of the trees shook when sudden gusts caught at them.

As she followed Blanche up the stairs, Christine tried to imagine what the woman might have been like as a little girl, in the days when she'd come to the Hôtel Saint-Pol with her mother. Surely the child had wandered around the palace investigating hidden passages and out-of-the-way places, just as she herself had once done. She wondered what secret hide-aways her companion had found, but before she could ask, they reached the top of the staircase and Blanche hurried down a short passageway to the queen's bedchamber.

Blanche went into the room, handed the gowns to one of the queen's chambermaids, and stood answering her questions about how they could be repaired. Another chambermaid came to the door and told Christine she should approach the queen, who was slumped in her chair by her fireplace, holding the gold ball filled with hot coals. Ludwig was with her, and Christine wondered how he'd gotten there so quickly. He looked up when he saw her, and slunk away to the other side of the room.

She entered and knelt.

'Have you the mandrake?' the queen asked. Her eyes were red, her face was puffy, and she looked very tired.

'I am sorry to tell you, *Madame*, Alix de Clairy knows nothing about it.'

'She knows all about it. My brother has told me he saw her use its juice to poison her husband.'

Christine looked at Ludwig, but he refused to meet her gaze.

'I have not wanted to believe Alix de Clairy is a murderess,' the queen said. 'Now I know it is true. But at least, now that she has used the poison, she could let me have the mandrake back. It will restore health to the king.'

'She doesn't have it, *Madame.*'

'My brother has told me you would try to protect her.'

'I have information to prove she is innocent.'

'You have received the information from a prostitute. My brother says you will even take yourself into a brothel and ask there an old harlot if she sold the poison.'

'I have other proof, *Madame.*'

Ludwig came to the queen's side and whispered something in her ear. Christine started to speak, but before she could, the queen raised her hand and hurled the gold ball with the hot coals into the fireplace. With a brittle crash, the ball broke apart, and the coals dropped, sizzling, into the flames. She glared at Christine. 'Leave now, before I have you thrown into prison for trying to protect a murderess.'

Christine knelt quickly and hurried from the room, nearly falling as she tripped over the queen's greyhound, which stood quivering by the door. Feeling faint, she leaned against the wall with her eyes closed while the world whirled around her – until she heard the rustle of a gown and sensed that someone was standing in front of her. She opened her eyes, expecting to see Blanche again, and was surprised to find the Duchess of Orléans, leaning on her crutch and breathing heavily. She put her hand on Christine's arm, and said, 'I heard everything, my dear. That was disgraceful of Isabeau. But you must forgive her. She is distressed because of the king's illness. She listens too much to her brother, and she does not know what to believe.'

Speechless with amazement, Christine stared at the old woman, remembering her previous encounter with her. Her sense of wonder increased when the duchess asked, 'Why did you not tell me you had information that would prove Alix de Clairy did not poison her husband?'

'I received the information from a prostitute, *Madame*. I thought you would not approve – or believe.'

'Do you think I am such a terrible old woman? It does not matter who gave you this information. What matters is that if it is true, we must save her.'

'It *is* true, *Madame*. I will tell you why. But I think you should sit down.' She took the old woman's arm and led her to a high-backed bench. The duchess eased herself down, wheezing and trying to catch her breath. With a motion of her trembling hand, she indicated that Christine should sit beside her.

'Now you must tell me everything,' she said, and she listened carefully as Christine told her why she knew Alix de Clairy was innocent.

The duchess rose, with difficulty, and picked

up her crutch. She said, 'I believe you. I will do all I can to help save her.'

Christine said, 'Please be careful, *Madame*.'

'You must not worry about me. It's you who must be careful.' She started to walk down the passageway, but then she turned. 'Be assured, I will make the queen understand that she should not believe the lies she hears.'

Hoping she wouldn't meet anyone else, Christine walked back the way she'd come with Blanche and went slowly down the spiral staircase in the tower. In the little courtyard with the empty flowerpots, the wind slapped her face, and in the narrow passageway leading to the great gallery, it blew clouds of dust around her. In the deserted gallery, a sudden current rocked the tapestries on the walls and set them jangling on their metal hooks. She looked up and found a pack of devils, monkeys, and satyrs leering down at her. She shook her fist at them, though they were only the sculpted supports under the ceiling beams.

Out in the street, she slumped against the wall of the palace courtyard – until she saw Marion coming toward her from the stables across the way. She stood tall, in a vain attempt to appear braver than she felt.

'What's the matter? Have you seen the *loup-garou*?' the girl asked in her husky voice.

'It wasn't the werewolf. I tried to tell the king what you saw, but he wouldn't listen to me. The queen's brother was there, and he claimed he saw Alix de Clairy give her husband the poison.'

'The dirty liar!' Marion spat into the street and pummeled the air with her fists.

'We do have someone on our side. I told the Duchess of Orléans everything, and she says she will do all she can to help save Alix. But she warned me to be careful.' Christine braced herself against the wall again and put her head in her hands. 'I hope I have the courage to go on with this.'

'Stop acting like a coward. You *have* to save Alix de Clairy now, because if you don't, all those grand people at the court will see that you're burned at the stake with her. You'd better wash the milk off your liver.'

That was an expression Christine had told Thomas not to use, but now it restored her courage. That and the edge of the duke's letter to the provost grazing her arm as it shifted around in her sleeve. She wrenched herself away from the wall.

Marion said, 'I spoke to Margot. You can go and see her. It's late now. Go tomorrow. Her hut is right behind the brothel.'

Marion walked home with Christine, taking her almost to her door and then hurrying away. Francesca came out of the kitchen as soon as she heard the door close. 'What did the king say to you?' she asked when she saw her daughter's face. Without waiting for an answer, she hurried off to get one of her herbal concoctions.

For once, Christine drank it without complaining. 'I'll tell you about it later. Please don't ask me any questions now.'

'You will feel better if you have some supper,'

Francesca said, taking her arm and drawing her into the kitchen.

The children were gathered around the table. Unable to face them, Christine retreated into the pantry and tried to master her troubled thoughts among the baskets of onions, sacks of flour, and jugs of oil. When she finally joined the family, she could only pretend to eat. Sensing her distress, Marie came to her side and put her arm around her, but Thomas was rowdier than ever, throwing pieces of bread at Jean and Lisabetta and shouting out proverbs his grandmother had taught him. Finally, Christine had had enough, and she announced, 'Here's another proverb for you to consider, Thomas. "The ass that brays the most eats the least."'

Thomas just looked puzzled, but Jean tried to make peace. 'Tell us about Brother Michel, Mama,' he said. 'Why isn't he in the monastery all the time? I thought the monks were supposed to stay there and pray.'

'Why don't you ask him yourself?'

'Really, *Cristina*. That would not be polite,' Francesca said. She looked at her daughter's plate. 'Why are you not eating?'

Christine choked down some food, and it made her feel sick. She left the table, went up to her room, and crawled into bed. But although she was deathly tired, she lay staring into the darkness until it was nearly dawn. Then she fell into a deep sleep.

When she opened her eyes again, it was midday, and the bells at Sainte-Catherine's were chiming sext. She dressed quickly and went downstairs.

She could hear the family in the kitchen, eating the midday meal. She wanted to go in and scold her mother for not waking her earlier, but the smell of onions and cabbage turned her stomach. She put on her cloak and boots and snuck out of the house.

The wind nearly blew her off her feet as she turned down the rue Tiron. She looked up and down the street for Marion, but the girl wasn't there. She crept along the overgrown path toward the brothel, still hoping to see her. But no one was outside.

She hurried past the brothel and came to a tiny hut. Its walls were formed of wooden slats barely held together by rusty nails and with such large gaps between them that they couldn't possibly keep out the wind. A crude wattle fence marked off a plot where brown stalks poked through the bare earth, obviously the garden where, in summer, Margot cultivated the plants she used in her potions. Christine thought of all the poisonous herbs the woman could grow – henbane, hemlock, nightshade. And wolfsbane.

She knocked on the door of the hut. When there wasn't any answer, she looked through the slats and saw a faint glow coming from a small fireplace. She knocked again, louder this time. Still no one came. She tried the door and found it unlocked, so she pushed it open and stepped inside.

The one-room hut was empty except for a few dried herbs hanging from the ceiling, a barrel seat, a table lying on its side, and broken jars spilling dusty herbs and foul-looking liquids onto the floor. The fire had died down to a few embers, and the place was icy cold. In one corner, a smoke-blackened curtain hung from the ceiling. 'Margot,' she called out, thinking the old woman might be behind the curtain. A nasty gust of wind darted through the open door and snatched at the cloth, pushing it aside for an instant so she could see what looked like a heap of pillows on a straw mattress. She picked up her skirt, squeezed between the barrel seat and the overturned table, and pulled back the curtain. The heap of pillows was an old woman, sitting with her back against the wall, like a discarded doll. Small and gray-haired, she wore a ragged brown chemise and had a crutch lying across her knees. Christine couldn't see her face, and she had no desire to do so. Margot's head was bent down at an impossible angle. She'd been strangled.

Twenty-Seven

What does it matter if you are lying on a little pile of dung or living in a wretched and miserable hovel where you have nothing to make you comfortable? This will last only a short time, because a blessed home, more beautiful and delightful than anything else, awaits

She let the makeshift curtain fall and stood in
shock, hardly able to breathe, her heart pounding.
When her breathing returned to normal, she
pushed the cloth aside again and knelt by
Margot's body, aware that she was alone in a
hut with a dead woman – a woman who lived
with prostitutes and might have sold poison to
a murderer. She heard a sound and rose to her
feet, her heart beating wildly again. The door
to the hut had swung shut in the wind. Now it
slowly opened, squeaking on its rusty hinges.
She reached down, seized the old woman's
crutch, and turned around, swinging it over
her head.

'The plague take you!' Marion cried. 'Don't hit
me!' Imposing in a large crimson cloak, her thick
red hair hanging loose over her shoulders, she
stood stock still in the doorway, her eyes wide
with astonishment.

Christine set the crutch on the floor. 'Forgive
me. It wasn't for you. Come over here and you'll
understand.'

Marion closed the door with her foot and
stepped in warily, keeping her eyes on Christine
as she crossed the room. Then she saw Margot.
'God's balls,' she whispered, and she bent down
to touch the old woman's cheek.

'Do you know who could have done this?' Christine asked.

'No one here. We all liked her. She told us when the stars were lucky, and which plants to use for pain, and what days were right for . . . well, you know.' Marion's eyes glistened with tears, and she bowed her head to hide them. 'At least now she's in a better place than this miserable hut.' She stroked Margot's cheek gently. Then she stood up, put her hands on Christine's shoulders, and asked, 'Who knew you were coming here?'

'Just you, and a friend of mine – a monk from the abbey of Saint-Denis.' Then she remembered her conversation with the king. The duke, Ludwig, and Guy de Marolles had all heard her say she was going to visit the old woman at the brothel. Ludwig had told the queen, which meant the queen's ladies would have heard, and by now any number of other people would be aware of what she'd intended to do. She shivered, and it wasn't because of the icy gusts that burst into the hovel through the holes in its flimsy walls. 'Actually, a lot of people know,' she said.

Marion turned away and stalked to the other side of the room, her crimson cloak swirling around her. She came back and grasped Christine's shoulders again. 'Someone killed Margot so she couldn't talk to you. Someone who wants to make certain you never find out who poisoned Hugues de Précy.'

'I am aware of that,' Christine said.

'For now, we must be the only ones besides the

murderer who know Margot is dead. We have to leave before someone finds us here.'

Marion went to the door, opened it, looked around, and stepped out. In a daze, Christine followed. The wind blew the door shut behind them.

'Over here,' Marion yelled, pulling her onto a narrow path winding through tall brushes behind the hut. 'This will take us to the street.' They pushed their way through thorny branches, and when they came to an opening, Marion darted out. Then she flew back. '*Merde!* Someone's coming!'

Christine recognized the bowed head and the black habit. 'It's Brother Michel, the monk I told you about.'

'Pretend you don't see him!'

'He's a friend,' Christine shouted over the wail of the wind. She stepped into the street before Marion could stop her.

Michel raised his head. 'What are you doing here, Christine?' He took her arm to draw her away.

Christine shook his hand off. 'This is Marion.'

He blushed. 'Marion . . . yes . . . Marion.'

'I went to ask the old woman about the poison. But she's dead.'

'What did you say? I can't hear you because of the wind.'

'The old woman in the hut behind the brothel. Someone strangled her.'

Michel looked at Marion. 'What have you to do with this?'

Marion drew herself up to her full height,

towered over him, and roared, '*Trou de la Sybille!* I didn't kill her!'

He backed away. 'God, give me strength. I didn't say you did.'

'No one else knows Margot is dead,' Marion raved. 'I have to take Christine home. Out of the way, *porc de Dieu.*'

'But if the woman has been killed, we must tell the authorities, and we must do it without delay.'

'No, you dullard! Someone killed Margot so she wouldn't talk to Christine. That person may try to kill Christine.'

Marion tugged on Christine's right arm. Michel stood dumbfounded for a moment, then he pulled on her left arm, saying, 'Yes, yes. We must take her home.' The two of them started to drag her down the street, Marion's crimson cloak and Michel's black habit flapping in the wind. The wind propelled them along, while frenzied birds wheeled over their heads and a stray dog ran after them, yapping and nipping at their heels. Christine pulled back. 'Stop! Anyone who sees us will know something is wrong. We must be calm and think.'

'You're right,' Michel said. 'But it is not wise to stand here while we think. Not wise at all.'

'Marion,' Christine said, 'you must not go back to the brothel. Someone there may know what's happened, and you'll be in trouble. Go to your lodging house. Tell no one what you've seen. Michel, you come home with me.'

'He won't be able to protect you,' Marion said. 'He's not worth the handle of a bucket.'

'Don't be deceived by appearances,' Christine said.

Marion scowled at the monk, made him a little curtsy, and flounced down the street toward the center of the city.

'How do we know we can trust her not to tell all her friends what has happened?' Michel asked.

'You don't know her. I do. Where are you coming from?'

'I've been at the court. The last of the men burned at the masquerade just died. Everyone is distressed. And the Duke of Orléans told me about your audience with the king. But somehow you succeeded; the king has asked the provost to let Alix de Clairy live for a few more days.'

Twenty-Eight

My happy mother gave me my name, nourished me, and cherished me so much that she breastfed me herself as soon as I was born.

Christine de Pizan, *Le Livre de la Mutacion de Fortune*, 1403

They walked in silence for a while, battling the wind. Then the monk said, 'It is deplorable that you have discovered another murder, Christine. Deplorable.'

'Matters are even worse than you know. The queen is very angry with me.'

'What reason has she to be displeased with you?'

'It concerns the mandrake she lost. There's no time to tell you about it now.'

The wind gave them a last angry shove, and they arrived at the door of Christine's house. They went inside, and Christine took off her cloak and started to go into the kitchen to look for her mother, but Michel stopped her. 'Have you considered the implications of what has happened, Christine?'

'Of course I have. But the sergeants from the Châtelet will find out who murdered the old woman, and I'll be safe.' She tried to sound unconcerned.

'They haven't found out who stabbed the man behind the chest. How much effort do you think they will expend trying to learn who murdered an old harlot? You are in peril, Christine, great peril, and it is time you ceased hiding it from your mother.'

'Why should I worry her?'

'There is no way to keep it secret. Think of her distress should she hear about it from someone other than you.'

Christine was reluctant to admit it, but she knew he was right. 'I suppose you think I should tell her about Marion, too.'

'You must.' He stood lost in thought. 'Perhaps one day we can turn Marion away from sin.'

'That is my hope. But it will be difficult. Believe me, I've tried.'

The monk shook his head. 'All things change, and we change with them,' he said, adding sadly, 'Although I suppose that is not always true.'

Christine looked up to see her mother standing in the doorway. 'Where have you been, *Cristina*? You left without telling me. And why are you here, Michel?'

'We must go in and sit down, Francesca. Christine has something to say to you.'

'I am sure it concerns Alix de Clairy.' Francesca looked frightened.

'Be calm, Mama,' Christine said, putting her arm around her mother's shoulders and drawing her into the kitchen. Georgette had been making candied orange peel. The table was covered with honey.

'The foolish girl has gone to the market. She was supposed to clean this up first,' Francesca said.

Christine sat down at the table, took a piece of orange peel, and nibbled on it. She didn't know where to begin, and Michel wasn't helping; he stood by the fireplace, warming his hands, his back toward her.

Francesca sat beside Christine and folded her arms across her chest. 'Well?'

'I know Alix de Clairy didn't poison her husband.'

'So you have told me. But what can you do?'

'I can try to save her. Michel is willing to help me.'

'Is that true, Michel?' Francesca asked.

The monk turned and faced her. 'Yes, it is.'

Francesca scowled at him. 'You are as fool-hardy as my daughter.'

'If God is with us, there is nothing to fear,' he said.

'There is someone else who wants to help,' Christine said. 'She's a good girl at heart, Mama. You must believe that when I tell you who she is.'

'Is it someone I know?'

'Do you remember Beatrix, the maid you dismissed?'

'Her daughter was raped and became a *prostituta*.' Francesca thought for a minute, and then she shook her finger at Christine. 'How many times have I told you not to go out after dark?'

Christine almost laughed. 'That's not the point, Mama. The daughter's name is Marion. You must remember.'

'Yes. I am sure it was not necessary for her to become a *prostituta*.'

'Have some compassion. It was the only thing she could do.'

Francesca made a clucking sound with her tongue, and Christine looked at Michel in despair. He wiggled his fingers at her, indicating that she should continue.

'You don't walk on the rue Tiron, Mama,' Christine said, 'because of the brothel. But I do. I often meet Marion there, and I talk to her. She's not a bad person.'

Francesca rose and paced around the kitchen, running her hands over bowls and platters, setting trivets upside down on the hearth and then turning them right side up again, lifting a

205

towel from the pole where she'd hung it to dry and running it through her hands, jabbing a knife into an onion lying on the table. 'First you go out to work, and I do not think that is respectable for a woman, and now you are talking to prostitutes. What would your father say? What would Étienne say?'

Michel went to the table and stood beside Christine. 'I think they would be proud of her, very proud. She has discovered the truth about Hugues de Précy's murder, and she has the courage to do something about it.'

Francesca stopped pacing. 'What does Marion have to do with this?'

'Sit down and I'll tell you,' Christine said.

Francesca sighed and lowered herself onto the bench again.

'It was Marion who told me Alix de Clairy didn't murder her husband. She was outside the palace that night, and she saw someone else give Hugues de Précy the poison.'

Francesca stood up and went to the fireplace. 'How can you believe a *prostituta*?'

'She wouldn't make up a story like that.'

'Then why does she not go and tell the provost?'

'You know Jean de Folleville wouldn't listen to her.'

The front door banged, and Georgette came rushing in, spilling the turnips and carrots she was carrying in a basket. 'There's been another murder!' she cried.

'Who has been murdered now?' Francesca asked.

'An old woman at the brothel on the rue Tiron. I heard the sergeants from the Châtelet talking about it in the street.'

'You see, *Cristina*. You must not walk on the rue Tiron.'

'I'm afraid it's too late.'

Georgette threw the basket onto the table and went to the hall to take off her cloak. Michel said, 'Send the girl out on another errand, Francesca. One that will take some time. I do not want her to hear what Christine is about to tell you.'

'*Dio buono.*' Francesca put her hand on her breast. When Georgette returned to the kitchen, she said, 'Go out and buy some cheese. And draw water at the well.'

'But there's cheese in the pantry. And I just took off my cloak.'

'Never mind. Do as I say.'

Georgette walked sullenly back to the hall. The front door slammed.

'Sit down again, Mama,' Christine said, and she sat beside her and told her everything. Francesca stared at her in horror and disbelief, uttering not a word, while Michel – who had not yet heard how the queen had thrown Christine out of her chambers because she had not been able to recover the mandrake, or how the duke had written another letter to the provost thinking she would be able to find out from Alix where the missing book was – walked around the room, shaking his head.

'The situation is more grave than I thought,' he said. But when he realized he was adding to

207

Francesca's alarm, he went to her and took her hands in his. 'Be strong, Francesca. God will keep Christine safe. But we must help.'

'It is not proper for a woman to be looking for murderers. I cannot believe you are encouraging her in this, Michel.'

'Who else will help Alix de Clairy, if I don't?' Christine asked. 'She will burn at the stake for something she didn't do. Is that what you want, Mama?'

'Why can you not be like other women?'

They heard the front door open. 'Here's a proper woman for you,' Christine said as Georgette came charging into the kitchen, waving a large slice of Brie above her head and spilling water from the bucket she carried.

'Put the cheese in the pantry before you drop it. And mop up the water immediately,' Francesca snapped at the girl. Then she went into the hall and called the children down to supper. 'You may as well stay, Michel.' It was not her usual gracious invitation. The monk looked pained.

While the children slurped their soup, Francesca, Michel, and Christine stared into their bowls. Marie and Jean tried to break the silence by starting a conversation about books, and Thomas, who'd just heard all the details of Margot's death from Georgette, thought he could make them laugh by pretending to be strangled.

'*Basta, Tommaso.* One fool in the house is enough,' Francesca said, looking at Christine. Then she said to Jean, 'You wondered what monks do when they are not in their monasteries. Why

208

do you not ask Michel? He seems to be very busy outside his.'

'What would you like to know, Jean?' Michel asked calmly.

'I thought monks were supposed to stay in their monasteries all the time and pray,' Jean said.

'A logical inference. But the abbot of Saint-Denis wants me to write down everything that happens during the reign of our present king, and that means I have to be out in the world to see what is going on.'

'Does the abbot expect you to meddle in everything, too?' Francesca asked.

'That's enough, Mama!' Christine said.

'Why did you become a monk?' Marie asked.

'I heard God calling me, when I was a boy.'

'Sometimes boys become monks when they don't want to,' Jean chimed in. 'Like the provost's nephew. I've heard that the provost is going to make him go into a monastery. He doesn't want to go.'

Michel sighed. 'I have heard about that. It is a shame Jean de Folleville should compel his nephew to become a monk if the boy has not received a call from God.' He bowed his head and sat without speaking for a while. Then he looked up and said, 'Did you know, Christine, Jean de Folleville and I were neighbors at one time, long before he came to Paris and became provost?'

'Where did you live?'

'In a village close to Amiens.'

'Alix de Clairy comes from that region, too,' Christine said.

'Yes. Her family was well known there. That is another instance of a boy being forced to take the cowl against his will.'

'What happened?' Francesca asked.

'It is a sad story that turned out well in the end,' Michel said. 'For generations, the lords of Clairy owned large estates in that part of the country, until Alix's grandfather lost most of them to Jean de Folleville's family in a property dispute. There wasn't much left for him to leave his two sons. Alix's father, the late Lord of Clairy, got what there was, and his younger brother had to go into a monastery.

'Did he hate being in the monastery?' Thomas asked.

'He certainly did. So much so that when he was old enough, he left.'

'How could he earn his living?' Jean wanted to know. 'You can't learn anything useful in a monastery.'

'Ah, but you can. He learned to be a scribe. Perhaps you know him, Christine. He's here in Paris. He calls himself Henri Le Picart.'

'That is the name I was trying to think of!' Francesca burst out, forgetting she was angry with everyone. 'Remember, *Cristina*, we were talking about the tin figures your father buried in the gardens at the Hôtel Saint-Pol? That was the friend who helped him. Henri Le Picart.'

'So you know him, Francesca,' Michel said. 'Well, he's Alix de Clairy's uncle.'

'Why did he change his name?' Marie wanted to know.

'It amused him to do so, I suppose. He likes to

210

confuse people. Many people in Paris know who he really is.'

'I've seen him in the library at the Louvre,' Christine said. 'And working in a booth next to Saint-Jacques-la-Boucherie.'

'Yes. He has a house near the church.'

'It's hard to believe such a disagreeable person is Alix's uncle.'

'It seems you've taken a dislike to him. You'll be interested to know that Jean de Folleville dislikes him, too. As a matter of fact, Jean dislikes everyone in Alix de Clairy's family, because while Henri was in the monastery, his brother – Alix's father – went to court and retrieved all the property his family had lost, shortly before Alix was born. When her father died last year, Alix inherited everything.'

Christine said, 'I gather from what you told us before, Michel, that being a scribe is only one of the ways Henri Le Picart makes a living.'

'He doesn't have to worry about money. He may have been unhappy in the monastery, but he studied the books in the library and gained knowledge of astrology, magic, and alchemy. It is rumored he has discovered the secret of turning base metals into gold. I don't know whether that is true, but he's done well for himself, very well indeed. In fact, he has made so much money he can afford to lend some of it to other people, including the king's brother. I saw Henri at the palace just this morning, and that may be why he was there. So you see, Thomas, it is not wise for you to turn up your nose at books. Not wise at all.'

'If he has so much money, why doesn't he leave the copying for those of us who really need the work?' Christine asked.

'No one knows the answer to that. Did I mention that in addition to all his other accomplishments, he is a poet?'

'He sounds like an interesting man,' Marie said. Christine glared at her.

'You would not appreciate his poems, Christine,' Michel continued. 'They are most unflattering to women.'

'I know very well he dislikes *me* at least. You should have seen the way he scowled at me when I disturbed him in his booth.'

'Perhaps you just imagined it,' Marie said, smiling at her with a knowing look on her face. Jean giggled.

'I certainly did not!'

Michel said, 'Henri would not like to think a woman might be a better scribe than he is.'

I'd probably be a better poet, too, Christine thought. *I must try sometime.*

Francesca asked, 'Do you truly believe he knows how to make gold, Michel?'

The monk shrugged his shoulders. 'There are a thousand probabilities about what goes on in that house of his near the church, but no one knows the truth.' He picked up his spoon. But before he ate, he said, 'Not every question should have an answer, and that is especially true of questions concerning Henri Le Picart.'

Twenty-Nine

Huguet de Guisay was a man lost in vice, considered a wretch by all honest folk. He hated the little people, whom he called dogs, and his perversity was such that he often forced them to imitate barking. Also, at dinner he made them hold up the table, and if one of them had the misfortune to displease him, he would make him lie on the ground, and he would climb on his back and strike him with his spurs until he drew blood . . . When his coffin was carried through the streets of Paris, nearly all those along the way cried out what he himself was wont to say: 'Bark, dog!'

The Monk of Saint-Denis,
Chronique du Religieux de Saint-Denis, contenant le règne de Charles VI de 1380 à 1422

Christine and her mother spoke few words to each other that evening. Christine was sorry Francesca was vexed, but she was relieved that she finally knew everything. Telling her had revived her courage. That and Marion's admonition to wash the milk off her liver.

213

Early the next morning, Francesca said, 'I am going to Mass at the cathedral, *Cristina*, and I want you to come with me. You must ask the Lord to protect you. You might also pray for help from Saint Dorothy; it is her feast day.'

Christine had planned to go to the Châtelet with the duke's letter, but as it was still very early, she decided to appease her mother and accompany her to Mass. It was not a happy decision.

A cold, dense fog shrouded the city, rolling through the streets, clinging to their cloaks, and muffling every sound. The cathedral's towers were hidden in gloom; its portals were so dark that the sculpted saints were hidden, and the interior was even less welcoming, because the windows, so bright with color when the sun shone, were as dull and gray as lead. Christine and her mother knelt before the statue of Saint Thomas, then crept along the nave, their way lit by flickering candles, and joined the other shivering worshipers. The priest processed through the half-light to the altar, accompanied by the voices of a choir that sounded hollow and flat, and although the thurifer swung his censer mightily, the heavy, damp air kept the incense smoke from rising, and it hung like a dense cloud within the sanctuary.

Chilled, tired, and annoyed with herself for coming, Christine leaned her head against her mother's sturdy shoulder and, while the priest droned on, stared up into the dark vaults. She saw figures moving down toward her. First came Saint Dorothy, carrying the red roses that symbolized her martyrdom. Queen Isabeau followed her. She was dressed in a red houppelande covered with rubies that popped off and fell like drops of blood, and Ludwig, who walked beside her, reached down to retrieve them. The queen's padded hair towered above her ears, and when she turned her head, pins flew out and circled around, squealing like bats. Cupped in her fingers, her hand warmer glowed, the coals burning crimson through the gold.

Next came the queen's ladies-in-waiting. They carried the long train of her houppelande, and in it lay the body of Hugues de Précy. His eyes popped out of their sockets and rolled down his cheeks, and his swollen tongue had grown so large it covered his body like a fleshy pink shroud. The queen's dwarf lumbered along behind the cortege, holding on one side the hand of a hairy little man with a long tail dangling between his legs, and on the other, the hand of Blanche the seamstress, who towered over her, carrying a basket of blood-stained gowns. Behind the dwarf shuffled old Margot, dragging her head on a string, and, at the end of the procession, enveloped in flames, came Alix de Clairy and the four wild men who had died at the masquerade. Alix, her hair blazing and the blackened tatters of her silver-brocaded dress writhing and twisting like pieces of burning parchment, came close to Christine, stared into her eyes, and mouthed the words, *Help me!*

Christine cried out, 'Yes, Alix! I will!'

Francesca turned with a start. 'Wake up, *Cristina*!'

Christine was shivering uncontrollably. 'I want to go home.'

Francesca put her arm around her shoulders and led her through the crowd of worshippers to the central portal of the cathedral. The fog had lifted, the sun blazed in a blue sky, and the air was cold and crisp. Christine rested against the stones of the portal and breathed deeply. 'I thought I saw Alix de Clairy. She was burning.'

'That is a very bad sign!'

'Christine does not believe in signs,' came a voice from one of the side portals.

'Michel!' Christine cried. 'What are you doing here?'

'Waiting for you. Georgette told me where you were. What frightened you?'

'I saw Alix burning. I know it was only a dream, but it was terrible.'

They heard shouting. Men staggered up the rue Neuve, carrying a black coffin and followed by an angry mob.

'Who is in the coffin?' Francesca asked.

'Huguet de Guisay,' the monk said. 'The last man to die from the burns he suffered at the masquerade. Poor soul. He never learned what it is to be merciful.' The pall bearers set the coffin down before the cathedral, whereupon several people kicked it and shouted, 'Bark, dog!'

Francesca turned her back on the coffin, and cried, '*Malvagio tiranno!*'

'Don't say that, Mama!' Christine admonished her. 'He was an evil tyrant, but he died horribly!'

'I cannot do otherwise. He was so cruel.'

'All the more reason to pray for his soul.'

'Humph.' Francesca took Christine's arm. 'We must go home.'

'I will come with you,' Michel said.

The streets were deserted, but when they came to the rue Saint-Antoine, the Duke of Orléans, resplendent in a beaver hat and a crimson cape with a wide ermine collar, galloped by on a black stallion, accompanied by some of his knights. 'They are going to the cathedral to protect Huguet de Guisay's coffin,' Michel said. Christine noticed that Guy de Marolles was not with them, and she wondered why; the duke never seemed to go anywhere without him.

The house was empty. There was no school that day, and the children had gone to the market with Georgette, but Christine was surprised that Goblin didn't come to greet them. She left her mother and Michel in the front hall and went upstairs to look for him. Although she remembered opening the shutters in her study before going out, they were closed, and the room was dark, the only light coming from the fireplace, where the flames pitched and tumbled as if possessed. In front of the flames, a figure writhed. At first she thought she was having another dream. But it wasn't a dream this time. There *was* something there, a grotesque figure, an evil little man with a knob where his head should be, leg-like appendages, and something that looked like a long tail.

She cried out. Her mother and Michel hurried up the stairs and into the study. Christine pointed to the fireplace. Her mother gasped, and Michel began to pray.

Holding back her fears, Christine looked closer. A stone projected from the fireplace mantle, and a rope had been slung around it. There was something hanging from the rope. She reached up, slipped the rope off the stone, and took the object down. It was the mandrake.

No one spoke for several moments. Christine opened the shutters to let in the light, and whispered, 'This is the mandrake the queen lost.'

'How do you know?' Michel asked in a hoarse voice.

'I got a good look at it in the queen's chambers.' She dropped the root. It landed against a book she'd left lying on the floor and sat there like a malevolent doll.

'It is another terrible sign,' her mother said. 'What can it mean?'

'Nothing mysterious,' Michel said. 'Someone put it there.'

'An evil spirit. There is evil all around, and now it has come right into our house.'

'No. A real person put it there. A real person who wanted to frighten Christine and who must have been watching, waiting until everyone had gone out.'

'Maybe it was Georgette,' Francesca said. 'She's the only other person who could have been in the house.'

'That's ridiculous, Mama. How could she have stolen it from the queen?'

They heard Georgette and the children talking downstairs. 'I can prove to you she didn't do it,' Christine said. She picked up the mandrake, hung it back on the stone, and stood in front of the fireplace. Then she called, 'Come up here, Georgette. Leave the children downstairs.'

Georgette ran up the stairs and into the study. Christine stepped aside so she could see the mandrake. The girl screamed and tried to run away. 'Stop her! She'll fall down the stairs,' Christine called out to her mother. Francesca caught the girl just in time, and pushed her down onto a bench.

The children bounded in. Lisabetta ran to Francesca, the boys went to the fireplace and gaped at the mandrake, and Marie hovered around Georgette, who was sobbing. Francesca said to Jean, 'Go down to the pantry. There is a box with valerian on the top shelf. Put a spoonful in a cup of wine and bring it here quickly.' Thomas gave his brother a shove, and Jean hurried to do as he was asked.

'I should not have frightened her,' Christine said. 'But at least we can be sure she was not the one who brought the mandrake. She would never touch it.'

Before Thomas and Marie could start asking questions, Michel went to the fireplace, took down the mandrake, and held it out to them. Georgette sat up straight on the bench and whimpered. Christine put her arms around her.

'It is only a root,' Michel said. 'Because it is shaped like a man, people fear it.' The children backed away. 'But as with most things we are afraid of, the fear is worse than the thing that's feared.'

Jean came running into the room. He wasn't carrying valerian and wine. He was carrying Goblin.

'What happened?' Christine cried. She released

Georgette, who nearly fell off the bench, ran to Jean, and took the dog from him.

'He was in the kitchen, tied to one of the table legs. He nearly choked, but I don't think he's hurt.'

Goblin coughed, licked Christine's face, and tried to jump out of her arms. She set him on the floor, and he stood up.

'I'll go down for the valerian,' Christine said. She started to move away and found Lisabetta clinging to her skirt. She unfastened the child's fingers one by one.

'I will go with you,' Michel said, setting the mandrake down gently on Christine's desk.

On the kitchen floor, they found the rope that had tied Goblin to the table leg. It was just like the rope tied to the mandrake. They went into the pantry to get the valerian and felt a draft. The oiled parchment that covered a small window was torn away, and the shutter behind it had been forced open.

'Now we know how the intruder got into the house,' Michel said.

'Let's hope he got out again,' Christine said.

'We'll look.' Michel found the valerian, scooped some into a cup of wine, and told Christine to follow him as he searched all the rooms in the house. No one was there.

When they went back upstairs, Georgette was sobbing again, but Goblin had stopped coughing and lay resting by the fire. 'The dog is well enough, but I wonder about this poor child,' Francesca said, as she held the cup to Georgette's trembling lips. The girl swallowed,

220

choked, and spit out some leaves. After a few minutes, she asked, 'Who put that horrible thing there?'

'Someone who wanted to frighten me,' Christine said. 'Someone who knew we weren't home.'

The girl sobbed more loudly than before.

Christine had been wondering how they could prevent her from telling everyone in Paris about the mandrake. Now it came to her. 'I'm sorry you were frightened, Georgette,' she said, going to her and putting her arms around her. 'But if you want to continue working here, you must promise not to tell anyone about this. Not your mother or your father, not your sisters and brothers – especially not Colin. Will you promise?'

Georgette nodded, wiping the tears from her eyes.

'Good. Now go and start dinner. My mother will be down soon.' She helped the girl up from the bench. 'Everything will be fine as long as you keep the secret.'

Georgette stumbled out of the room, keeping as far away as she could from Michel, who was holding the mandrake again.

'That was clever, Christine, very clever,' the monk said. 'But it surprises me that she would want to stay here after the fright she's had.'

'She would have a hard time finding a job anywhere else,' Francesca said.

Lisabetta stayed close to Christine, but Jean, Thomas, and Marie stood near Michel, staring at the root. 'What about you children?' he asked. 'Can you keep the secret?'

Without taking their eyes off the mandrake, they all nodded.

He dangled the root in front of their noses. 'If you promise not to tell anyone about this, I'll take you to the abbey and show you how we brothers live. Would you like that?'

'Yes,' they breathed in unison.

'But if you tell anyone, anyone at all, I won't take you there, and I'll whip your hands just as your teacher does when you don't attend to your lessons, only harder, much harder.' He made the mandrake jump up and down like a puppet. 'Do you promise to keep the secret, all of you?'

'We promise,' they whispered.

'And remember, I know your teacher and the parents of your friends at school, and just about everyone else in Paris. So if you tell, I'll find out. Now go down and play. Take Lisabetta and Goblin with you, and don't leave the house.'

When they'd gone, Michel said, 'I'm sorry if I frightened them, but no one else must know about this, no one.'

Francesca bustled around the room, tidying up the books and papers Christine had left scattered about. 'It is easy for anyone to know this is your room, *Cristina*. But who would want to frighten you?'

'Someone who thinks I've been asking too many questions.' Christine sat down at her desk and held her head in her hands.

Michel picked up the mandrake. 'What do you plan to do with this, Christine?'

She knew she should take it to the queen. But she'd had enough of the horrible root, and she had the sinking feeling that if she gave it back to her, it would cause more trouble. 'Throw it into the fire,' she said.

'No!' her mother shrieked. 'You must not burn a mandrake. We will all become ill. The house will burn down. The children will die.'

'God in Heaven!' Christine cried. 'That's the problem. All those ridiculous beliefs. Don't you see, Mama? Whoever brought the mandrake here thinks I'll be frightened and give up trying to find out who murdered Hugues de Précy.'

'That may be so. But I will not let you throw the mandrake into the fire.'

'Our infirmarer at the abbey would like to have it,' Michel said.

'I'm sure he could put it to good use,' Christine said, remembering what her father had told her about doctors numbing their patients' pain with the juice of the mandrake root.

Francesca looked at her and sighed. Then she turned to the monk. 'I will only lend it to you, Michel. It is bad luck to give away a mandrake.'

'It was left here for me, Mama,' Christine said. 'I'll decide what to do with it, and I've decided you can have it, Michel.'

The smell of something burning came up the stairs. 'What has the girl done now?' Francesca cried, rushing from the room. Michel laid the mandrake on the desk, directly in front of Christine.

'Do you have to put it there?' she asked.

'It can't hurt you.'

'I know it can't.'

'But the person who came into your house and hung it in your fireplace can. Do you really want to go on trying to find out things you aren't supposed to know?'

'I can't believe you asked that, Michel.'

'I ask because the situation has become extremely dangerous, and I am sorry I encouraged you in this. I am very afraid for you now, Christine.'

'Do you expect me to sit in a corner, shaking with fear like Georgette, or like a foolish old woman?' She picked up the mandrake. The rough skin was warm, like human flesh. The thing felt alive in her hand, but she held onto it nevertheless, and she shook it in Michel's face. The knob that looked like a head bobbed up and down, and the tail jerked between its legs. 'Perhaps I won't let you take it to your infirmarer. I'll keep it. I'll bath it in wine, bake it in the oven, dress it in silk, feed it communion bread . . .'

The monk wiggled his fingers at the mandrake as if he hoped it would disappear.

'You're not afraid of it, are you, Michel?'

He smiled. 'As I've said before, Christine, I always wondered how Étienne could tolerate your sharp tongue.'

Thirty

One sees so many women who, because of their husbands' cruelty, live miserable lives in the shackles of marriage where they are more badly treated than the slaves of the Saracens.

Christine de Pizan, *Le Livre de la Cité des Dames*, 1404–1405

Francesca returned. 'The leeks are burned, but we may eat what is left of the dinner. You must stay, Michel.' She looked at the mandrake in Christine's hand. 'Why have you not given that to him?'

'He'll take it with him when he leaves.'

Francesca went back downstairs, and Michel followed. But before going down herself, Christine shut the mandrake in a chest at the foot of her bed so her mother and Georgette wouldn't have to see it again. She pushed the lid of the chest down firmly, hoping that she, too, might be able to forget about the detestable root for a while.

But of course no one talked of anything else while they were eating. Georgette hovered around the table, hanging on every word.

'Who put it in the fireplace?' Thomas wanted to know.

'Someone who wanted to frighten me,' Christine said. 'But it's nothing more than a root with an odd shape.'

'It is not just a root,' Francesca said. 'Your father knew. There is a little demon in it. You do not want a mandrake in your room at night. It will shine in the dark.'

Georgette nodded agreement, and said, 'Witches use them as lamps.' Lisabetta moved closer to Jean.

'That's enough, Georgette. Bring more wine,' Christine said.

The girl skulked off to the pantry, and Christine said to her mother, 'You're encouraging her in those ridiculous beliefs. And you're frightening the children.'

Michel drank the last of his wine and rose from the table. 'No one will find out whether the mandrake glows in the dark, because it is going with me to the abbey.'

Christine followed him to the hallway, and whispered, 'Please leave the mandrake here for now and come with me to the Châtelet. I'm taking the duke's letter to the provost.' She put on her cloak and boots.

Francesca came to the doorway. 'You must not go out, *Cristina*.'

'Don't be afraid, Mama. Michel is coming with me. Keep the children inside, and I'll be back soon.' She hurried out the door, and the monk followed.

Near the old wall, they found Marion, stamping her feet and waving her arms around to keep warm. 'I've been waiting for you.' She curtsied to the monk.

'This one has a devil in her,' he muttered under his breath.

'How long have you been here?' Christine asked her.

'Ha! You didn't see me. I hid when I saw you coming home from Mass with your mother.'

'Did you see anyone near my house this morning?'

'No one in particular, except the Duke of Orléans, looking especially fine in a crimson cape. Why do you ask?'

Christine looked at Michel. 'Should I tell her?'

'It may prove the truth of the old saying, "A bad beginning leads to a bad ending." But I suppose you'd better.'

Marion made him another little curtsy. 'Empty-headed monk.'

Before Michel could retort, Christine said, 'While I was out, someone broke into my house and left a mandrake hanging in my fireplace.'

'We have to find out who it was,' Michel said.

'I'll help.'

Michel studied the girl in her crimson cloak, swinging her embroidered purse. 'I suppose we must employ desperate means,' he muttered under his breath. He said to her, 'Perhaps one of your friends knows something about it. But therein lies a difficulty. You must ask questions without saying why you are doing so.'

'I'm not as stupid as you think. Someone on the rue de la Truanderie may know. I'll go there.'

Michel shook his head and said something about the derelicts who lived on the street of the vagabonds.

'Where did you find this blockhead?' Marion whispered in Christine's ear.

They walked to the Châtelet in silence, and when they arrived, Marion made a face at the monk and sauntered off with her nose in the air.

Michel and Christine went to the entrance of the prison. Christine gave the duke's letter to the wart-nosed guard, and, as before, the man disappeared into the provost's side of the building. Soon he returned, bringing with him the jailer with the defective teeth, who looked at the monk and said, 'I'll admit only the lady.'

'I'll wait right here for you, Christine,' Michel said.

The jailer gave Christine a nasty smile, and led her to the dingy room where she had spoken with Alix before. The stout guard named Hutin opened the door. He, too, smiled at her, but his was a kindly smile.

Alix stood listlessly by the grimy window, still wearing the tattered dress and the little red cape, now covered with grime. Her hair was so dirty it seemed to have turned gray. When Christine spoke her name, she turned and said, her voice barely a whisper, 'How far away the light is. I hope they burn me soon.' She swayed and clutched at the wall to keep from falling. Christine went over to support her, and said to Hutin, 'She needs something to sit on.' He left, came back with a stool, and eased Alix down onto it. Then he reached into a pouch, brought out a tart that smelled of pork and herbs, pressed it into her hand, and went out.

Alix sat hunched over on the stool, holding the

tart. 'Please eat it,' Christine said. Like a dutiful child, Alix nibbled at it.

'I know they've tortured you,' Christine said.

Alix held up her arms to show the marks of the cords. She tried to smile. 'It could have been worse. They already thought I was guilty, so they didn't try too hard.' She shifted her weight on the stool and nearly slid off.

Christine feared she was too weak to tell her what she wanted to know, and she was surprised when Alix sat up straight, and said, 'The Duke of Orléans disliked Hugues – the king was too fond of him.'

Christine said, 'I don't think the duke could have killed Hugues. He was at the masquerade.' She spoke these words, but at the same time she knew the duke could have commissioned one of his men to do it. Guy de Marolles, for example. She hadn't forgiven Guy for knocking her down in the courtyard.

Alix spoke again. 'I don't really think the duke did it. It's more likely the queen's brother did. Hugues found out something about him. I was the one who told him.'

Christine felt a bit of hope. 'Tell me about it.'

'Ludwig took something that belonged to the king – a sapphire set in a gold band. The queen had it in her room one day, and I saw Ludwig take it. I shouldn't have said anything to Hugues about it, but I did.'

Christine remembered Michel saying the king had lost a valuable sapphire that was supposed to cure diseases of the eye. Georgette had said Colin had discovered a secret. *That must be it,* she thought. Ludwig stole the gem and Colin found out. Ludwig had bought the boy's silence with a new knife, but a knife wouldn't have been enough for Hugues. 'What did Hugues do?'

'He told me he made Ludwig give him money so he wouldn't tell the king. Ludwig was worried the king would send him back to Bavaria.

'Now I understand why Ludwig lied to the king.'

'What do you mean?'

'He told the king he saw you give your husband the poison. It's quite understandable that he would tell such a lie, if he himself murdered Hugues because Hugues was black-mailing him.'

A furry shape scuttled up the wall. Alix didn't notice it, but Christine cringed and looked away. Everything about the room was foul. A weak ray of sunlight barely penetrated the dust covering the window, and drops of water oozed from the mold-encrusted walls. She couldn't bear to think what might be hidden under the filthy piles of straw on the floor. She stood behind Alix with her hands on her shoulders to keep her from toppling off the stool and looked into the corner where she'd imagined seeing Étienne smiling at her on her previous visit to the prison. He wasn't there. She was alone with this unhappy young woman who had no family except for a disagreeable little man who probably wouldn't care whether she lived or died.

Or perhaps he would care, she thought. *Perhaps there would be money for Henri Le Picart if Alix died.*

'What do you know about your father's brother?'

'He's in a monastery.'

'No longer. He's here in Paris. He calls himself Henri Le Picart, but he's still your uncle. If you die, he could inherit your property.'

Alix covered her face with her hands. 'Then he should have just killed me.'

'In order for him to obtain your property, your husband would have to die before you. He did, and now if you die, the property could go to Henri.' Or so Christine thought. She was often in court fighting for the money owed her from her husband's estate, but beyond that, she had to admit to herself, she had limited knowledge of the laws of inheritance as they applied to royal chamberlains like Hugues de Précy.

Alix started to slip from the stool once again, so Christine knelt on the floor and held her. Dust and bits of straw caught on her cloak, and she tried to forget the rat she'd seen. She said, 'The last time I was here, you told me the night Hugues was poisoned, he had a book he was going to give the queen.'

Alix sat straight up on the stool. 'Please don't ask me about the book! I don't know where it is.'

'You must know something about it.'

Alix looked up at Christine, anguish in her eyes, and then she fell against her, sobbing.

Christine understood. 'Hugues killed the man behind the chest, didn't he, Alix – to get the book.'

In a barely audible voice, Alix said, 'I recognized his dagger. It was an old one he kept in a

231

chest at home. He never wore it. No one else could have known it was his.'

'How did you know it was the same book he was going to give the queen? Did you see it?'

'I guessed. He told me he'd found a book of magic somewhere. He thought he could use it to gain the queen's favor. Hugues would do anything to get what he wanted. He deceived everyone. I am so glad my father didn't live to see it.' She shook uncontrollably as she said this.

To take Alix's mind off the terrible truths she had just revealed, Christine said, 'Tell me about your father.'

'He was kind, but he was always busy with his estates. My mother died when I was six, and he didn't want me to be lonely, so he let me have a companion – my old nursemaid, Gillette.'

The old nursemaid who was foolish enough to give her a mandrake, Christine thought. 'Where is Gillette now?'

'She's here in Paris. I know she would come here to visit me if she could.'

Christine wanted to find out more about this old woman. 'Would you like me to go and see her?'

'Oh, yes! She lives with her cousin Maude on the rue Beaubourg. The last house before the old wall.'

Keys rattled, and the door opened. Hutin had come to take Alix away. As they left, Alix turned and said to Christine, 'I'm going to die. Tell Gillette it's better that way.'

Michel was pacing back and forth in front of the prison, ignoring the guards, who looked as though they feared he might attack them. When Christine came out, they made a great show of sniffing their fingers.

'What is the meaning of that?' Michel asked.

'They're mocking me. The last time I was here I brought Alix a sprig of my mother's rue.'

'*Audendo magnus tegitur timor*,' Michel announced in a loud voice. The guards raised their cudgels.

'Michel! What did you say to them?'

'I told them a show of bravery usually conceals great fear. But I'm sure they don't know any Latin.'

'I don't care whether they do or not. We'll come to grief if you say any more.' She hurried away. Michel laughed and followed.

'Did you learn anything from her?' he asked when he caught up with her.

She looked back over her shoulder at the guards. The bald man with the harelip was staring at them with a blank look on his face, and the giant with the warty nose was giving them the fool's finger. She took Michel's arm and led him down the street and into the church of Saint-Jacques-la-Boucherie. In the dark, deserted nave, silence settled around them like a comforting blanket, and after a few minutes, she felt at peace for the first time that day. Michel knelt to pray, and she knelt, too, thankful for this man of God who thought she was right to try to save Alix de Clairy and was willing to jeopardize his own safety to help. She whispered, 'I know for certain it was Hugues de Précy who stabbed the man behind the chest and stole the book.'

'She told you that?'

'Yes. And she also told me that the night Hugues was poisoned, he was bringing the book to the queen. He said it was a book of magic.'

Michel shook his head. *He knows very well what sort of book it is*, Christine thought.

'The duke must suspect Hugues killed the man,' the monk said. 'That's why he thinks Hugues's wife knows where the book is.'

'What's in the book, Michel?'

He just shook his head. 'It would be unwise for you to go back to the palace. It would be better for me to tell the duke you have learned nothing about the book.'

They both understood what would happen then. Once the duke believed Alix really didn't know anything about the book, he'd see no reason why she should be kept alive.

'What more did you learn from her?' Michel asked. 'Did she mention anyone who might have wanted to kill Hugues?'

'It could have been the queen's brother. Hugues was blackmailing him. He'd discovered Ludwig had stolen the gem the king lost – the sapphire you told us about, the one that is supposed to cure diseases of the eye.'

Michel shook his head. 'I'm not surprised to hear that about Ludwig, not surprised at all.'

Christine looked around the church. Rays of the setting sun streamed in through the colored glass windowpanes, and carved saints smiled down at them from the pillars. It pained her to think of what Alix de Clairy was suffering in the prison while she and the monk sat in such a peaceful place.

Desperate to save Alix, she found herself devising an impossible plan. She said to Michel, 'Tell the duke Alix is so confused she can't remember where the book is. Tell him she may be able to think more clearly in a day or two. Ask him to write another letter to the provost for me, so I can talk to her again. That will give us more time.'

'Can't you think of anything better than that?'

'Don't make me more discouraged than I am already.'

'If it weren't for you, she'd be dead by now. That might have been the best thing, if we aren't able to save her.'

'That's what she said. "Tell Gillette it's better that way."'

'Who is Gillette?'

'Her old nursemaid. She lives with her cousin Maude on the rue Beaubourg. I promised Alix I'd go and see her.'

They left the church and went down a side street. Michel pointed to a large house and said, 'Henri Le Picart lives there.' Christine half expected to see an angry little man in a black cape and long hood come out, but the thick wooden door, decorated with carvings of dragons and serpents, remained firmly shut. She waited until they were on the rue Saint-Martin and then asked Michel, in a whisper, 'If Alix de Clairy dies, won't Henri Le Picart inherit her father's property?'

'If Alix de Clairy is put to death for murdering a man who was a faithful knight and a royal chamberlain, her property will be confiscated by the king.'

'Is there no way Henri could obtain it?'

'Well, sometimes the king gives a criminal's property to a relative, but that is unusual. Henri could ask for it, I suppose. But I doubt he would, or that the king would think he needed it. Henri already has a surfeit of money. He is a strange man, Christine, and I know you have taken a dislike to him, but I don't think he's a murderer. No, I don't think so.'

Maybe he doesn't need money, but he might want the book, Christine thought.

When they arrived at her house it was dark. Francesca was waiting at the door. 'I cannot endure this much longer, *Cristina*. Something terrible will happen, I know it.' The sound of something crashing to the floor came from the kitchen, and she rushed out to see which of her treasures Georgette had broken.

Christine asked Michel, 'Will you go to the duke and ask him to write another letter?'

'I do not think he will, but I will try. Tomorrow. I will come and tell you what he said.'

'You said you'd take the mandrake and give it to your infirmarer. I'll go up and get it. I don't want it in the house overnight.'

Michel hesitated. 'I'll have to leave it with you for now. I'm not going back to the abbey just yet.' He hurried down the street.

Disappointed, Christine went back inside, climbed the stairs to her study, and opened the door. The fire was almost out and the room was dark except for a soft glow that seemed to be coming from the chest at the foot of her bed. Georgette and her mother would have said it was the mandrake.

Thirty-One

I beg you ladies, never be charmed by any man, for they are all deceivers.

Christine de Pizan, *Ballade*, c.1410

Christine knew the mandrake was shut up in the chest, but long after she had gone to bed she lay awake imagining it leering at her from a corner of her room. When she finally fell into a troubled sleep, she dreamed of it dancing through fire with the dragons and serpents she'd seen on Henri Le Picart's door, swinging its hairy tail and mocking her with red eyes and a mouth full of worm-eaten teeth.

Late the following morning, Michel came with disappointing news: he hadn't been able to speak with the duke. He tried to reassure Christine that as long as the duke believed Alix de Clairy knew the whereabouts of the book, he would make sure she was kept alive. He promised he would speak to him the next day, but Christine's mind was not at ease.

'Then let's go and visit the old nursemaid,' Michel said. 'She may be able to tell us something about Alix that will help.'

Francesca hovered in the doorway. 'You do not know this person, *Cristina*. She may do you harm.'

'There's nothing to worry about. She's an old woman,' Christine assured her, though she was not entirely confident that a nursemaid who had given her charge a mandrake presented no threat.

They walked down the rue de Paradis beside the old wall until they came to a small house at the corner of that street and the rue Beaubourg. A hunchbacked woman in a faded brown cloak dragging on the ground came out of the house and lurched toward them.

'Gillette?' Christine asked.

The woman shook her head.

Michel smiled. 'Then you must be Gillette's cousin Maude. Can you tell us where to find her? We are friends of Alix de Clairy.'

The woman gazed at the monk suspiciously. Finally she said, 'She'll be in the chapel of Sainte-Avoie, on the rue du Temple. There's a shortcut – take the alley by my house to a path through the orchard.'

They turned down the alley, stumbling over stones and piles of dung. Christine looked back and saw Maude watching them. Michel turned too, tripped, and nearly fell. As he reached out to steady himself, he caught at a ledge under a window of Maude's house, and stopped. He seemed to be examining his hand.

'Did you hurt yourself?' Christine asked.

'No, no. Just steadying myself.'

They came to a grove of ancient apple trees and a muddy path leading to a cottage that Michel said was a hospice for widows. Beside the hospice stood the chapel of Sainte-Avoie, a shabby, unadorned building with a narrow bell tower. Inside they found an old woman in a patched woolen cloak kneeling before one of the altars. Christine called out softly, 'Gillette?'

Slowly, the woman rose to her feet. She was tiny, frail, and trembling. Her pale skin was almost translucent, the strands of hair that escaped from under her grey hood were pure white, and even in the gloom of the chapel, her eyes glowed sapphire blue. Christine had been imagining Gillette as a malevolent spirit exerting an evil influence over Alix de Clairy. This woman looked like a saint.

Christine said, 'We've come about Alix de Clairy. We're her friends.'

'She has no friends here.'

'I know it appears so, but we want to help her. Could we speak at your cousin's house? It's cold here.'

'We can't go there.'

'Then perhaps the sister in charge of the hospice will let us sit inside where it's warm,' Michel said.

Christine took Gillette's arm, and they followed the monk to the cottage next to the church, where Michel spoke to a tall attendant who showed them to a room with a large fireplace. They sat on a bench and stretched their hands out to the flames. The warmth did not stop Gillette's hands from shaking.

Christine looked into the woman's startlingly blue eyes and said, 'I've been to the Châtelet to see Alix.'

'I went to see her, but they wouldn't let me in.' Gillette's eyes filled with tears. 'I've been told she has been condemned to die. Why? Alix wouldn't harm anyone. How can they believe those terrible things about her?'

Christine said, as gently as possible, 'People think her a witch, because she brought the queen a mandrake. You gave her the mandrake. Where did you get it?'

Gillette bowed her head and covered her eyes with her quivering hands. In a voice so low Christine could hardly hear, she said, 'From my cousin, Maude. I didn't think it would do any harm. Maude said it would restore the king to health.'

'And you believe that?'

'If you are kind to the little spirit in a mandrake, it will do what you ask.'

Christine sighed, sorry they had come to see a superstitious old woman, not to be feared, and not worth talking to, either. But Michel, who'd been sitting quietly, staring into the fire and seemingly paying no attention to the conversation, looked up and said to Gillette, 'Tell us about Hugues de Précy.'

Gillette raised her head and looked at him. 'He was cruel to Alix.'

'Why?'

'He knew something about her.' She shifted uneasily on the bench. 'I shouldn't have told you.' Her hands trembled violently. 'I promised I would keep the secret. It has nothing to do with Hugues de Précy's murder.'

'You can't be sure.' Michel's voice was gentle, and he seemed to have shrunk; his shoulders were hunched, his eyes blinked rapidly, and his hands were hidden in the sleeves of his black habit. Christine had never seen him look so meek. 'You may trust us,' he said.

On a chain around her neck, Gillette wore a small wooden crucifix. She clutched it and looked into the fire. A falling log sent a whirlwind of sparks up the chimney with a crackling noise that shattered the silence of the quiet room.

'He was cruel because he knew that Alix isn't who she thinks she is,' she said.

Astonished, Christine leaned forward and was about to speak, but Michel raised his hand to stop her. 'Go on,' he said to Gillette.

'I may have done a great wrong.' She sat in silence for a long time. Then she said, in a hushed voice, 'A lady who was about to give birth hired me as a nursemaid. I was there when the child, a girl, was born. It was dead.' She put the wooden crucifix to her lips.

'There was a midwife. Her name was Macée. She took me to her house and showed me a newborn baby in a basket. "It's a girl," she said. "She was born this morning. Give her to the lady, because she won't be able to have any more children of her own."'

'Where did she get this baby?' Michel asked.

'She wouldn't tell me. She just said I should give it to the lady. I felt sorry for the lady, so I agreed. I took the baby to her and placed it in her arms. Her husband, a great lord, hardened his heart and looked away, but she pleaded with him to let her keep it. I had something to say, too. I pointed out that his wife would not be able to conceive again and he needed a child to inherit his property.'

Christine realized that the old woman wasn't as simple as she seemed.

Gillette continued, 'Finally, the lord agreed they would raise the child as their own. But he had to make sure no one would ever know the baby was not his.'

'To make sure she would inherit his property,' Michel said.

Gillette nodded. 'He secretly buried his own baby, and his wife and I were sworn to secrecy. Macée as well – the lord sent me to her with money to buy her silence. He retained me as a nursemaid, and later as a companion for the little girl, because his wife died when the child was six.'

'And the abandoned baby was Alix?' Christine asked.

'Yes. She never had any reason to think the Lord of Clairy and his lady were not her true parents. They loved her as if she were their own child.'

'No one else knew of this?'

'No. But Hugues de Précy found out when he was in Amiens with the king. It had to have been Macée who told him. Hugues also knew the Lord of Clairy had a large amount of property and Alix would inherit it.'

Christine sighed. She knew what was coming next.

'Hugues went to the lord and threatened to reveal the secret of Alix's birth unless he had assurances that he could marry her when she was old enough – she was only eight at the time. He had the lord in his power. He returned eight years later and married her.'

'Did the Lord of Clairy know it was Macée who had revealed the secret?' Christine asked.

'He did. But she left Amiens, and he could never find her.'

'Do you think Macée told the secret to anyone besides Hugues?'

'I can't believe she would have done so. She lives here in Paris now. I see her sometimes, and I know she is truly sorry she betrayed Alix. Poor soul – she's had the pox, and it has disfigured her face. These days, women come to her in secret, because she does things other midwives refuse to do.'

Gillette looked up with tears in her eyes. 'Hugues de Précy never loved Alix. He only married her for the property she would inherit. Before they were married, he treated her like a princess – all smiles and kindness, giving her gifts and pretending to be gentle. Alix was completely deceived. I'm glad her father did not live to see how cruel Hugues really was.'

'I wonder why he treated Alix so badly,' Christine mused.

'I suspect he despised her because he knew she was not of noble birth.'

'All this must have caused you great sorrow.'

'It did. God help me, I could have poisoned Hugues myself, and I'm sorry I didn't.' Gillette pushed herself to her feet, shaking uncontrollably, and cried, 'I'll tell the authorities I was the one who did it. Then I can die in Alix's place.'

She stumbled against the side of the bench and nearly fell.

'They wouldn't believe you,' Michel said, as he rose and steadied her.

'He's right,' Christine said. 'But there's someone else who might have had good reason to poison Hugues de Précy. Do you know Alix's uncle, the man who calls himself Henri Le Picart?'

'I've seen him here in Paris.'

'Perhaps he has discovered the secret, and now he wants to use that knowledge to his advantage.'

Out of the corner of her eye, Christine could see Michel gesturing at her, but she ignored him. 'Preposterous,' he said in a loud voice.

Bewildered, Gillette looked at him, then back at Christine. But before either of them could say anything more, the tall sister who had showed them in reappeared and asked them to leave, because it was time for the midday meal she served to the women who lived at the hospice.

Michel and Christine helped Gillette to her feet, and they went out. When the old woman realized they intended to walk back through the orchard with her, she said, 'Leave me now. I can go by myself.' She waved them away and shuffled along the path to Maude's house. Before she had gone very far, she turned and called out to Christine, 'I will speak with Macée. Perhaps she'll tell me something that will help Alix. If she does, I'll come to you. Tell me where you live.'

'Not far from here. Outside the old wall after you pass the King of Sicily's palace.

Look for a house just beyond the first three market gardens.'

Gillette nodded, walked on, and was soon hidden by the trees.

Michel and Christine walked for a while in silence. Christine thought the monk was angry because of what she had said about Henri Le Picart, but he muttered, 'It is strange. Very strange.'

'If you mean what Gillette told us, it's more than strange. It's terrible.'

'I mean the things I saw through the window of Maude's house.'

She remembered how he'd tripped and steadied himself against the window ledge. 'The window was covered with linen,' she said.

'The linen was torn. I could see inside. There were herbs hanging from the ceiling.'

'That's how everyone dries herbs.'

'And little figures made of wax and clay. I think Maude practices witchcraft.'

'Do you think Gillette does, too?'

'I don't know. But she wanted to keep us away from Maude's house. And she believes in the power of the mandrake.'

Thirty-Two

Early in the morning, order your chambermaids to sweep and clean the entrances to your house – the hall and other places where people enter and stay to talk. Have them dust the footstools and shake out the bench cloths and coverings.

From a book of moral and practical advice for a young wife, Paris, 1393

Michel left Christine at the door of her house. 'I really do not believe the duke will write another letter, but I'll ask,' he said as he turned down the street. 'I'll come tomorrow and tell you what he says.'

Christine went to the kitchen to look for her mother and, not finding her there, climbed the stairs to her study. Michel still had not taken the mandrake, and she had the disquieting thought that perhaps he didn't really want it. But then she discovered her fire had gone out, and she forgot about the mandrake as she ran back downstairs, planning to give Georgette a good scolding. The girl was in the front hall, where she was supposed to be sweeping. Instead she was leaning on her broom, crying. Colin was with her, and he looked about to cry, too.

'What ails you two?' Christine snapped. 'Does my mother know you're here, Colin?'

'No,' he muttered, not looking at her.

'Your mother went out with the children,' Georgette said, wiping her eyes with her apron.

'She won't be pleased to see you like this. Finish your work. And you should go back to the palace, Colin.'

'I can't. The queen sent me away. That seamstress, Blanche, told her I'd done something bad.'

246

'What did you do?'

'Nothing. I don't even know what Blanche said it was.'

Christine thought about Colin's stealthy habits, always watching, always listening. She wondered what he'd discovered about Blanche.

The hall was cold, so she took Georgette and Colin into the kitchen. The fire there was nearly dead, too, so she put Georgette to work reviving it with the bellows. Colin sat down on a bench by the table, sniffling. He picked up a knife Georgette had forgotten to put away and fingered it, his bony wrists protruding from sleeves much too short for his long, skinny arms.

'When my mother comes home, we'll see if we can find something for you to do here,' Christine said. 'I already have a job for you. The fire in my room has gone out. You can go and start it again.'

Before she could tell him which room was hers, he bounced off the bench, ran into the front hall, and clumped up the stairs. At that moment, Georgette worked the bellows too hard, sending ashes flying around the kitchen, and Christine forgot about everything except making sure the girl swept up the mess. Georgette hadn't finished the job by the time Colin came back, so Christine gave him a broom, too, and when her mother and the children arrived, with Goblin dancing around at their heels, everyone was busy sweeping. Goblin growled when he saw Colin and ran back into the hall.

Francesca placed her basket on the table, stood with her hands on her hips, and stared at

247

the boy. Christine took a tart from the basket and ate it while she told her about his mysterious dismissal from the palace. 'He needs work,' she whispered. 'I'm earning a little more money now. Surely we can afford to hire him for small chores.'

Her mother watched Colin sweep ashes into a corner. 'He is just like his sister!'

'I know. But we can endure it for a while.'

Francesca threw up her hands. To divert her attention from Colin, Christine said, 'I learned something from the old woman Michel and I visited. Alix de Clairy's birth mother gave her away the day she was born. Alix doesn't know.'

'How could a mother do such a thing? Who was she?'

'No one knows.' Francesca was watching Colin, and Christine said quickly, 'There's something else I want to talk to you about. How well do you know Henri Le Picart?'

'He was a friend of your father's. I did not like him. Why do you ask?'

'Remember what Michel told us? He's Alix de Clairy's uncle.'

'Then why does he not help her?'

'Perhaps because he is Hugues de Précy's murderer. I wonder about him.'

'You said you saw Henri in the library at the Louvre. Why do you not ask Gilles Malet about him?'

'Gilles is angry with me.'

'I cannot believe he is so angry he will not answer a few questions.'

Christine took another tart and thought for a

moment. 'Perhaps you're right. I'll go and speak with him tomorrow.'

When Michel hadn't arrived by sext the next day, Christine didn't have the patience to wait any longer for him. She asked her mother to tell him to meet her at the Louvre, put on her cloak, and started out the door. Then she remembered the mandrake. Not wanting to have it in the house for another night, she ran up to her room, retrieved it from the chest, and threw it into her leather pouch, vowing not to forget to give it to Michel the next time she saw him.

It was a bright day, unusually warm for that time of year, and the sun had turned the streets into rivers of mud that splattered up onto her cloak every time a horseman galloped by. She expected to see Marion around somewhere, and she wasn't disappointed; the girl was waiting for her at the corner of the rue Tiron, wearing a turquoise mantle, open to show off a lavender blue surcoat with a band of bright orange-and-yellow flowers embroidered down the front. She took hold of Christine's arm to prevent her from stepping into a particularly foul-smelling puddle.

'Where are you going, Lady Christine?'

'To speak to the librarian at the Louvre.'

'You shouldn't be walking on this muddy street. I'll go with you and show you a better route.'

The street Marion chose was even dirtier than the one Christine had been on, so they decided to go over to the Grève. When they arrived at the sandy open space, where they were

249

jostled by men carrying casks of wine and vagrants looking for work, Marion began to describe a beheading that had taken place there the day before. Christine couldn't bear to think about executions. She put her hands over her ears and hurried along.

'Why the rush?' Marion asked.

'I want to find out all I can about Henri Le Picart.'

'That man frightens me. But he knows how to get my friends out of the Châtelet.'

So besides lending money to the king's brother, Henri rescues prostitutes from prison, Christine thought. *Just as Marie said – an interesting man.* 'He's Alix de Clairy's uncle,' she said.

'So why doesn't he help her?'

'That's what I want to know.'

'Come on, then. Let's walk beside the river.' Marion ran off, and Christine hurried after her. The ice on the Seine was breaking up, and the thawing river smelled like a sewer, but that was nothing compared to the stench they encountered when they reached the area near the Châtelet. Marion held her nose and pronounced the odor worse than all the farts in Paris. She took Christine's arm and pulled her down the street toward the Louvre.

When they came near the building, Christine said, 'Why don't you go to the secondhand clothes market and wait for me there, Marion. Perhaps some of the queen's ladies-in-waiting have discarded the dresses they wore to Catherine de Fastavarin's marriage ball.'

'I know I can't go into the library with you,

Lady Christine. But you shouldn't go by your-self. There are too many hiding places for the murderer – all those books.'

'I won't be alone. Brother Michel is coming to meet me.'

'If you think that monk friend of yours will be able to protect you, you're as thickheaded as he is.' Marion closed her mantle tightly and started to walk away, with her nose in the air. 'If you don't get attacked by the murderer, you might pass by the clothes market on your way home and look for me. Perhaps I'll still be there.'

Thirty-Three

A virtuous woman is rarer than a phoenix or a white crow.

Jean de Meun, *Le Roman de la Rose* (Part II), c.1275

Do not think me, a mere women, foolish, arrogant, or presumptuous for daring to criticize an author of such refinement whose work is much praised when he, just one man, dares to defame and censure without exception an entire sex.

Christine de Pizan, Letter to Jean de Montreuil, 1401

In the library, Christine found Gilles sitting at his desk looking so agitated she was tempted to retreat back down the stairs. She dropped the pouch with the mandrake onto a bench just inside the door, laid her cloak on top of it, and waited for him to notice her. But instead of looking up, he shuffled the books on his desk, causing one of them to fall to the floor. She walked over and picked it up. It was only then that he realized she was there. He seized the book from her hands.

'Why are you here, Christine?'

She had never seen him so overwrought. Nevertheless, she was determined to get the information she had come for. 'I want to speak to you about Henri Le Picart.'

Gilles looked toward the door. 'I have no time. The Duke of Orléans is here.'

She turned and was dismayed to see Louis, with Guy de Marolles right behind him. The duke stepped into the room, swept off his big beaver hat and made her a deep bow. 'So, my little emissary. I trust you have learned something from Alix de Clairy.' He removed his crimson cape and handed it and the hat to Guy.

Michel hasn't spoken to him, she thought. Too disconcerted to say anything, she merely shook her head.

The duke started to pace around the room like an animal on the prowl, all the while keeping his eyes on her face. Behind him, Guy snickered. Then Louis stood in front of her. 'I want that book, Christine.'

'Alix was too confused to think clearly about it, *Monseigneur*.'

'Then you did not speak to her properly. I thought better of you, Christine. Surely you could have devised a way to make her tell you what I want to know.'

'Perhaps I could, if it were possible to visit her again.'

He resumed pacing, frowning and clasping his hands behind his back. Then he said, 'Very well. But I warn you: this is your last chance. All will not be well with you if I do not have that book tomorrow.' He looked at Gilles. 'Give me something so I can write a letter.'

Moving as if in a trance, Gilles laid a piece of parchment on his desk, took an inkwell and a quill from a cupboard, set them beside the parchment, and stood to one side, looking at the floor.

The duke went to the desk and sat down. 'You're not yourself, Gilles.'

Gilles said nothing. He merely put a hand on a corner of the parchment to hold it steady while Louis wrote. For once, his bushy eyebrows were still.

Louis sat with one leg thrust out, the hand that wasn't writing resting on his hip. No sign of anger clouded his handsome face, and for a moment Christine breathed easily, telling herself his threat had not been serious. But she could hear Guy snickering, and she realized that, as usual, more went on with the duke than met the eye.

Louis finished the letter, stood up, and handed it to her. He took his cape and hat from Guy and motioned to Gilles. 'Come with me to the rue de la Harpe. I want your advice about a breviary I'm thinking of buying.'

As if waking from a dream, Gilles, who seemed to have forgotten Christine was there, picked up his cloak and followed Louis out the door. Guy made her a mocking little bow and hurried after them.

Alone in the library, Christine stood by Gilles's desk, holding the duke's letter. Sun streamed in through the glass-paned windows on the other side of the room, but she was not warmed; the perspiration that ran down her back was icy cold. She knew she would never be able to obtain the information the duke wanted. She wouldn't be able to save Alix de Clairy. Alix would forgive her, but the duke wouldn't.

For a long time, she stood in a daze. When she became conscious of her surroundings again, she was surprised to find she was still holding Louis's letter in her hand. She folded it and put it in her sleeve. She looked at Gilles's desk and saw the book she had picked up from the floor. It was a book her husband had told her about, *The Romance of the Rose*. She had once remarked to Étienne that, from its title, it sounded delightful. 'You wouldn't think so if you knew what was in it,' he'd said, laughing. To distract herself from her troubled thoughts, she sat down and started to read. As she skimmed through the first part, an allegory of love, she decided the book was pleasant enough. But that was only the first part. There were two authors, and when the second one took up the story, he turned it into a diatribe against women. She began to read in earnest. The author's attitude toward women appalled her. In one place he wrote, 'A virtuous woman is rarer than a phoenix or a white crow,' and in another, 'A woman is an animal full of wrath, waspish and fickle.' And then, 'A woman has no understanding at all.' She was so infuriated, she scarcely noticed a fluttering sound on the other side of the room. But as the noise went on and on, she closed the book and went to investigate.

She remembered Gilles telling her the wire mesh on the library windows was deteriorating, and now she could see why that worried him. One side of a double window was open, and because the mesh behind it had fallen away, a bird had flown in and become trapped behind the glass on the other side. *Perhaps a phoenix, or a white crow*, she thought angrily. But it was only a tiny sparrow, flapping around in desperation as it tried to find the way out. The base of the window was above her head, so she found a stool and stood on it. When the sparrow saw her, it hopped into the corner and remained perfectly still as she put her hand in and picked it up. She held it for a moment, feeling the beating of its heart under its soft feathers. But when she tried to stroke its head with her finger, it struggled so hard she was afraid it would hurt itself. She opened her hand and let it fly away.

She stayed on the stool and gazed out the open window, looking over barren gardens to the Porte Saint-Honoré, whose round towers with their pointed roofs rose above King Charles the Fifth's new wall. She was well aware that just on the other side of the wall was the *Marché aux Pourceaux*, and she tried not to think about it, for it was to the pig market that criminals condemned to be burned alive were taken. She concentrated instead on the scene farther to the north – brown fields and vineyards on a hill dotted with windmills and topped by the church of Saint-Pierre and the convent of the nuns of Montmartre. The air was turning colder, and black clouds cast long shadows over the fields. Another winter storm was on the way. She imagined she could see the nuns in the convent garth, perhaps collecting laundry they'd hung outdoors to dry, and she thought about how peaceful the sisters' existence was compared with hers. Then she remembered the book on Gilles's desk. Why did men write those things about women? Some of them deserved it, she supposed – those who thought mandrakes had little demons in them. But to say that women have no understanding at all!

She stepped down from the stool, and as she did so, her foot struck the wood paneling just above the floor. One of the panels fell away, exposing a large opening in the wall. Noticing something brown inside the opening, she bent down, looked in, and recoiled in horror. She thrust the panel back into place, dashed to the other side of the room, scooped up her cloak and the pouch with the mandrake, and started out the door. Gilles was there, and she nearly bumped into him. He started to speak, but she brushed past him and forced herself to walk slowly down the spiral staircase. Then she ran.

Thirty-Four

Please tell me why so many authors revile women in their books.

Christine de Pizan, *Le Livre de la Cité des Dames*, 1404–1405

She raced across the moat and up the rue Saint-Honoré, sloshing through puddles and slipping in mud, until she reached the rue de l'Arbre-Sec where, struggling to get her breath, she sank down onto a step at the base of the stone cross. The vegetable sellers were still hawking their produce, and the corpse was still rotting on the gallows, but she noticed nothing.

Suddenly, Michel ran up to her, panting and flinging his arms about. 'I've been looking everywhere for you,' he gasped, as he lowered himself onto the step beside her.

'Didn't my mother tell you I'd be in the library?'

'Of course she did. But you aren't in the library, are you? It's just luck that I came this way.' He was puffing so hard he could barely speak, but he managed to ask, 'What are you doing here? Why do you look so distressed?' He put his hand out to steady himself and overturned a basket one of the vendors had placed on the step.

'I hope a canker rots you, *porc de Dieu*!' cursed the old woman. She seized her onions and turnips, threw them into the basket, and moved away.

'This is not a pleasant place,' the monk said.

'I need to talk to you, Michel.'

'If it's about the duke's book, I have disappointing news for you. I wasn't able to speak with him. I'm sorry.'

'It doesn't matter now. I've found the book. It's in the library at the Louvre.'

At first, the monk looked at her without comprehending. Then he laughed. 'Well, well, after all this excitement. In the library. That is the best place for it.'

'You don't understand. The book is *hidden* in the library.'

'What are you saying?'

'It's hidden in an opening at the bottom of a wall. A panel fell away, and I saw it there.'

'How do you know it was the right book?'

'I saw the symbols on the cover. The duke has more confidence in me than you do; he described the book to me.'

The monk looked pained. 'Does Gilles know you found it?'

'You really do doubt my intelligence, don't you?' She put her hands over her face. 'Oh, Michel, what shall I do? Gilles has always been good to me.'

'People aren't always what they seem. Didn't it ever occur to you that Gilles would do almost anything for a book?'

'I can't believe it. Gilles must have found it

258

somewhere after Hugues de Précy was murdered.' She turned to the monk, and asked angrily, 'Why won't you tell me what's in that book?'

'It is best you don't know.'

She jumped up and stood in front of him with her hands on her hips. 'I've had enough of this, Michel. You act as though I have no understanding at all, as though I were a waspish phoenix, or a wrathful crow, or any fickle woman.' Her voice rose as she garbled the insulting descriptions of women in *The Romance of the Rose*.

The vegetable sellers were staring at them. 'We can't talk here,' Michel said. 'Come with me.' He led her down the rue de l'Arbre-Sec to the church of Saint-Germain-l'Auxerrois and made her sit on a stone bench in front of the main portal. The seat was still warm from the morning sun, but the sky had turned gray, and the air felt cold. Gusts of wind sent dry leaves and debris spinning around their feet.

Michel sat beside her and tucked his hands into the sleeves of his habit. 'Now, about fickle women and waspish crows.'

'You wouldn't understand.'

'Oh, I've read *The Romance of the Rose*.'

'Then perhaps someday you'll tell me why one of the authors of that book felt it necessary to write those terrible things about women. But let's forget about *The Romance of the Rose* now. I want to know what's in the other book, the one everyone is so eager to have.'

Michel glanced around to make sure they were alone, and then he leaned toward her. 'I'm sure you know about all those charlatans who claim they can restore the king to health. Well, there was one who was even more evil than the others. He styled himself a monk, but he was no monk. He was a demon from Hell!' He turned his head and spat onto the ground. 'Because he was as thin as a skeleton, and his filthy clothes hung on him like rags, everyone thought he had mortified his body through pious devotions. That was a disguise; the only creature he was devoted to was the Devil. He succeeded in this deception because it is in the nature of many people to wish to be deceived. The Duke of Orléans is among those people; he was going to let him practice his vile magic on the king. Abominable! Abominable!'

Christine shivered. 'The man I found behind the chest?'

'Yes. And the book he was carrying contains instructions for working magic spells and conjuring demons, rituals that can supposedly be used to cure the king. Hugues de Précy killed him and stole the book so he could give it to the queen, to gain favor for himself.'

'The duke suspects this about Hugues, yet he hasn't told the king?'

'The king loved Hugues de Précy. Even his own brother would be reluctant to tell him Hugues was a murderer and a thief.'

'Tell me more about this book.'

Michel sighed. 'It's not what's in the book. It's what many people *believe* about the book. They think it will give whomever possesses it power over everything on earth and in heaven.' Christine felt a chill go down her spine; Michel's voice was as solemn as her father's had been the day he'd told her about mandrakes.

'So you don't believe the book by itself has any kind of evil power?'

'Of course not. I would never give credence to such nonsense.'

'What about the omens and signs you and my mother are always talking about?'

'That is not the same. God speaks to us through signs. This book has an altogether different significance, altogether different. By itself it could have no effect on anything. But some of the people who think it does are evil beyond measure, and if the book falls into the wrong hands, there's no telling what could happen. Don't you understand? Hugues de Précy killed a man to obtain it. Someone seems to have killed Hugues for the same reason. Imagine all the other terrible things that may occur because of that book.'

'And if the duke gets his hands on the book, what do you think he will do with it?'

Michel shook his head. 'No one can tell.'

'Do you really think I could come under its spell? Is that why you don't want me to know what's in it?'

Michel blushed. 'Forgive me. I don't think that at all. It's just that this book can cause so much trouble, and I don't want you to be involved in it. You're certain Gilles doesn't know you found it?'

'Almost certain. But I can't believe Gilles is the murderer.'

'If you want to save Alix de Clairy, you have to entertain every possibility.'

'It could have been Henri Le Picart. He uses the library. And you told us he knows about magic and alchemy and how to make gold. Someone like that would certainly want to have such a book.'

Michel shook his head. 'You are making no sense. Even if Henri had stolen the book, why would he hide it in the library?'

Christine rose and walked around the bench. The sky had grown threatening, and the wind pulled angrily at her cloak. Michel stood, too. 'You must inform the Duke of Orléans about the book without delay, Christine. I don't know what he intends to do with it, but he has to be told. No good will come of this, however. I wish that damnable book would disappear forever.'

'And now that the book is found, there is no way to save Alix de Clairy,' she moaned.

Michel put his hand on her arm. 'A wise man once said, "While a man has life, there's hope." The same goes for a woman.'

Large drops of rain began to fall. Christine was tired and hungry, and now she feared she would be drenched. 'I must go home,' she said.

'You can't go home just yet. With all this discussion of the book, I forgot to tell you, the Duchess of Orléans is very ill, and she is asking for you.'

'But I spoke with her the other day and she was no more frail than usual. I told her what I've learned about Hugues de Précy's murder, and she said she would help save Alix de Clairy.'

'She was all right early this morning, too. I saw her in the courtyard talking to that boy, Renaut.

But later she fell down some stairs. No one knows how it happened. She is ailing badly. She has something to say to you, and you must go to her immediately. After that, you can tell the duke about the book.' He picked up her pouch. 'I'll carry this.'

'It's for you, anyway, Michel. It's the mandrake.'

He slung the pouch over his shoulder and whispered, 'Damnable thing.' The pouch bounced up and down against his black robe as they hurried up the street.

Thirty-Five

Many perils come from talking too much.

From a book of moral and practical advice for a young wife, Paris, 1393

After Marion left Christine at the library, she didn't go to the secondhand clothes market. Instead, she went to the church of Saint-Jacques-la-Boucherie and looked into all the booths where the scribes worked. The scribe she was looking for wasn't there. She walked around the streets near the church until she came to a house with sinister-looking carvings of dragons and serpents on its door. Henri Le Picart stepped out and walked across the street, dressed in his customary black cape with the long black hood and the ermine collar. *He looks as evil as his house*, she thought.

Henri went over to the church and into one of the booths. She crept up and looked around the corner of the little compartment. He was busy writing and didn't seem to see her. She wondered whether any of the other scribes could tell her something about him, but she didn't want to ask them; she felt more comfortable with the thieves, beggars, and loose women who frequented that part of Paris, so she walked to a narrow cul-de-sac where she knew she would find her friends and asked if anyone knew Henri Le Picart.

A prostitute named Hélène laughed. 'He got me out of prison.'

'How did he do that?'

'I got caught stealing a gold belt from one of the shops on the Grand Pont. He paid some men to come to my trial and swear I'd been somewhere else at the time. The provost had to let me go.'

'So Henri is a friend of yours?'

'I hardly know him. He only helped me because he wanted to annoy the provost.'

Some of the other vagrants were eager to volunteer information. 'Henri owns a lot of houses,' said a thief who was taking coins out of his sleeve and counting them. He made a face when Marion said she lived in one of those houses. 'I wouldn't rest easy in a house belonging to that man.' He spat into the gutter.

'He scares me, too,' said a beggar with his arm in a sling and a patch over one eye.

'What about all those weird carvings on his

264

door?' another of the thieves said. 'They'd frighten anyone. But I tell you this. Henri Le Picart is rich. He knows how to make gold.'

A beggar in filthy, gore-stained rags had come into the cul-de-sac. He smeared blood from a dead cat onto his tattered clothes, then reached into the gutter for some foul-smelling muck and added it to his costume. When he'd completed his disguise, he said, 'I was in that house the other day. Henri had a job for me. He paid me to pump a bellows under a fire in a little brick oven. He had glass vials with colored liquids. Lots of books, too, with strange symbols on their covers. And roots and dead plants hanging from the ceiling. It was scary.'

Marion shuddered. She remembered the book stolen from the murdered man behind the chest at the palace, and the mandrake root hanging in Christine's fireplace. She hurried out of the cul-de-sac, eager to find Christine and tell her she'd learned more from her friends than anyone would ever learn from some dusty old librarian.

She turned the corner, and ran right into Henri Le Picart.

'You and your friends talk too much,' he said. 'I suggest you learn to hold your tongue.' He walked away.

I'm not going to let him frighten me, Marion said to herself, wondering how much he'd heard. It had started to rain, but she scarcely noticed. Keeping well behind and ducking into doorways to avoid being seen, she followed him.

Thirty-Six

The princes of the realm had sincere affection for the Duchess of Orléans. They regarded her as the most honorable and magnificent lady of the kingdom, and during her lifetime they always respected her like a mother.

The Monk of Saint-Denis,
Chronique du Religieux de Saint-Denis, contenant le règne de Charles VI de 1380 à 1422

Long before Christine and Michel reached the palace, the storm broke with driving rain and a fierce wind that tried to hold them back as they struggled along the slippery streets. By the time they arrived at the queen's residence, they were soaked through. When Michel told Simon they were on their way to see the Duchess of Orléans, Simon looked at their wet clothes and shook his head.

'You can't go to her in that condition.' He led them to the little room with a fireplace where the palace guards sheltered from the cold and told Christine to remove her cloak and spread it out on a trestle in the corner.

Michel hung the pouch on a nail protruding

266

from the wall and opened it partway. 'I want the mandrake to dry out before I give it to the infirmarer,' he explained. Christine wished he'd leave the pouch closed.

They sat on a bench before the small fireplace and warmed their hands over the flames. Simon had returned to his post, but his sack lay in the corner, and Christine wondered whether it contained anything to eat. Then Renaut bounced into the room, dived into the bag, brought out a slice of gingerbread, and stood in front of her munching it. 'You can have some, too,' he said as he reached back into the bag and produced another piece.

Christine didn't hesitate to take the gingerbread. 'Do you think Simon will mind?' she asked Michel.

'Surely not. The boy can do nothing wrong in Simon's eyes. He and his wife have no children.'

When Renaut had finished his gingerbread, he went to a corner of the room, sat on the floor, and took his little red top out of his sleeve. 'Why are you here?' he asked as he set the top spinning.

'We're going to speak with the Duchess of Orléans,' Michel said.

'She's about to die. My grandmother told me. You can ask her about it yourself.' Renaut picked up his top and slipped it into his sleeve as Blanche strode into the room.

'Is it true the duchess is dying?' Michel asked her.

'That is what I've heard.' She stuffed Renaut into his red jacket and pulled him out the door, leaving the faint odor of cloves behind.

Michel went to the trestle, lifted Christine's cloak, and spread it out again. 'It is still damp,' he said. 'We'll have to come back and get it later. We cannot delay going to the duchess any longer.'

They went into the courtyard, where Christine was horrified to see Gilles Malet and the Duke of Orléans coming toward them, followed by Guy de Marolles. *The duke will ask me about the book*, she thought. *And right beside him is the person who has it, the king's librarian.*

But Michel spoke first. 'We're on our way to the duchess,' he said, as he hurried Christine across the courtyard.

'Thank you, Michel,' she breathed when they were well out of earshot.

'It is only a short reprieve,' he said. 'You will have to tell the duke about the book as soon as you have spoken with the duchess.'

In her cold room, the duchess lay motionless on her hard bed, attended by one of the king's physicians, as well as the queen and her ladies-in-waiting, who looked like peacocks stranded in a monk's cell. The old lady's eyes were closed, but she opened them when Michel said, 'You asked for Christine, and here she is, *Madame*.'

Christine knelt by the bed. 'You wished to see me, *Madame*?'

The duchess attempted to sit up, but she fell back against her pillow.

The queen stepped up to the bed. With a little motion of her trembling hand, the duchess waved her away. Michel said, 'Should everyone but Christine leave, *Madame*?' She nodded.

Michel said to Christine, 'Sometimes when she tries to speak, no words come. Be patient.'

Alone with the duchess, Christine continued to kneel, shivering on the cold floor. She said, 'I know you have something to tell me, *Madame*. Does it have to do with Hugues de Précy's murder?'

The duchess nodded and tried to smile.

'Do you know who poisoned him?' The duchess nodded again. She put one trembling hand to her throat and with the other pointed to a book lying at the foot of the bed. Christine got to her feet, glad to give her knees a rest, and picked it up. The duchess moved her hand in the direction of a stool by the fireplace and nodded approval when Christine brought it near the bed and sat on it.

Christine held the book, an illuminated Book of Hours with an inscription identifying it as the queen's, close to the duchess's face and turned the pages. The old woman watched the colorful illustrations, and when the calendar page for the month of February appeared, she raised her shaking hand and pointed to a picture of snow-covered houses clustered around a small church.

'Are you trying to tell me someone who lives in a village poisoned Hugues?' Christine asked.

The duchess shook her head and motioned for her go on. She showed no interest in any of the following illustrations until they came to the image of a Cistercian monk. Here she raised her hand again.

Christine looked puzzled, and the duchess sighed.

At last they came to the Office of the Dead and a scene of the first horseman of the Apocalypse. With great difficulty, the duchess lifted her hand until it touched the flank of the white horse. Christine could only stare at the picture, realizing she'd failed. 'I'm so sorry, *Madame,*' she said, taking the duchess's hand in hers. A slight pressure of the old woman's fingers indicated forgiveness. The duchess lay back against the pillow, closed her eyes, and seemed to sleep. '*Madame?*' Christine asked. There was no answer.

Christine went into the hallway. The queen, tapping her foot and glaring at her footmen, stood rubbing her hands together over one of the moveable stoves her footmen wheeled around the cold corridors of the palace whenever she left her apartments in the winter. All her ladies had left, but Michel and the doctor were there. The queen went into the duchess's room, and the doctor followed her.

'Why does she seem so angry?' Christine asked the monk.

'One of her rings has disappeared. She thinks someone stole it. But tell me, what did the duchess say to you?'

She looked around. Several sergeants-at-arms leaned against the wall. She drew Michel away from them, and whispered, 'She knows who murdered Hugues de Précy. But she couldn't talk, so she tried to tell me who it was by pointing to the illustrations in a Book of Hours.'

'What illustrations?'

'A village in the snow, a Cistercian monk, and

the first horseman of the Apocalypse. I was too dim-witted to understand what they meant.'

Michel drew his hands into the sleeves of his habit and studied the floor. 'It makes no sense to me, either,' he said. 'Perhaps God will speak to me about it. But in the meantime, you must tell the duke about the book in the library. You will find him at the Celestines. He has gone there to pray for the duchess.' That did not surprise Christine, who knew that whenever Louis was in one of his penitent moods, he went to the church of the Celestines, next to the Hôtel Saint-Pol. 'And to beg forgiveness because he is convinced he caused the tragic fire. He is more upset than you know,' Michel added. 'I will go with you.'

When they returned into the guards' warming room, they were surprised to find Renaut curled up asleep with his head on his red jacket. 'Blanche was about to take him home, but she changed her mind and left him here,' Simon said. 'I can't imagine what she is doing here at this late hour.'

Renaut opened his eyes, looked at Christine, and reached for Simon's sack. 'Do you want more gingerbread?'

Christine's stomach growled obligingly. 'I hope you don't mind,' she said to the *portier*. 'I was not home for dinner.'

'I have something better.' Simon went to a small cupboard in the wall, brought out a loaf of bread, a wedge of strong-smelling cheese, and a flask of wine, and set the small feast on a bench. Michel was as hungry as Christine, and, with Renaut's help, the food was soon gone. Then the boy stretched out in front of the fire and fell asleep again.

Michel helped Christine into her cloak, and they went out. It was almost dark, and the storm, which had been gathering strength all afternoon, raged. 'I know a path to the Celestines that won't take us into the street. It's quicker, and we won't get so wet,' Christine said, leading the monk toward a path through one of the palace gardens. Only then did she realize something was missing.

'Michel! You forgot the pouch with the mandrake!'

He stopped and clapped his hand to his head. 'So I did. It can't have been on the nail where I left it, or I would have remembered it.'

'You don't seem to want it. Otherwise you'd have taken it back to the abbey long before this.'

Michel thought for a moment. 'You may be right, Christine. I'm not so sure it's wise to carry a mandrake around.'

Christine smiled to herself and didn't feel so ashamed of her own thoughts about the horrible root. She said, 'Nevertheless, somebody must have taken it. We have to find out who it was. Mandrakes are dangerous. We should go back and ask Simon.'

'Not in all this rain. I'll find out later what happened to it,' Michel said.

It was night now, and since they hadn't brought torches, they had to make their way along the path in nearly complete darkness, clinging to each other as the rain beat down and the wind blew against them. They came to the orchards.

The trees, black silhouettes against the gray sky, strained and shuddered as the gusts tore away branches that crashed to the ground.

'Do you know where you are going?' Michel shouted.

'This path should come out at the church,' Christine shouted back.

Suddenly, the rain relented, the darkness lifted, and for a moment, they could see shadows moving through the trees. Then night closed in again.

Christine took Michel's arm and pulled him along the path until they came up against a large obstacle blocking their way. She groped around and felt the bark of a fallen tree. When she turned aside to go around it, she lost the path.

'Great God in heaven! Where are we?' Michel cried.

'I don't know.'

'Have patience and endure,' the monk muttered to himself.

The rain poured down again, and the wind whipped their wet clothes around their legs. Christine tried to hang onto the monk's arm, but he shook her off and walked away. She heard him bump up against something.

'What is it?' she called out.

'Wooden palings,' he called back.

She heard a roar, and she knew what he'd found. 'Michel! That's the lions' stockade!'

'A plague upon it! The gate is open.'

'Get away from there, Michel!' Christine cried. But it was too late; the lions were out.

She could sense huge shapes padding toward her, and she cowered against the trunk of the fallen tree, listening to throaty, grunting sounds as they plashed past her through puddles and mud. Their wet fur smelled heavy and rank, like dung and rotting hay.

She stayed perfectly still, and Michel must have done the same, for she could no longer hear him. She wondered how many lions there were, but it was too dark to count them. Sometimes one roared, and she waited to feel sharp teeth closing around her arm, or claws digging into her throat. She closed her eyes and prayed.

After a while, all she could hear was the rain, and she thought the beasts had gone. She was about to step away from the tree when she saw a light floating toward her and a woman ran past, an apparition dressed in rags, her long auburn hair – so thick and disheveled it obscured her face – shining in the glow of her lantern. The wind died down, the rain fell softly, and the lions, driven by the spectral woman, came slinking back, grunting and grumbling to themselves. They filed past, and then all was quiet, until Michel shouted, 'Christine! Are you safe?'

She sloshed through the mud toward the sound of his voice. The darkness abated, and she could see him, hitching his habit up to his knees and stamping his soggy feet. Her boots were waterlogged, too. 'I'm safe, but I'm wet and cold, and I'm going home,' she wailed. 'I'll speak with the duke first thing in the morning.' Something moved in the shadows.

Christine grabbed the monk's arm. 'We have to get out of here!'

'Are you afraid of me, too?' Marion said, as she stepped up to them.

Christine let go of Michel's arm. 'What are you doing here, Marion?'

'Looking for you, of course. You're easy to find, you make so much noise.'

I should have known, Christine thought, remembering the Hôtel Saint-Pol was not fortified, and there were many ways to get in. And in any case, the girl probably knew most of the guards.

Marion said, 'You seemed awfully scared of those old lions.'

'Of course we were scared,' Michel huffed.

'Of those old things? They're so fat and lazy they can hardly move.' Marion slapped her thigh and laughed. 'They get out all the time. I'd be more afraid of the woman who looks after them.'

'Do you know Loyse?' Christine asked.

'Nobody does. But I've seen her with the lions.'

'How did you know we were here?'

'You were in such a rush, you didn't see me standing at the corner of the rue Tiron. You didn't even know you were being followed.'

'What's that you're saying?' Michel asked. Alarmed, he lowered his voice. 'Somebody's following us?'

'Henri Le Picart. He was behind you all the way to the palace. He went in just after you did.'

'Did he come out again?' Christine whispered.

'I stood by the main entrance for a long time,

275

and he didn't come out there. Then I went around another way and saw you two wandering through the gardens. Somebody was behind you. I think it was Henri, but it was so dark all I could see was a black cape.'

Thirty-Seven

Remember, dear ladies, how deceptive flatterers think you are weak, fickle, and easily swayed, and how they try to catch you, using all kinds of outlandish and deceitful wiles – just as they lay traps for wild animals. Flee, flee, my ladies. Have nothing to do with these men, for their smiles hide agonizing, virulent poisons.

Christine de Pizan, *Le Livre de la Cité des Dames*, 1404–1405

The rain stopped, the wind died down, and the moon floated through scattered clouds. The earth was deathly still, awash in the moon's light and mysterious shadows.

'Where did the person in the black cape go, Marion?' Christine asked.

'Along another path. That path turns back this way, so you should come away from here.'

'Let's go to the rue de Pute-y-Muce,' Christine

said. By the light of the moon, she could see Michel's face, and she could tell from his expression, he'd had enough of her directions. Nevertheless, she started out, calling back over her shoulder, 'From there we can easily get to my house.'

'I'll stay close to you,' Marion said, as she hurried after her. 'If you two milksops are afraid of those old lions, you'll go all to pieces if someone's really after you.'

'There is nothing to jest about. Three people have been murdered. We don't want Christine to be the fourth,' Michel called out as he reluctantly followed. When he caught up to them, he drew himself up to his full height, as if to show he was perfectly capable of providing all the protection they needed. He was still shorter than Marion, and Christine was glad to have the girl's company.

They walked quickly to the rue de Pute-y-Muce, a narrow, muddy street behind the palace where Marion, much to Michel's disgust, waved to some of the prostitutes for which the street was named. Then they turned down the rue Saint-Antoine and made their way to Christine's house. Marion stayed close to her companions all the way to the door, but she hid in the shadows while they went in. They could hear her laughing and muttering to herself, 'Saint Matthew's ulcer! Afraid of those old lions!'

When Christine and Michel went into the hallway, Francesca emerged from the kitchen and fussed at them. 'Where have you two been? Do you not have enough sense to take cover from the rain? Go and put on dry clothes, *Cristina.* You come into the kitchen, Michel.'

Christine lit a candle and went upstairs. Goblin was there, guarding the sleeping children, and he jumped up and raced around while she changed, then danced along beside her as she went back down to the kitchen. Michel sat before the fire with his boots off and a blanket around his shoulders, rubbing his hands together to warm them. As soon as Christine appeared, he went to the table and looked hungrily at steaming bowls of soup Francesca had set out. But before he had a chance to eat, someone banged on the front door. Francesca went into the hall. Michel and Christine hurried after her.

'Don't unlatch it, Mama,' Christine said.

'I knew it! They have come to murder us!' Francesca cried.

A voice shouted, 'Christine! *Merde!* Open the door!'

'It's all right, Mama,' Christine said. 'It's Marion. It must be important if she's willing to face you.'

'Murderers. Prostitutes. Why have you not invited all the criminals in Paris?' Francesca marched back to the kitchen.

Christine opened the door and was surprised to find that Marion was nowhere in sight. Instead, she found Gillette and a woman she had never seen before.

Gillette said, 'I've brought Macée. She has something to tell you.'

'Where's Marion?'

'Is that her name? We were wandering

278

around looking for your house, and she jumped out at us and wouldn't let us go until we told her we had come with information that will help Alix.'

Christine saw a movement in the shadows. 'It's all right, Marion. They're friends,' she called out.

'Shut the door!' Francesca shouted from the kitchen.

Christine drew the two women into the house. It was cold in the hallway, and she could see that Gillette was shivering, so she led them into the kitchen.

'Who are these people, Christine?' Francesca asked impatiently.

'This is Gillette, Alix de Clairy's nursemaid. And this is Macée, the midwife who delivered Alix.' Christine took Gillette's arm and drew her over to a bench by the fireplace. The midwife stood to one side, not looking at anyone. She was a tall, thickset woman with a face so disfigured by pockmarks, it was impossible to guess her age. Christine put her hand up to the pockmark on her own face and shuddered.

Michel touched Christine's arm, and whispered, 'I saw that woman years ago, in Amiens. She was pretty then, but she was involved in things that – well, I don't want to speak about them.'

'She's a midwife, Michel. I know about all the things midwives do. We can't concern ourselves with that. She may be able to tell us something that will help Alix.'

Macée stood twisting her hands together, and

Francesca kept her distance on the other side of the room.

'What have you to tell us, Macée?' Christine asked. The woman just tugged at her thin gray hair.

Christine looked at Gillette. 'Why doesn't she speak?'

'She's afraid.'

Christine suddenly grew angry with the woman with the pockmarked face who stood hunched, staring at her with dark, sunken eyes. 'Why should we care about your fears, Macée, after the suffering you've caused?'

Macée cringed and turned away. Gillette rose from the bench and went to Christine's side. 'We must try to forgive her. Drink made her says things she shouldn't have, many years ago.'

Christine could picture how it had happened – the lusty countrywoman, shrewd at her work as a midwife but ignorant of the ways of gentle-folk, sitting in a smoky tavern with a dashing young knight, her tongue loosened with wine. The knight was Hugues de Précy, sleek and cunning, hoping to hear something he could use to his advantage.

'She wants to make amends,' Gillette said. 'She thinks she knows who poisoned Hugues de Précy.'

'If she knows, why hasn't she said something before this?'

Gillette crept back to the bench and sat down. 'She will tell you.' She held her trembling hands clasped in her lap.

Macée strode to the fireplace and stared into

280

the flames. Then she turned and faced Christine defiantly. In the flickering light, the pits in her face became ugly craters, and her eyes seemed to be set in deep sockets. 'I found out today who the lady in the dungeon is.' Her voice was loud and grating. 'I want to help her.'

Out of the corner of her eye, Christine saw Michel start toward her, but she waved him away.

The midwife looked into the fire again. Keeping her eyes on the flames, she began her story. 'Two weeks ago, a lady came to me. She'd discovered she was going to have a child. She didn't want the baby, and she was in agony, because she'd tried to do away with it by herself. I could do nothing to help except give her something for the pain. The herbs put her to sleep, and in her dreams she cried out her secret. The baby's father was not her husband. She said the real father's name. I knew that name.'

The room was quiet except for the occasional crackle of a flame. 'Who was this lady?' Christine asked.

'The wife of a knight, Guy de Marolles.' Christine pictured Guy's ugly face and couldn't help thinking it was no wonder his wife had found a lover.

'After the woman went home,' Macée continued, 'she was very ill. She feared she would die, and she confessed her sin to her husband. But she refused to tell him who her lover was. So he found out where I lived and came to me. I told him I had nothing to do with the injury his wife

281

had inflicted on herself, but he didn't believe me. He knew about certain things I'd done in the past, and he said he'd have me thrown into prison if I didn't tell him who the father of the baby was.'

'So Guy de Marolles learned from you who had seduced his wife?'

'Yes.' She spat into the fire. 'He swore he would kill that man, and I was glad.'

Macée turned and looked at Christine. Her face was ghastly, but Christine dared not avert her eyes, for fear she would stop speaking. She knew that her mother and Michel were standing like statues near the table; she knew that the soup she and Michel had not eaten was cooling in the bowls; she knew that Gillette sat on the bench holding her trembling hands together; she knew that no one breathed. Even Goblin sat perfectly still.

'Who was the wife's lover?'

'The knight Hugues de Précy.'

'When did Guy de Marolles come to you and learn his name?'

'The day Hugues de Précy died.'

Christine felt a wave of relief sweep over her. Guy had killed Hugues because he had learned Hugues had seduced his wife. That meant Gilles was innocent. She looked over at Michel. He nodded. He'd heard.

'You were right to tell me this, Macée.'

The midwife turned away and gazed into the fire again, tugging at her hair and muttering to herself, '*Cochon! Diable!*' Christine's vision of a tavern where Hugues plied Macée with drink shifted to an image of a squalid room where he made love to this simple woman, to learn her secrets.

Macée was speaking again. 'He was very sly, Hugues de Précy, all those years ago. He deceived me with his handsome face, and I told him about Alix de Clairy's birth. But I didn't tell him everything.'

Christine looked where she did, into the fire. A flame leapt up. She heard Étienne say, *She must know about Alix de Clairy's mother.*

'Why did Alix's birth mother abandon her, Macée?'

'She had to. So her husband wouldn't find out there were two of them.'

'Two of what?'

Francesca was standing close now, her curiosity overcoming her aversion to the midwife. 'You know, *Cristina*. Twins.'

'That's just a foolish belief, Mama!'

'It may be a foolish belief,' Macée said, 'but her husband was a violent man. He would have killed her if he'd found out there were two babies.'

Christine felt like murdering someone herself. Alix had been rejected because of the absurd idea that if a woman has twins she must have lain with two men.

'What did the mother want you to do with the baby, Macée?'

'She told me to give it away. So I asked Gillette to take it to the Lord of Clairy and his lady, because their own baby was born dead.'

'And the birth mother never wanted to know what had happened to her baby?'

'No.'

'Did you tell Hugues de Précy who Alix de Clairy's real mother was?'

'No, but he assumed that since she had been given away, she was not of noble birth.'

Gillette crept over and stood beside the midwife. 'There's more.' Her blue eyes glistened in the light of the flames.

Macée hung her head and pulled at her hair. 'Yes, there's more.' Her rasping voice sank to a whisper. 'The birth mother kept the wrong baby.'

'The wrong baby?' Christine asked in astonishment. 'How could there have been a right and a wrong baby?'

'The one the mother kept was possessed by demons. The mother blamed me. She sent the child away for a while, but then she took her back, and for years after that she taunted me with the sight of the accursed girl. Then Hugues de Précy went to the Lord of Clairy and told him what he knew. I ran away.'

'Where is the mother now?'

'She's here in Paris.'

'And the baby she kept, was it a girl?' Christine asked with a sense of foreboding.

'Yes.'

'Is she in Paris, too?'

'Yes. The devil-ridden girl helps the king's lion keeper.'

Christine's head felt light, and her knees buckled. She sat down on the bench. She recalled Simon telling her that Blanche had lived in Amiens after her marriage. She thought of Alix's auburn hair, and she remembered Loyse's auburn

284

hair shining in the lantern light as she ran after the lions. She could believe Loyse was Alix de Clairy's twin sister, but the thought that Blanche was Alix's mother stunned her.

Gillette spoke up. 'She's telling the truth. She wants to help save Alix.'

Christine asked Macée, 'How is it possible Blanche never wanted to know where her other daughter was?'

'While her husband was alive, she tried to forget the second baby had ever existed. But her husband is dead now. When she saw the woman who played her harp and sang for the queen, she wondered about her, because she looked so much like Loyse. She would have come to me sooner to ask whether I knew anything about her, but it took her a while to find out where I live. A few days ago she came to my house – I live not far from the palace. And I told her. Yes, now Blanche knows for certain the lady in the dungeon is her daughter.'

Thirty-Eight

It was generally said that the king's strange malady was caused by witchcraft. I don't know whether this is true. I only know that the rumor was founded on the weakening of his faculties. At first he still recognized his friends and family, the lords at the court, and all the people in his household. But eventually his mind was lost in such gloom that he forgot everything and by a strange and inexplicable oddity claimed he wasn't married and didn't have any children. He even forgot his own person and his title of King of France.

The Monk of Saint-Denis,
*Chronique du Religieux de
Saint-Denis, contenant le règne
de Charles VI de 1380 à 1422*

Francesca grabbed Christine's hands, pulled her to her feet, and hugged her. '*Che miracolo, Cristina!* Alix de Clairy is saved. It is no longer necessary for you to trouble yourself about the killer.'

Michel wasn't smiling. He drew his hands into the sleeves of his black habit, studied the floor, and said, 'Alix de Clairy's salvation is not so easily accomplished.' He went to the fireplace and asked the midwife, 'Are you willing to go to the Châtelet and tell the provost that Guy de Marolles swore he would kill Hugues de Précy?'

The woman's eyes grew wide with terror.

Christine looked at Michel. He was frowning, and she understood why. They might know the truth, but what use could they make of it?

The monk paced around the room, mumbling to himself, not noticing that the children, wrapped in their bedclothes, had crept into the room. Marie looked at the midwife, went to her mother, and stationed herself at her side.

286

'She won't harm us,' Christine whispered to her.

Jean lifted Goblin into his arms and held him so tightly the dog yelped. Thomas and Lisabetta hid behind Francesca. 'Why are you children not in bed?' their grandmother wanted to know.

'How can we sleep when everyone is talking down here?' Jean asked. 'Who are these women?'

'They're here to help us. Or, rather, to help Alix de Clairy,' Christine said.

'Why do you want to help the lady in the dungeon?' Marie asked. 'She poisoned her husband.'

'She didn't poison her husband. These women think they know who did, and they are brave enough to come here and tell us about it. You children have no manners. Either be silent or go back to bed.'

The children went to the table and sat down. Jean let Goblin lap up a bowl of cold soup. Francesca, who was staring at the midwife, didn't notice.

Michel stopped pacing around the room and sat with the children, resting his head in his hands, setting his hair on end around his tonsure. Goblin, who'd climbed onto the table, licked Michel's bald spot.

'What's the matter?' Jean asked, setting Goblin on the floor again.

'Do you see that unfortunate woman by the fireplace?' Michel asked. 'What do you think would happen if she went to the provost and told him she knows who poisoned Hugues de Précy, and it wasn't Alix de Clairy?' Jean shook his head. 'Well, that is our problem. He would not believe her, and she would be in grave danger.'

'You could tell him. He'd believe you, wouldn't he? You're a monk.'

'He would want to know how I found out, and I would have to admit I learned it from her.'

'Tell him you found out some other way. Do you have to always tell the truth, if you're trying to save someone's life?'

Michel thought for a moment, and then he slapped his hand on the table. 'There is wisdom in what you say, Jean. Sometimes it *is* necessary to tell a falsehood. Yes, I will go to the provost.'

'Does that mean the lady in the dungeon won't burn at the stake?' Thomas sounded disappointed.

Michel stood up, prepared to leave immediately for the Châtelet.

Francesca said, 'You cannot go now. It is the middle of the night.'

He sat down again. 'So it is. I will stay here by the fire until the first light of day, and then I will go.'

Goblin dozed at Michel's feet, the candles burned low, and the children's eyes were closing with sleep. 'It's too late for Gillette and Macée to be out in the street,' Christine said to her mother. 'They can sleep in my bed.'

The front door slammed shut. They looked around and saw only Gillette.

Francesca sighed. 'Will you be comfortable here in the kitchen, Michel?'

The monk looked at the remaining bowl

of soup. 'Do you think you could reheat this, Francesca?'

'Is there more?' Christine asked.

'I will make it ready for you,' her mother replied.

Christine took Gillette and the children upstairs, put Gillette in her bed, and went down to a long-delayed supper. Then she and her mother left Michel yawning by the fire and settled down in Francesca's bed for what remained of the night.

Francesca snored gently, unaware that Goblin was curled up beside her, but Christine lay awake asking herself questions. It had seemed so simple: Alix would go free because Guy de Marolles was the murderer. But was he? Why would Hugues de Précy drink from a flask given to him by the husband of a woman he'd seduced? There was more reason to suspect the queen's brother, Ludwig, who had something to hide and who'd lied about being outside the palace the night of the murder. And what about Gilles? How had he obtained the mysterious book, and why had he hidden it in the library? She turned over and thought about Henri Le Picart, the evil-looking little man with the black beard and black cape who glared at her and followed her to the palace. She thought *him* capable of committing any number of murders – perhaps not for money, but certainly for a book that would give him unlimited power.

She tossed and turned so much that her mother complained in her sleep, and Goblin spent the rest of the night on the floor.

* * *

289

In the morning, long before daybreak, Christine rose, dressed, and went down to the kitchen to find that Michel had already left for the palace.

She built up the fire. Then, by the light of a candle, she heated water and washed the bowls they'd used the night before. After that, she found some vegetables and started to chop them to make soup. She had carrots and onions in little pieces on the table and was about to attack some parsnips, when a voice called from the doorway, '*Cristina?*'

She jumped, and the knife came down on her thumb. 'You startled me!' She sucked her bleeding finger.

Her mother held up a candle, examined the wound, and pronounced it not serious. 'What did you think you were doing?'

'I thought I'd start another soup for you.'

'It is not good to work with knives in the dark. Especially when you do not know how to use them because you never do any cooking.'

'I was trying to keep myself busy while I wait for Michel to return from the palace.'

The front door slammed, and Georgette and Colin burst into the kitchen. 'They're going to burn her this morning!' Georgette screeched.

'It can't be true!' Christine cried.

'It is. And everyone's afraid the king is about to lose his mind again. He says he feels arrows pricking him. The queen wants to go to him, but he won't see her.'

The front door slammed again, and Michel appeared, his pale blue eyes blinking uncontrollably, and his hands clasped so tightly his knuckles turned white.

'Are they really going to burn Alix this morning?' Christine asked.

'I'm sorry to tell you, they are.'

'Didn't you tell the provost about Guy de Marolles?'

'The provost is not in Paris today. I wasn't able to speak with him.'

There was a sound at the doorway. Gillette was standing there, and with a little cry, she slumped to the floor. Francesca ran to her, lifted her head, and slapped her cheeks gently. 'Bring some water, Georgette,' she said. The girl filled a pitcher from the water vat, and Francesca sprinkled a few drops onto the old woman's face. Gillette sat up and leaned against the wall, weeping.

The children came down the stairs and into the kitchen, followed by Goblin, who turned and raced back up when he saw Colin.

'We heard,' Jean said. Christine looked at him and started to say something, but no words came. Marie put her arms around her. Thomas sat on the floor and studied his feet. Little Lisabetta knelt beside Gillette, and begged her not to cry.

Christine sat down on the bench by the table, and Michel stepped over to her. 'There is still something you can do, Christine. Remember what you discovered yesterday.'

She looked at him blankly.

'*The Romance of the Rose* must be right,' he said. 'Women have no understanding whatsoever.'

She jumped up, her face burning. Then she saw he was smiling. 'That's better,' he said. 'You mustn't go to the Duke of Orléans in tears. You must be calm when you tell him about the book hidden in the library.'

'Book? What book? *Non capisco,*' Francesca interrupted.

'You're right, Michel,' Christine said. 'No understanding at all. How could I have forgotten?'

'What book?' her mother asked again.

Michel said to Christine, 'The duke will surely want to question Gilles about the book. Perhaps he'll convince the provost to let Alix de Clairy live until he does so.'

Christine ran into the hall, followed by Michel, and grabbed her cloak. The children crowded around her, hopping up and down in excitement. Goblin ran about in circles. Gillette clung to the doorjamb, and Georgette and Colin stood and stared. Francesca came out of the kitchen and thrust into Christine's hand a sprig of vervain. 'I do not know what you two are talking about, but take this. It should bring you good fortune, whatever you are about to do.'

Christine and Michel sailed out the door. Everyone else followed and stood in the street watching them rush toward the palace.

Thirty-Nine

Because men believe women embody every
abomination, they condemn them all.

Christine de Pizan, *Le Livre de la*
Cité des Dames, 1404–1405

It was a cold, bright morning, and the streets, wet and slippery from the rain the day before, glistened in the early sun. Christine and Michel pushed their way through feverish throngs – noblemen, street vendors, merchants, little children, housewives, beggars, all hurrying toward the pig market to see Alix de Clairy burned at the stake. A group of knights on horseback galloped through the crowd, scattering the thrill-seekers in all directions and causing a hunchbacked old crone toting a basket of eggs and a sack of squawking chickens to stumble and fall against Christine, nearly knocking her down. 'Damnable fools,' the woman called after the horsemen. Then she noticed Michel, crossed herself, and walked away smiling.

'They truly believe that,' he said.

'Believe what?'

'Has your mother not told you? You will have good fortune if you meet a Benedictine in his black habit in the morning. Of course, if I

293

were a Cistercian in a white habit, that would portend misfortune, and the woman would have cursed me.'

Christine stepped over a pile of manure, slipped, and nearly fell. 'I'm glad I can rely on you for good fortune, Michel,' she said, 'because I just dropped the sprig of vervain my mother gave me.'

The courtyards of the Hôtel Saint-Pol teemed with commoners milling around and clamoring for news of the king. Christine lost Michel in the crush and made her way alone to the entrance of the king's residence. She had hoped to find Simon there, but an unfamiliar *portier* blocked her way.

'I must speak with the Duke of Orléans on a matter of great importance,' she said. The man shook his head. Then Michel reappeared. Recognizing the monk, the guard moved aside.

In the palace, all was confusion. Knights paced back and forth, sergeants-at-arms looked around anxiously, footmen cowered in the corners. Michel disappeared a second time, and as Christine stood by herself wondering what to do, the queen came in, surrounded by her ladies-in-waiting, who cried out that the king wouldn't let his wife near him. The queen's face was distorted with pain and anger, but she walked proudly, holding her head high – until, with a little sigh, she sank to her knees, weeping.

Michel reappeared. 'What shall I do now?' Christine asked.

'Wait for me here. I'll try to find the duke.'

The ladies-in-waiting helped the queen to her

feet, but she looked at them as though she had never seen them before. Christine moved away – and bumped into Ludwig. Horrified, she hurried through the gallery. When she turned to see whether Ludwig had followed her, she saw instead Henri Le Picart coming toward her. She pushed open the first door she came to and stumbled into a small, sparsely furnished room.

Guy de Marolles jumped up from a bench near a fireplace, drew his sword, and rushed at her. 'Servant of the devil! Satan's whore!'

She backed away. 'What harm have I done you?'

'You are a woman. All women are evil.'

She took another step back. Guy followed and was almost upon her when the Duke of Orléans burst into the room, followed by Michel. The duke grasped Guy's arms, seized his sword, and forced him down onto a bench. Howling in anguish, the knight dropped his sword and tore at his hair. Louis sat beside him and stroked his hands, murmuring reassurance, as though he were talking to a child.

Nearly fainting with fright, Christine let Michel draw her out of the room and help her to a chair standing against a wall of the gallery. 'I am sure that man is capable of murder,' he said. 'But I do not believe the duke is prepared to hear it.' He tucked his hands into the sleeves of his habit and thought for a moment. Then he said, 'Rest here a bit, and then make your request of the duke, as you planned, Christine.'

Christine leaned back in the chair and breathed deeply. After a while she looked up at Michel and said, 'I'm ready.'

They went back into the room. The knight sat on the bench, his head in his hands, and Louis stood gazing sadly down at him.

'Christine has something to say to you, *Monseigneur*,' Michel said.

The duke turned to Christine and smiled. 'Oh, yes, my little emissary. You never did find out about the book, did you?'

She opened her mouth to speak, but no sound emerged. Michel moved close and whispered into her ear, 'Remember what *The Romance of the Rose* says about women, Christine. Prove you are different.'

She took a deep breath. 'I've found your book, *Monseigneur*. It's in the library at the Louvre. Please let Alix de Clairy live until you ask Gilles Malet how it came to be there.'

'Ha! You think you can save your friend, but your plan is of no use. I already have the book.'

She felt the blood drain from her face. 'How is that possible?'

'Gilles brought it to me this morning.'

'But he hid it in the library!'

'I am aware of that. He was not eager for me to have it, because he, like everyone else, is afraid its secrets will harm the king. But Gilles is an honorable man. He brought the book to me, along with a lecture on how not to use it. I'm certain Brother Michel would be happy to deliver a similar lecture.'

'You can be sure of that, *Monseigneur*,' Michel said. 'I'd take that book and burn it if I could.'

Christine was aghast. Surely the monk had gone too far. But the duke merely laughed and

296

slapped him on the back. 'Will you never leave off admonishing me, my friend?'

'Not while evil is present, *Monseigneur*. But tell me, how did Gilles obtain the book?'

'He found it in a shop on the rue de la Harpe. Someone had sold it to a bookseller there.'

'That was the person who murdered Hugues de Précy!' Christine cried. 'Alix de Clairy couldn't have sold it. She was in prison.'

Michel touched her arm. 'Be careful, Christine,' he whispered.

The duke sneered. 'You told me, Christine, the prostitute Marion saw someone else outside the palace on the night of the murder. That person must have taken the book. Not knowing its worth, the fool sold it for a pittance. I will concede, your friend is not the thief. But she is a murderess. She will die at the stake this morning.'

She started to protest, but the duke raised his hand. 'Why do you persist in your efforts to save Alix de Clairy?' He narrowed his eyes and looked at her suspiciously.

Michel tightened his grip on Christine's arm and hurried her from the room. 'You cannot change his mind, Christine. I know his nature. To persist now would be to put your own life in danger. Think of your children, your mother. They would be in danger, too.'

'And Alix de Clairy will burn at the stake for a murder she didn't commit!'

'There is no way to help her now. But there is still something you can do.'

'What are you saying? There is nothing more, once she is dead.'

'But there is. To honor her memory, you can still try to discover the identity of the real murderer. As a start, you can go to the bookseller on the rue de la Harpe and ask who sold him the book.'

The monk's words had no effect. Nothing could have made an impression on her at that moment. She didn't even notice Henri Le Picart standing nearby. She merely bowed her head and wept.

Michel led Christine out of the palace, and they stumbled down the street, pushing their way through the mob rushing to see Alix de Clairy's execution. Christine pulled her cloak over her ears to block out the bloodthirsty cries of the crowd. But as they drew closer to her house, she and the monk were alone, except for a flock of crows croaking overhead and a few dry leaves tumbling along ahead of the wind, like small wounded animals. It seemed as though everyone in Paris had gone to watch the spectacle Christine had tried so hard to prevent.

Everyone except her mother. Francesca had sent the older children off to school with Georgette, and she was waiting by the door. One look at her daughter's face told her what had happened. She said, 'You did all you could to save her. Now you must rest.' She removed Christine's cloak, led her to her room, where she'd built up the fire and turned down the bed, and made her lie down. Then she went to the kitchen, where she found Michel standing by the fireplace, his head bowed and his lips moving in prayer. She prepared one of her herbal drinks and took it up to Christine.

'Where's Gillette?' Christine asked.

'In my bed. I gave the poor soul a strong dose of valerian so she would sleep.' She handed her daughter a beaker. 'This contains valerian, too. Drink all of it.' Christine did as she was told, and then lay back against her pillows.

She closed her eyes, and she saw everything. She watched as Alix de Clairy, tied to a wooden lattice and dragged through the streets behind a horse, was brought to the pig market. She watched as she was placed against the stake and bound to it with chains. She saw the pyre – straw and sticks at first, then logs to keep the fire going. She heard the words of the priest; they offered no comfort. She watched men approach with torches and touch them to the straw, and she shuddered as the flames caught and snaked through the sticks and logs, snarling and snapping as they caught at Alix's once beautiful dress with its silver brocade. She watched frenzied men throw log after log onto the fire, and she could feel the dress falling away from Alix's body as the flames devoured it. She smelled Alix's burning flesh and hair. She screamed.

'*Cristina!*' Her mother stood over her.

'I saw it! I saw Alix burning!'

Francesca sat on the bed and stroked her daughter's feverish forehead. Then the valerian did its work, and Christine slept.

When she awoke, her mother sat by the fire, watching her.

'How long have I slept? What time of day is it? Where's Michel?'

'It is mid-afternoon, long past dinnertime. Michel went back to the palace some time ago.'

A loud knock sounded on the front door, and Francesca hurried down to answer it. She didn't return, and Christine nearly went back to sleep again. But when she heard voices downstairs, she sat up and listened. Francesca was talking to Michel. At first she sounded happy, then she became angry, and Christine heard her say, 'Not in my house!' She couldn't make out any more of their words, but she could hear her mother grumbling and Michel remonstrating. Suddenly there was silence. She thought the monk had left. Then she heard footsteps on the stairs, and Marion, her unbound hair streaming around her shoulders, appeared. She ran to the bed, fell to her knees, and buried her face in the covers, shaking as though she were sobbing.

'I'm so sorry, Marion,' Christine moaned. 'I tried to save her, but I couldn't.'

Marion looked up, her eyes shining. She wasn't sobbing. She was laughing. 'She isn't dead, Lady Christine.'

'What are you saying?'

'Alix de Clairy isn't dead. They didn't burn her.'

'I don't believe you.'

'It's true.'

'How do you know this?'

'Everyone in Paris knows it. There wasn't any burning. Alix de Clairy disappeared.'

'No one just disappears.' Christine was suddenly angry at what she thought was a horrible jest.

Michel and Francesca stood in the doorway. The smile on the monk's face seemed to light up the room. He said, 'It's true, Christine.'

Francesca was fingering her prayer beads. 'A miracle!' she said.

Christine was incredulous. 'How is it possible?'

'All I can tell you is, she escaped,' Michel said. 'No one knows where she went, but she is still alive, of that I am sure.'

'No one could escape from the Châtelet. But even if she did manage it somehow, sooner or later, she'll be found. They'll torture her more cruelly than before, and then they'll burn her.' Christine lay back against her pillows. Instead of elation, she felt despair.

The door downstairs slammed: Georgette had brought the children home. 'The lady in the dungeon got away!' they shouted as they raced up the stairs, followed by Goblin. They all burst into the room and stood around the bed, waiting for Christine to speak. Instead, she lay with tears streaming down her cheeks. Thomas leaned down and rubbed his hot cheek against hers. 'Why are you crying, Mama? She got away.'

Michel said, 'Remember the phoenixes and the crows, Christine. A woman with understanding would not be crying.'

She opened her eyes and the room spun around. 'What good is understanding now?'

'It will help you find the true murderer. Don't you see? You have been given another chance to save Alix de Clairy.'

Forty

You should pity fallen women. Pray for them. Give them a chance to reform.

Christine de Pizan, *Le Livre des Trois Vertus*, 1405

Christine tried to sit up. 'That's better,' Michel said. 'Much better than lying there weeping.'

But she sank back against the pillows again. She felt tired and defeated, not the strong and courageous woman she wished to be.

Marion put her hands on her hips and leaned over her. 'You can do it, Lady Christine. I know you can. You're clever enough to make a dead donkey fart!'

Marie put on her primmest face, Jean laughed, Thomas fell to the floor whooping with delight, and Lisabetta looked puzzled. Even Francesca was trying not to smile.

Michel said, 'What has become of your wits, Christine? Do you not remember what the duke told us about the book?'

'What book?' Francesca asked.

Christine's head ached; she couldn't manage a long explanation. She said, 'The book that was stolen from the dead man I found at the palace. Hugues de Précy had it, and his murderer took it.

The Duke of Orléans has it now. Gilles found it for him.'

Francesca shook her head in confusion. 'Where did Gilles get it?'

'From a bookseller. Of course! The bookseller on the rue de la Harpe.' She leapt off the bed so quickly she nearly fainted. Marion held her so she wouldn't try to lie down again.

Michel grinned at her. 'You do remember.'

'Yes, I remember. We must find the bookseller.' But then she was overwhelmed with despair. 'There are so many booksellers,' she said, and she slipped out of Marion's grasp and fell back onto the bed.

Francesca stood over her, her eyes sparkling. '*Cara Cristina*, do not give up now!'

Her mother had joined her battle, just as she was about to abandon it. She got up again, more slowly this time.

'*Brava*,' Francesca said. 'But you must not go to look for the bookseller immediately. It is late and it is getting dark.'

'We will go first thing tomorrow morning,' Michel said. 'No matter who the bookseller is, he won't forget who brought him *that* book.'

'We must have something to eat,' Francesca said, and she went down to the kitchen, followed by Goblin and the children.

'Keep Marion here for a moment,' Christine whispered to Michel, and she went after her mother.

The children were sitting at the table watching their grandmother set out bowls of the soup Christine had started that morning. 'I have

303

improved this, *Cristina*,' Francesca said. 'Carrots, onions, and parsnips are not enough to make a tasty soup.'

'I'm not interested in recipes for soup,' Christine said. 'Where is Gillette?'

'The dose of valerian I gave her was very strong. She is still asleep. She does not yet know Alix has escaped.'

'Then we should let her rest,' Christine said. 'But let Marion have supper with us.'

Francesca started to object, but Thomas got up from the table, went to his grandmother, and put his arms around her. 'She's Mama's friend.'

Francesca looked over at the other children. 'Brother Michel brought her, so she can't be all bad,' Jean said. 'I think she should stay.' Marie nodded in agreement.

Francesca sighed. 'All right. But if she is going to talk, I hope she will choose her words wisely.' The children giggled.

Christine went to the foot of the stairs and called to Michel and Marion. When Marion came down, she admonished her to be careful what she said in front of the children, but the girl merely lowered her head, looked at her through her eyelashes, and said, 'From what I've seen of those children, I don't think there is much I could say that would unsettle them.' She took off her crimson cloak and hung it in the front hall where it perched next to the family's old black and brown cloaks like a brightly colored bird that had flown off course. What she wore underneath the cloak was just as dazzling – a red-and gold-trimmed emerald green dress with long, pinked sleeves and a turquoise belt embroidered with blue and yellow griffins and centaurs. When she entered the kitchen, Francesca took one look at her and spilled some of the soup she was ladling into a bowl. Goblin crept under the table, and the children stopped eating, spoons in midair. Georgette stood with her mouth open until Christine told her to go somewhere else, and the girl retreated halfway into the pantry.

Once everyone had settled down, they made short work of the soup. Francesca had added ground almonds, ginger, and various spices, and she pronounced the result acceptable. Georgette stood peering through the door of the pantry, not missing a word of the conversation.

Francesca leaned across the table and asked Christine, 'Now will you explain about the book?'

'I found it hidden in the library at the Louvre.'

'*Mio Dio!* Who hid it there?'

'Gilles. Naturally, I thought he'd murdered Hugues de Précy to get it.' Francesca shook her head. 'I know,' Christine said. 'But would you have thought differently if you had found it there?'

'I certainly would not have suspected Gilles. Many strange people must come into the library. It could have been one of them.'

'You know nothing about libraries. You don't even like books.'

'By the bellies of all the apostles!' Marion cried. 'Stop arguing and tell us about the book.'

'Yes, tell us,' said Georgette, who'd crept into the room.

'Gilles bought the book from a bookseller on the rue de la Harpe. We don't know which one. Then he hid it for a while because he didn't want the Duke of Orléans to have it.'

'Why did he not want the duke to have it?'

Michel said, 'You're wrong about most books, Francesca, but this one is truly evil. Gilles knows. It is his business to know about books.'

'What's in it?' the children asked in one voice.

'Do you remember what I said about the mandrake your mother found in her room?' the monk asked them.

'We didn't tell anyone,' Jean said.

'I know you didn't. But the same restriction applies to the book. It is more evil than the mandrake. We must not discuss it.'

Something nagged at the back of Christine's mind, something she knew she should remember but couldn't. Before she could think what it was, her mother said, 'Finish the story, *Cristina*.'

'Gilles finally realized it was necessary to take the book to the Duke of Orléans. When I went to the duke this morning, he already had it. That means Gilles isn't the murderer.'

'I should think not.'

'So who *is* the murderer?' Jean asked, pushing his hair out of his eyes and looking just like his father.

That is what your mother is going to find out, Christine heard Étienne say.

'The book was stolen from Hugues de Précy the night he died, so whoever sold it to the bookseller must be the murderer.'

306

Marion sat quietly, her soup uneaten. 'Was it a book with strange symbols on the cover?' she asked in a low voice.

Michel looked at her. 'Yes, it was. Do you know something about it?'

She avoided his gaze. 'One hears about such books.'

She does know something, Christine thought. *But she'll never admit it to Michel.*

'Is the murderer not the angry husband the midwife told us about last night?' Francesca asked.

'It may be,' Christine said. 'But I'm not so certain it was Guy de Marolles. There are other people who wanted to get rid of Hugues de Précy.'

'Henri Le Picart isn't one of them,' Michel said.

She scowled at him. 'For goodness sake, Michel, why won't you admit there could be profit for Henri in this?'

'What kind of profit? He doesn't need money.'

'What about the book?'

'Why do you dislike this Henri le Picart so much, Mama?' Jean asked.

Christine felt herself blushing. 'Wouldn't you dislike someone who follows you around all the time and glares at you?'

'How do you know he follows you around?'

'He does,' Marion said. 'I've seen him. On the rue Saint-Antoine. He was probably even there when she almost got eaten by the lions.'

'What lions?' Francesca cried.

'Michel and I lost our way near the lions'

307

stockade at the Hôtel Saint-Pol,' Christine said. 'But we didn't get hurt.'

'They were scared to death,' Marion said.

'Those lions are too old to hurt anyone,' Thomas said. 'Besides, they're locked up.'

'Actually, for a while last night they weren't,' Christine said.

'What were you doing near the lions' stockade?' her mother wanted to know. 'Where was the lion keeper? And the woman the midwife told us about, his assistant?'

Christine said, 'We were on our way to speak with the Duke of Orléans at the church of the Celestines. And the woman put the lions back in their stockade. That's enough questions for now, Mama.'

Michel got up from the table. 'I must go to the palace. The Duchess of Orléans may be asking for me. I do not think she will live through the night.' He looked at Christine and said, 'I forgot to tell you. The queen knows Alix de Clairy did not steal the mandrake. When I was at the palace this morning, I told her about how it had been hung in your fireplace.'

It was then that Christine remembered what had been at the back of her mind earlier. She said, 'We never found out what happened to the mandrake, Michel, after it disappeared from the guards' room.'

Forty-One

Many cowardly men have large, strong bodies.

Christine de Pizan, *Le Livre de la Cité des Dames*, 1404–1405

Marion left Christine's house and went across the Île to the left bank of the Seine. She was friends with many of the students from the university who frequented that area, but for once she didn't stop to talk to anyone. She hurried along the rue Saint-Jacques and down the rue des Écrivains, into the district where manuscript painters, bookbinders, parchment makers, and copyists worked. Along the way, she passed bookshops with painted signs above their doors, but she ignored all those establishments; she knew what she was looking for would not be in any of them. By the time she had reached the rue de la Harpe, it was night, and she could barely see where she was going.

A group of noisy, drunken students in hooded gowns lurched toward her through the darkness, and she shrank back into a doorway. Most of the students seemed oblivious to her presence, but one short fellow limping along behind the others turned her way as they went by. She suspected he had seen her, so she waited until all the raucous youths were far away before she stepped into the street again. A cat darted out from an alley and yowled as it ran over her boots, its green eyes glinting in the light of a candle in the window of a house across the way. But then the candle flickered and went out, and there was no light save that from the oil lamps burning by the tower gate at the end of the street near the Porte Gibart. She heard a faint crunching sound, like footsteps on pebbles. Before they came close enough for her to discover who it was, she ran to a shabby building without a sign, pushed open the door, and darted in.

Immediately, she was enveloped in dust, in a room illuminated by only the feeble glow of one small oil lamp hanging from the ceiling. She could see through the gloom well enough to know that a few worm-eaten manuscript pages were strewn about, but she wasn't interested in those. She walked to a heap of moth-eaten clothes and mangy fur pelts in a corner, almost stumbling over a scrawny brown dog that had hollowed out a nest for himself at the bottom of the pile. Then she went to another corner and inspected a stack of chipped bowls, broken crockery, and dented cooking pots. She lifted several of the pots and found what she was looking for.

A huge man with an angry red scar on his cheek emerged from behind a curtain at the back of the room. 'What are you doing there, whore?'

'Wouldn't you like to know, you lousy cutpurse.' She walked up to the man and stood in front of him with her hands on her hips. 'I want to know about a book you bought and then sold to the king's librarian.'

The man shrugged his shoulders.

'It had symbols on the cover – a circle and a sword and a lot of crosses.'

The man gagged. 'What business is it of yours?'

'That book was stolen from the Duke of Orléans.'

Even in the dim light, Marion could see that the man's face went white and the cicatrix turned a darker red. 'I don't know anything about it.'

'The plague take you! That was no ordinary book. I know you had it, and I want to know who brought it here.'

'Suppose I did have it? I wouldn't tell you about it, you stinking slut.'

Behind him, a hand pushed aside the filthy curtain, and a woman wearing a tattered chemise and carrying a naked baby slouched into the room. The man shook his fist at her, and croaked, 'Go to the devil, bitch.'

The woman ducked to avoid the blow. Bouncing the baby from one hip to the other, she pushed a strand of greasy hair away from her face and stared at Marion with insolent black eyes. 'Get out!' the big man said, as he shoved her back through the curtain. Then he came around the table, put his hands on his hips, and thrust his face close to Marion's. 'Filthy whore! Go back to your dunghill.'

Marion stepped back and spat into the moldy rushes on the floor. 'Don't order me around, devil's scum. Tell me what I want to know, or your wife back there will have a crow to pluck.'

The man raised his hand as if to strike her, but Marion just laughed. 'You don't frighten me, donkey pizzle.' She stepped up to him again, even closer this time. 'I saw you steal a silver candlestick on the Grand Pont last week, and I know where it is.' She looked over at the stack of worthless crockery. 'The sergeants at the Châtelet would be glad to hear about it, and they will, if you don't tell me who brought you the book.'

The veins in the man's forehead throbbed. 'You didn't see anything in that pile of junk,' he whimpered. He slumped back against the table until he was almost sitting on it. Marion started to walk toward the heap of crockery. 'Wait!' he cried. 'I'll tell you. The miserable book wasn't worth anything, anyway. I was lucky to be quit of it.'

'Who brought it here?'

'A little boy. I don't know his name.'

'What did he look like, then?'

'Nothing special. He had a lot of tawny hair. He was wearing a red jacket and a red cap. I can't tell you anything more.' Beads of sweat rolled down his cheeks as he watched to make sure she didn't go near the corner junk pile.

Marion was certain he'd told her all he knew. The big man was too terrified to hold anything back; he looked as though he was about to faint with fright. She went to the door and stepped out into the street. But before the door swung shut, she looked back and saw that he was still standing by the table, staring after her. She curtsied and raised the fool's finger at him. *I really scared that bastard*, she said to herself as she started back toward the river.

Footsteps sounded behind her, and she walked quickly to the Île, where groups of noisy students hurried to the public houses. She ducked into a tavern, dashed across a room crowded with young men drinking at long wooden tables, pushed aside a heavy leather curtain, and ran into the back room. The tavern owner, who was drawing wine from a cask, looked up. 'How goes it with you, Marion?'

Without answering, she peered through a hole in the curtain. Another group of students came in, and with them was Henri Le Picart. She remembered the students who'd passed her on the way to the bookshop. The one who'd turned to look at her must have been Henri. *Clever of him to pretend to be limping*, she thought.

Henri stood beside a great stone fireplace that seemed to be throwing off more smoke than heat and stared at the curtain. Marion jumped back. Now there was no doubt in her mind that he was the murderer. She could almost feel his hands around her throat. But when she looked again, she saw that he was leaving. She waited a while, then went into the other room and asked four unsteady youths to accompany her home. *They're so drunk they can hardly stand*, she thought, *but they'll make enough noise to frighten him off. We may be arrested by the night watch, but anything is better than being accosted by Henri Le Picart.*

Forty-Two

Even the most wicked of women do not follow you into your house and rape you.

Christine de Pizan, Letter
dated 1400–1401

Marion led the drunken students, who held torches in their unsteady hands and brayed bawdy drinking songs, to the other side of the river and along the streets to the old wall near Christine's house. Henri Le Picart was nowhere in sight, so she took one of the torches, sent the young rowdies back to the tavern, and hurried on by herself.

Christine and her mother were upstairs preparing for bed when they heard a sound at the front door. 'It's probably the wind,' Christine said as she went down to investigate. But when she opened the door, Marion jumped out of the shadows and ran past her into the house. 'I've found your bookseller,' she said breathlessly.

'You?'

'Don't look so surprised. Do you want me to tell you about it?'

'Of course I want you to tell me.'

'Who is there?' Francesca called from the top of the stairs.

'Only the wind, Mama. Go to bed.' Christine took Marion's arm and dragged her into the kitchen. 'I've suspected all along you haven't been telling me everything you know.'

'Well, listen then. One of the girls at the brothel stole that book from a customer. He came to the brothel and stole it back, just before he went to the palace and got murdered. I saw the markings on the cover.'

'But how did you know which bookseller had it?'

'I know many things. But what's important is this: the bookseller told me a little boy with a lot of tawny hair and a red jacket and a red cap brought it to him. Do you know such a boy?'

'I do. A boy who looks like that comes to the palace with his grandmother, a seamstress who sews for the queen and her ladies.'

Christine remembered Simon telling her Renaut and his grandmother lived on the rue de la Harpe. The murderer must have enlisted Renaut to sell the book. 'I'll go to the palace at once and speak with the boy,' she said.

'Surely he won't be there at this hour.'

'The *portier* knows where he lives. I'll find him.'

'I forgot to tell you. Henri Le Picart is out there somewhere.'

'Then come with me. If we stay together, we'll be safe.' She lit a taper, went into the hall, and put on her cloak. Whispering to Marion that she should not make a sound, she drew her out the door before Francesca could call down to her again.

There was no sign of Henri Le Picart in the street. 'That doesn't mean he isn't here,' Marion said. 'It's dark, and he's very cunning.' There was no moon, but by the light of her taper and Marion's torch, they made their way along the deserted streets to the palace. Christine left Marion at the queen's stables, where she hoped she would be safe, and hurried across the street to the queen's residence. As soon as she entered the courtyard she heard the king's lions roaring. 'What's wrong with them?' she asked Simon, who, to her relief, was still there.

'They're hungry. The lion keeper is away. Loyse should be looking after them, but she has disappeared.'

'Doesn't her mother know where she is?'

'Blanche was here early this morning, but I haven't seen her since. The Duchess of Orléans is dying. Brother Michel is with her. Why are you here at this hour?'

'I'm looking for Renaut.'

'He should be home in bed, but he's still here, in the guards' room, waiting for his grandmother. She seems to have forgotten him.'

Occupied with something on the floor, the boy didn't look up when she came into the room. She stood in the doorway for a moment, wondering how to question him about the book without frightening him. Torches in brackets on the wall lit the room, and she could see that he was in tears.

'What's the matter?'

'My top. It's broken.'

She looked at the floor. Something red that

sparkled like glass lay in pieces on the boards. *What kind of a top would break like glass?* she wondered. She bent down and picked up the pieces. They *were* glass. She fitted them together, and she held in her hand an object the color of blood – the color of the flask the king had shaken in her face, the flask with the poison that had killed Hugues de Précy.

'This isn't a top!' she cried. 'It's a stopper for a flask! Where did you get it?' At the sound of her agitated voice, the boy wept bitterly.

She remembered she'd seen him hide his toy in his sleeve when Blanche entered the room. She knelt on the floor beside him. 'It's your grandmother's, isn't it?'

'I just borrowed it.'

She got up, staggered to a bench, and sat there, stunned, while Renaut stared at her, his eyes full of tears. Now she knew what the duchess had been trying to tell her with the illustrations in the Book of Hours. The snow, the Cistercian monk dressed in the habit of his order, the horse of the first horseman of the Apocalypse. All were white, like the name Blanche. The murderer wasn't Guy de Marolles, or Ludwig, or Henri Le Picart. The murderer was Blanche.

Renaut came over and stood in front of her, sobbing. 'Please don't be angry with me. I was going to put it back.'

'You're not the one I'm angry with,' she whispered, and she pulled him down on the bench, took him into her arms, and held him close, as if to protect him from the woman who had poisoned Hugues de Précy and who was willing

317

to let her own daughter die for the murder. Then she leapt up, told Renaut to stay where he was, and flew from the room, still holding the pieces of the stopper in her hand. She ran past Simon, crying, 'It was Blanche! I have to tell Michel!' and tore across the courtyard. She plunged through the first entrance she came to and was immediately lost.

She raced blindly down a dimly lit passageway, and burst into a cloister where everything was dark except for torchlights flickering in the hands of two people who stood arguing. She went toward the lights, thinking she could ask whomever it was to tell her which way to go to the duchess's chambers. As she drew closer, the voices grew louder, and she recognized them. It was the queen's brother Ludwig. And Blanche! She stepped behind a column and listened.

Ludwig was shouting at Blanche in his halting French. 'I will tell no more lies for you. You have made me say to the king that I saw Alix de Clairy poison her husband, but that is the last time I will do such a thing. And I will report to the queen that it is you who stole her ring.' Blanche started to protest, but he continued, more vehemently than before, 'The boy, Colin, knows. He saw you take it. He will not keep silent. You thought it was clever to say lies about him, to make my sister send him away. I do not know what is your purpose, but I will have no more part in it.'

Blanche growled, 'I know you stole the sapphire the king cares so much about. I will tell him.'

'I will give it back. My sister will make it right.'

There was a sharp sound as Blanche struck Ludwig across the face with such force that he fell, dropping his torch. 'We made a bargain,' the woman shouted. 'And you're going to keep it, or I'll kill you, just as I killed Hugues de Précy and the old woman at the brothel.'

Christine heard Ludwig gasp, and she realized he hadn't known it was Blanche who'd murdered Hugues. He retrieved his torch and struggled to his feet. Christine heard him come stumbling toward her, panting and crying with fear. Blanche cursed and began to hunt for him. She came near the column where Christine was hiding. Without thinking, Christine leapt out at her, shouting, 'Monster!'

Blanche screamed and raised her torch. Christine shrank back behind the column, but Blanche had recognized her. 'What are you doing here?' she snarled.

Christine thrust out her open hand. The pieces of the red stopper glittered in the light from the woman's torch.

Blanche backed away. 'Where did you get that?'

'Where I got it is of no importance. What signifies is that it was you who poisoned Hugues de Précy.'

'He had to die,' Blanche rasped, moving close to the column again. 'Because of Jehanne.'

Who was Jehanne? Christine thought the woman must be demented. She remembered what she'd done to Hugues and Margot, and she trembled. Ludwig seemed to have escaped, but she might not be so lucky. Her fingers curled tightly around the pieces of the stopper, and the broken glass dug into her hand as she moved farther back into the shadows. Blanche came near her again. There was nowhere for Christine to run: everything behind her was black.

Blanche held her torch close to her face. 'You think you know everything, haughty lady. But you don't know about my daughter Jehanne. I'll tell you. Hugues de Précy killed her.' Her voice seemed to come from a great height.

Christine remembered then what Simon had told her about Renaut's mother. 'I thought she died when Renaut was born,' she said.

'She did. Because Hugues de Précy raped her. He made her pregnant, and she died giving birth to Renaut. That is how Hugues de Précy killed my daughter.' Her voice grew louder and more shrill, and then horrible sounds penetrated the darkness, great gasping sobs that reverberated through the cloister as she stumbled back and forth, bumping into columns, cursing, falling to her knees, pulling herself up, falling again.

Christine put her hands over her ears to block out the noise and counted. Hugues had gone to Amiens with the king eight years ago. Renaut was seven. It must be true. Hugues was his father.

'Didn't Hugues know you were Jehanne's mother?'

Still sobbing, Blanche reached out for her, but her hand came up against the column instead. 'He never saw me in Amiens. But I knew who he was, and when he came back last year I recognized him.' The sobbing stopped, and her voice became as cold as ice. 'I followed him here so I could punish him for what he did to Jehanne.'

Christine felt the heat of the torch. *The woman may kill me*, she thought, *but I have to know everything.* 'You mourn that daughter, yet you care nothing for the daughter you gave away.'

'How do you know about that?' Blanche asked, growling like an animal.

'The midwife told me.'

'These things are not your affair.'

Christine heard the woman's labored breathing, felt her cloak brush against her. She moved back into the darkness. *If she wants to kill me, why doesn't she do it?* she asked herself. Frightened as she was, she persisted with her questions. 'When you gave Hugues the poison, what did you tell him it was?'

'I told the fool it was a love potion.'

'And then you put the flask under your own daughter's hand!'

Blanche moved close to her, grabbed her wrist, and held it firmly. 'It was dark. I didn't know it was my daughter.' The torch was so close to Christine's face, she could smell her hair scorching. Still she raged at the woman.

'You killed old Margot, didn't you?'

'I had to. You were going to find out she sold me the poison.'

'And you pushed the duchess down the stairs. She realized what Renaut's top was, and she confronted you.'

Blanche gripped her wrist so tightly, she cried out in pain. 'The old lady was going to die anyway.'

'And you put the mandrake in my fireplace.' She struggled to pull away, but the woman's fingers were like a vise.

'No. It was that stupid boy, Colin. One of the queen's ladies told him to do it, to punish you for being so superior.'

Christine cried out as Blanche gave her wrist a violent twist, sending a wave of pain through her body. Then everything went black as the seamstress raised her torch and brought it down on her head.

Forty-Three

In Isabella of Bavaria, reigning at present by the grace of God, there is no cruelty, greed, or any other vice. She has only sincere love and kindness for her subjects.

Christine de Pizan, *Le Livre de la Cité des Dames*, 1404–1405

Christine awoke in darkness. Her hands and feet were tied, and she was sitting on a cold, damp surface with her back against a large object she couldn't see. She struggled against the ropes binding her, but the effort only drove them more deeply into her flesh. Her head throbbed and exhaustion overwhelmed her.

After a while, she realized that someone was

sitting next to her – a woman, barely discernable in the gloom. At first she was too frightened to cry out. Then the woman leaned toward her. She felt her breath on her cheek, and she found her voice. 'Get away!' she cried. She fought the ropes, but they held fast.

The woman touched her forehead gently and said, 'Christine.'

The voice was so weak she didn't recognize it. 'Don't be frightened. Smell this. You gave it to me.'

Something brittle brushed against Christine's nose, and the acrid odor of rue burned her nostrils. 'Alix!' she cried.

'I thought you'd never wake up.'

'Where am I? How did I get here? Why are you here?' Christine asked, amazed and confused.

'I don't know where we are. Somewhere near the palace, I think. The seamstress who works for the queen and her ladies brought me here this morning. Later, she brought you.'

Now she remembered – the dark cloister, Blanche's hand gripping her wrist, the raised torch, the pain. Christine supposed she was fortunate to be alive: she'd been certain Blanche was going to kill her.

'I don't understand, Alix. How did you escape from the Châtelet?'

'The seamstress came and took me away. I'll tell you about it, but first I must rest.' For many minutes Alix's shallow breathing was the only sound Christine could hear in that dark place. It was very cold. She pulled her knees up toward her chest and put her arms around her legs in an effort to keep warm.

Then Alix said, 'The seamstress has lost her reason, just like the king. She thinks she's my mother.'

Now is not the time to tell her it's true, Christine thought. She asked, 'How did Blanche get you out of the prison?'

'She went to the queen and told her she was my mother and she should be allowed to see me before I died. The queen believed her, and she wrote a letter to the provost, telling him to let her into the prison.'

Alix coughed and seemed to be choking. But she managed to catch her breath, and she continued, her voice so low and hoarse that Christine had to strain to hear it, 'The seamstress brought a woman into the prison with her. The woman must have been given some kind of potion, because she seemed half-dead. The seamstress gave me something to drink, and after that I felt the same way. I was awake, but I was helpless.'

Christine remembered that doctors used the juice of the mandrake to numb their patients. She thought of the mandrake in her pouch, the mandrake that had disappeared from the guards' room. Blanche had taken it, and she had known exactly what to do with it.

Alix's voice trembled as she said, 'The seamstress put the woman's clothes on me, and my clothes on her, and she took me out of the prison and left the other women there to die.' She slumped over against Christine and wept.

Christine longed to put her arms around her and comfort her, but her hands were tied. All she could do was ask, 'You have no idea who the woman was?'

'She was dressed in rags and her hair was so disheveled, it covered her face. But I know her name, because as she was leaving, the seamstress said, 'Goodbye, Loyse.'

Christine gasped and was, for once, speechless. After a long while, she said, choosing her words carefully, 'Listen to me, Alix. That woman did not die. She got away.'

'How is that possible?' Alix gasped.

'No one knows. But I'm telling you the truth. She did not die.'

Her body shaking with sobs, Alix rocked from side to side, saying to herself over and over, 'Thank God. Oh, thank God.'

I've told her enough, Christine thought. *Someday she'll find out that Loyse is her sister, but not now.*

She waited until Alix was calmer, and then she asked, 'What is Blanche planning to do with you?'

'She says she wants to take me to a place far away. She has gone to get her grandson.'

'What is she going to do with me?' Christine asked.

'She told me she brought you here so you could write some documents that will allow us to get to another country where no one will accuse me of poisoning Hugues.'

She has no idea it was Blanche herself who murdered Hugues, Christine thought. *She doesn't know anything. And it's better that way.*

Alix's breathing was labored, her voice almost inaudible. Christine knew that she was very weak, but she thought there was something she might be able to do.

'Can you untie my hands, Alix?'

Alix leaned over and fumbled with the ropes, but she had no strength. Christine despaired. And then she heard footsteps and saw torchlight coming toward them. Objects took shape in the darkness, and she realized that she was surrounded by weapons of war, and that she was leaning against the carriage of a large battering ram. Blanche, carrying several large sacks, was picking her way through the engines of death, dragging a terrified Renaut behind her. She stood over her. 'So, *Madame*, you will now have a chance to put your learning to good use. I am going to take my daughter and my grandson away. You will write the necessary documents for me.'

Perhaps this is my chance to escape, Christine thought. She held up her fettered wrists.

'I don't suppose even you could write like that,' Blanche said. She bent down and undid the ropes binding Christine's wrists, but she did not untie the ropes around her ankles.

'What will I write with?' Christine asked in desperation.

'You're not the only one who is privileged to have these things,' Blanche said as she reached into one of the sacks and brought out a quill, some pieces of parchment, and an inkhorn. Christine wondered from which of the secretaries who worked for the king and his brother she had purloined them. The woman had thought of everything; she'd even brought a small board for her to write on. And something else. Blanche was holding before Christine's eyes a piece of sealing wax and the queen's ring so she could stamp the documents with the royal seal.

Blanche leaned down and placed the writing materials and the board on Christine's lap. Then she rose, backed away slightly, and stood holding her torch so Christine could see to write.

Christine didn't bother to ask the woman what she intended to do with her once she'd finished. She felt around on the ground and experienced a rush of exhilaration when her hand touched a club. Her fingers were stiff, but she was able to get them around it. When Blanche looked away, distracted by Renaut, who was crying and begging her to take him home, she took a deep breath, gripped one of the horizontal bars of the carriage of the battering ram, and heaved herself up. She couldn't stand, but she braced herself by throwing her arm over the bar and leaning against the side of the carriage. She lifted the club, thankful it was not too heavy, and swung it as hard as she could, hitting Blanche on the side of the head. The woman cried out in pain and lunged toward her, knocking her to the ground.

As she fell, Christine could see men approaching, men who lashed out with their own clubs and sent Blanche sprawling. Then she lost consciousness.

* * *

This time when she awoke, she was lying on a cushioned bench in a small, dimly lit room. By flickering candlelight and the glow of flames in a fireplace, she could see someone standing over her, someone with a black beard and black eyes, wearing a black cape. She struggled to sit up, but his strong hand on her shoulders restrained her. She looked around and was relieved to see many other people. *Surely, they won't let him kill me*, she thought.

'Lie there and rest,' Henri Le Picart said. She realized she had never heard him speak before. His voice was not unkind.

Michel stepped out of the shadows. 'I told you, you were wrong about him, Christine.'

She seemed to be waking from a dream. 'Where am I? Where is Alix de Clairy?' She was so exhausted she could hardly speak, and it was difficult to breathe because there were so many people in the small room. The air, thick with the smoke of candle wax and the wood fire, was suffocating.

The Duke of Orléans appeared. 'You are in the palace. Alix de Clairy is here, too. You don't need to worry about her. She won't be going anywhere.'

'How did I get here? Where did you find me? Where is Blanche?'

Michel leaned down to her. 'Too many questions all at once, Christine.' He knelt beside her and took her hands in his. 'To begin with, it is important for you to understand that Henri saved your life.'

Her head spun. 'I want to sit up.'

The monk placed soft pillows behind her back. 'Ludwig helped, too. He told the duke that Blanche was in the cloister, about to kill you.

He was still in the cloister while Blanche and I were raging at each other, Christine thought. *He must have seen her carry me off. But he wasn't trying to save me. He was trying to make sure Blanche got caught before she could kill him.*

Michel said, 'Simon told me that after you talked to Renaut, you rushed off calling Blanche's name. That was when I finally realized what the duchess had tried to tell you by pointing to pictures in the Book of Hours. Alas, she died before she could know we finally understood.' He bowed his head for a moment, then continued. 'Simon showed me which way you had gone, but when I got to the cloister, only the duke and Ludwig were there; Blanche had already taken you away. Fortunately, Henri arrived. He had heard the duke and Ludwig talking, and he had followed them.

'Ludwig didn't know where Blanche had taken you, but he thought he knew in which direction she had gone. Henri remembered something about that part of the palace. There is a tunnel under it that goes to the *Bastille*. A passage branches off from the tunnel. It runs beneath the field where the war machines are stored and opens into one of the sheds. He surmised that Blanche might have gone there. And he was right. That is where we found you.'

Christine gazed up at Henri, still suspicious of his motives. 'That is all very well, but why have you been following me all this time?'

Henri said, 'Listen to me, Christine. I believe Alix de Clairy is innocent. But if I interfere, it will only anger the provost. You, however, have been putting yourself in great danger, and Brother Michel has been unwise to encourage you. He thought he could protect you, but he failed to take into account the fact that one should never expect a woman to do the sensible thing.'

Christine started to protest, but she saw Michel shaking his head, and she held her tongue.

Henri continued, 'When I heard Michel talking to you at the palace this morning, urging you to continue looking for the murderer, I suspected you would be foolhardy enough to try to do it on your own. Your friend Marion was foolhardy, too, when she decided to go by herself to find that bookseller.'

'How did you know that was what she was about?'

'I guessed. Then I followed you both to the palace, but I lost you, after you talked to that boy, Renaut, and went running off after Blanche in the dark. I must say, even I was surprised at the recklessness of that.'

'I wasn't running after Blanche. I was looking for Michel!'

'You were a fool.'

'I found the murderer.'

His expression softened. 'Praise God.'

She turned to the duke. 'Where is Alix de Clairy?'

'She is here.'

She looked around the room. It was dark, but

she could see Blanche in one corner, bound to a chair, with Renaut standing beside her, crying. On the other side of the room two sergeants-at-arms held a woman dressed in dirty rags. A mass of tangled hair hid her face, but Christine knew it was Alix. Her hands were tied in front of her.

'Why is she bound?'

'She escaped once. You can be sure we won't let it happen again,' the duke said. 'Now she will die.'

'What are you saying, *Monseigneur*? Alix de Clairy didn't murder her husband. Blanche did. She admitted it!'

'The seamstress will be punished for helping her escape. She was cunning about it, I must say. If the guard who took the prisoner out of her cell hadn't noticed there were no cuts on her arms, the wrong woman would have died at the stake.'

Hearing this, Blanche cried out, 'I knew she wouldn't die. I knew they would realize they had the wrong woman.'

Of course, Christine thought. *Hutin would have told them. He knew about the marks of the cords on Alix's arms.*

'Tell them what you told me,' she said to Blanche. 'Tell them you killed Hugues, and why.'

'Of course I killed him. He raped my daughter.'

'Your daughter was his wife,' the duke snarled.

'Blanche had another daughter,' Christine said. 'That daughter died giving birth to a child conceived when Hugues de Précy raped her. Don't you think that might have driven a mother

331

out of her mind? Don't you think that might have driven a mother to seek a terrible revenge?'

The duke shook his head. 'She is lying, to save her daughter.'

'She is not lying. She poisoned Hugues. Marion saw her do it.'

'No one believes a prostitute.'

Henri moved closer to Christine, and said to her in a low voice, 'Why did you go running off in the dark after you talked to the boy?'

'I told you. I was looking for Michel. To tell him about the top.'

'What about the top?'

'Blanche kept the stopper to the flask. Renaut was using it as a top. It broke, and I picked up the pieces. I had them in the cloister.'

Henri was actually smiling at her. 'So you must have dropped the pieces there.'

She couldn't help smiling back. She looked at the duke. 'Please send someone to the cloister to look for them.'

Louis shook his head. 'You will say anything to prove your friend is innocent.'

There was a disturbance on the other side of the room, people making way for someone who swept in and strode up to Louis. It was the queen, wearing a plain blue cotte, her long black hair hanging loose around her shoulders.

She said to Louis, 'You will send someone to that cloister to look there for the pieces of glass.'

The duke faced her defiantly. 'I will obey only the king.'

'The king is not well, and he should not be

troubled with this matter. I speak for him. Send someone to the cloister.'

Simon stepped out of the shadows and knelt before the queen. 'Please allow me to go, *Madame*.'

'Do so,' she said. Louis started to protest, but she raised her hand. 'It is necessary to have the truth,' she said. 'If Blanche possessed the stopper, then she possessed the flask with the poison with which Hugues de Précy was murdered.' She stamped her foot. 'Tell those men to now release Alix de Clairy. She has had enough suffering.'

The duke made an angry motion to the sergeants-at-arms. 'Untie her. But stay close to her. Don't let her escape.'

Alix couldn't possibly run away, Christine thought. *She's too weak. Is he so determined to perceive her as an evil woman that he is blind to that?*

Simon took a torch from one of the sergeants, and left, smiling at Renaut as he went.

Some of the queen's ladies had come into the room, and they crowded together in the shadows, whispering among themselves as the sergeants unbound Alix's hands.

Finally, Simon reappeared. He knelt before the queen and opened his hand. In it were pieces of red glass. The queen took them and held them up for the duke to see. Then she looked at Renaut and said, 'Come here, child.'

Terrified, the boy clung to his grandmother. Simon went to him, gently pried him away, and led him to the queen. 'Now you must kneel,' he instructed the boy, and Renaut fell to his knees, shaking.

'You need not be afraid,' the queen said. 'I want only that you tell me what are these pieces of glass and where you got them.'

With tears running down his cheeks, Renaut stammered, 'It was my top. I didn't steal it. I found it in grand'maman's room. I was going to put it back, but it broke.'

'So you see,' the queen said to Louis. 'Blanche is telling the truth. She is the one who poisoned Hugues de Précy. Alix de Clairy is innocent.'

Forty-Four

Now let all those disparaging writers who attack women be silent.

Christine de Pizan, *Le Livre de la Cité des Dames*, 1404–1405

At dawn the following morning, Christine and Michel left the palace. As they walked down the street toward the old wall Christine asked the monk, 'What will happen to Alix de Clairy now that everyone knows she is not the Lord of Clairy's natural daughter?'

'The king may do whatever he pleases with the lord's property,' Michel said. 'I cannot believe he will leave Alix de Clairy destitute. No, I cannot believe that. The king may not be in his right mind, but he has always been compassionate.

I hope the queen will have a say in the matter. She is determined to make amends for all the suffering Alix has endured.'

'Tell me something else, Michel. How did Henri know about the passage to the shed with the war machines?'

'He told me he and your father discovered it years ago, when they were in the tunnel under the palace.'

'What were Henri and Papa doing down there?'

Michel smiled. 'Henri is a bit embarrassed about that. He says they were burying the tin figures of the Englishmen.'

'I thought they buried them in the palace gardens!'

'They did put most of them there. But they thought that if they buried some of them deeper, they would be more effective in making the English leave.'

'And men criticize women for their foolish beliefs!'

Christine tugged on the sleeve of Michel's black habit to make him hurry. She was eager to reach her house and tell her mother Alix de Clairy was free. But, for once, Francesca was not at the door waiting for her. She was in the kitchen, sitting on a bench in front of the cold fireplace, her eyes heavy with sleep.

Michel stirred the ashes and revived the fire while Christine gently shook her mother until she was fully awake. Francesca looked around, confused.

'Don't you want to know what happened. Weren't you even a little worried about me?' Christine asked.

Francesca smiled. 'I know what happened. Colin came and told us everything.'

Christine could picture Colin sneaking into the room in the palace where the truth had been revealed. He'd probably been there the whole time.

Francesca went upstairs to wake the others, and Michel and Christine rested by the fire until the children came bounding in, followed by Goblin, who jumped into Christine's lap. The children crowded around their mother. 'The lady in the dungeon is saved!' Thomas shouted. 'Now the seamstress will go to the dungeon.'

Francesca and Gillette came into the room. 'What will happen to Blanche's grandson?' Francesca wanted to know.

'The *portier* at the queen's residence took Renaut home with him,' Michel said. 'Simon loves the boy. He and his wife will care for him.'

'And the other daughter, the one who feeds the lions? What has happened to her? Is she really as strange as everyone says?'

Michel sighed. 'Loyse is already back with the lions. Nothing that has happened seems to have made an impression on her. Perhaps she is not aware of any of it, because of the mandrake juice Blanche gave her.'

The front door slammed. Georgette burst into the kitchen and stood looking at Christine with admiration in her eyes. Finally, Gillette, who had been waiting patiently, asked softly, 'Where is Alix now?'

'The queen took her to her chambers and put her to bed,' Christine said. 'She will rest, and

336

under the queen's care, she will recover.' She rose, went to the old woman, and led her to the bench by the fire. Sitting beside her and holding her trembling hands in hers, she said, 'I must tell you, Gillette, Alix is weak and confused. She refuses to believe Blanche is her mother – she thinks the seamstress has lost her mind – and I thought it best to let her continue in that belief. When the time comes, you will convince her of the truth.'

Gillette nodded. Then Christine told her how she had gone with Alix and watched as the queen's maids undressed her, took her to the queen's bath, and brought her back, dressed in one of the queen's chemises, looking clean and at peace, though nothing like her former self. But she would never tell Gillette, or anyone else, about the conversation she'd had with Alix when they were alone.

Alix had asked her, 'Do you think we could do something to help the seamstress?'

'Why should we? She killed two people, probably three.'

'Because she's lost her mind. But I am grateful to her. She saved me from burning at the stake. And from something worse.'

'What could be worse than that?'

'I could have been damned.'

'Surely not,' Christine said.

'I will tell you why,' Alix said. 'Do you remember that Hugues was limping?' Christine nodded, wondering why she would mention it. 'He had a cut in his foot that wouldn't heal. One day when he had been especially unkind to me,

I thought of taking some wolfsbane from Maude's house and making a powder to put in his shoe. I know what a deadly poison it is.'

'You were only thinking of it,' Christine said. 'I'm sure you would not have actually done such a thing.'

'Probably not,' Alix said. She leaned back against the luxurious pillows on the bed and fell asleep.

Christine awoke from the memory of this conversation when she realized Michel was telling her mother something about the Duke of Orléans. 'Once he knew what a tragic mistake he had made, he begged Alix's forgiveness and went to the church of the Celestines to pray,' Michel said.

I'm sure he even shed a few tears, Christine thought.

Someone pounded on the door, and Francesca went to unlatch it. There was no argument this time; Marion was conducted right into the kitchen. She went to Christine and made a little curtsey. 'I knew you could save her, Lady Christine. I've brought you a present as a reward.' She opened her purse, drew out a large embroidered belt, and laid it across Christine's lap. Christine gazed at it in awe. The belt was decorated with brightly colored flowers – roses, violets, snowdrops, and primroses. And with birds – warblers, goldfinches, and nightingales, so real she could almost hear them singing. Michel, who was sitting beside her, leaned over to get a closer look, and she handed it to him. He studied it for a long time. Then he looked

338

up at Marion and asked, 'Did you make this?'
She nodded.

*He's going to tell her she should give up pros-
titution and take up embroidery as a profession,*
Christine thought. *But now is not the time.* She
silently begged the monk not to say it.

He didn't. He just smiled and said, 'It is beautiful.
Very beautiful indeed.'

Acknowledgments

Many thanks to R. C. Famiglietti, for graciously answering my numerous queries about the court of Charles VI; Susan T. Newman, for many gifts of books about medieval Paris; Holly Domney and Emma Grundy Haigh, for skillful editing and copyediting; Josh Getzler, my wonderful agent, for unfailing help and encouragement; and my husband, Robert M. Cammarota, for constant support.